W9-AEM-054

Victory Over Japan

ALSO BY ELLEN GILCHRIST

The Land Surveyor's Daughter

In the Land of Dreamy Dreams

The Annunciation

Victory Over Japan

A BOOK OF STORIES BY

Ellen Gilchrist

Little, Brown and Company • Boston • Toronto

Third Printing

LIBRARY OF CONGRESS CATALOGING IN PUBLICATION DATA

Gilchrist, Ellen, 1935-
Victory over Japan.

1. Women—Southern States—Fiction. I. Title.
PS3557.I34258V5 1984 813'.54 84-11307
ISBN 0-316-31303-3

The characters and events portrayed in these stories are fictitious. Any similarities to real persons, living or dead, is purely coincidental and not intended by the author.

Permissions to quote from previously published material appear on page 279.

MV

Designed by Dede Cummings

Published simultaneously in Canada by Little, Brown & Company (Canada) Limited

PRINTED IN THE UNITED STATES OF AMERICA

For Bodie and Bob

☙☙☙

Contents

CRYSTAL

Rhoda

❧❧❧

Victory Over Japan

WHEN I was in the third grade I knew a boy who had to have fourteen shots in the stomach as the result of a squirrel bite. Every day at two o'clock they would come to get him. A hush would fall on the room. We would all look down at our desks while he left the room between Mr. Harmon and his mother. Mr. Harmon was the principal. That's how important Billy Monday's tragedy was.

Mr. Harmon came along in case Billy threw a fit. Every day we waited to see if he would throw a fit but he never did. He just put his books away and left the room with his head hanging down on his chest and Mr. Harmon and his mother guiding him along between them like a boat.

"Would you go with them like that?" I asked Letitia at recess. Letitia was my best friend. Usually we played girls chase the boys at recess or pushed each other on the swings or hung upside down on the monkey bars so Joe Franke and Bobby Saxacorn could see our underpants but Billy's shots had even taken the fun out of recess. Now we sat around on the fire escape and talked about rabies instead.

"Why don't they put him to sleep first?" Letitia said. "I'd make them put me to sleep."

"They can't," I said. "They can't put you to sleep unless they operate."

"My father could," she said. "He owns the hospital. He could put me to sleep." She was always saying things like that but I let her be my best friend anyway.

"They couldn't give them to me," I said. "I'd run away to Florida and be a beachcomber."

"Then you'd get rabies," Letitia said. "You'd be foaming at the mouth."

"I'd take a chance. You don't always get it." We moved closer together, caught up in the horror of it. I was thinking about the Livingstons' bulldog. I'd had some close calls with it lately.

"It was a pet," Letitia said. "His brother was keeping it for a pet."

It was noon recess. Billy Monday was sitting on a bench by the swings. Just sitting there. Not talking to anybody. Waiting for two o'clock, a small washed-out-looking boy that nobody paid any attention to until he got bit. He never talked to anybody. He could hardly even read. When Mrs. Jansma asked him to read his head would fall all the way over to the side of his neck. Then he would read a few sentences with her having to tell him half the words. No one would ever have picked him out to be the center of a rabies tragedy. He was more the type to fall in a well or get sucked down the drain at the swimming pool.

Fourteen days. Fourteen shots. It was spring when it happened and the schoolroom windows were open all day long and every afternoon after Billy left we had milk from little waxy cartons and Mrs. Jansma would read us chapters from a wonderful book about some children in England that had a bed that took them places at night. There we were, eating graham crackers and listening to stories while Billy was strapped to the table in Doctor Finley's office waiting for his shot.

"I can't stand to think about it," Letitia said. "It makes me so sick I could puke."

"I'm going over there and talk to him right now," I said. "I'm going to interview him for the paper." I had been the only one in the third grade to get anything in the Horace Mann paper. I got in with a story about how Mr. Harmon was shell-shocked in the First World War. I was on the lookout for another story that good.

I got up, smoothed down my skirt, walked over to the bench where Billy was sitting and held out a vial of cinnamon toothpicks. "You want one," I said. "Go ahead. She won't care." It was against the rules to bring cinnamon toothpicks to Horace Mann. They were afraid someone would swallow one.

"I don't think so," he said. "I don't need any."

"Go on," I said. "They're really good. They've been soaking all week."

"I don't want any," he said.

"You want me to push you on the swings?"

"I don't know," he said. "I don't think so."

"If it was my brother's squirrel, I'd kill it," I said. "I'd cut its head off."

"It got away," he said. "It's gone."

"What's it like when they give them to you?" I said. "Does it hurt very much?"

"I don't know," he said. "I don't look." His head was starting to slip down onto his chest. He was rolling up like a ball.

"I know how to hypnotize people," I said. "You want me to hypnotize you so you can't feel it?"

"I don't know," he said. He had pulled his legs up on the bench. Now his chin was so far down into his chest I could barely hear him talk. Part of me wanted to give him a shove and see if he would roll. I touched him on the shoulder instead. I could feel his little bones beneath his shirt. I could smell his washed-out rusty smell. His head went all the way down under his knees. Over his shoulder I saw Mrs. Jansma headed our way.

"Rhoda," she called out. "I need you to clean off the blackboards before we go back in. Will you be a sweet girl and do that for me?"

"I wasn't doing anything but talking to to him," I said. She was beside us now and had gathered him into her wide sleeves. He was starting to cry, making little strangled noises like a goat.

"Well, my goodness, that was nice of you to try to cheer Billy up. Now go see about those blackboards for me, will you?"

I went on in and cleaned off the blackboards and beat the erasers together out the window, watching the chalk dust settle into the bricks. Down below I could see Mrs.

Jansma still holding on to Billy. He was hanging on to her like a spider but it looked like he had quit crying.

That afternoon a lady from the PTA came to talk to us about the paper drive. "One more time," she was saying. "We've licked the Krauts. Now all we have left is the Japs. Who's going to help?" she shouted.

"I am," I shouted back. I was the first one on my feet.

"Who do you want for a partner?" she said.

"Billy Monday," I said, pointing at him. He looked up at me as though I had asked him to swim the English Channel, then his head slid down on the desk.

"All right," Mrs. Jansma said. "Rhoda Manning and Billy Monday. Team number one. To cover Washington and Sycamore from Calvin Boulevard to Conner Street. Who else?"

"Bobby and me," Joe Franke called out. He was wearing his coonskin cap, even though it was as hot as summer. How I loved him! "We want downtown," he shouted. "We want Dirkson Street to the river."

"Done," Mrs. Jansma said. JoEllen Scaggs was writing it all down on the blackboard. By the time Billy's mother and Mr. Harmon came to get him the paper drive was all arranged.

"See you tomorrow," I called out as Billy left the room. "Don't forget. Don't be late."

When I got home that afternoon I told my mother I had volunteered to let Billy be my partner. She was so proud of me she made me some cookies even though I was supposed to be on a diet. I took the cookies and a pillow and climbed up into my treehouse to read a book. I was getting to be more like my mother every day. My mother was a saint. She fed hoboes and played the organ at early communion even if she was sick and gave away her ration stamps to anyone that needed them. She had only had one pair of new shoes the whole war.

I was getting more like her every day. I was the only one in the third grade that would have picked Billy Monday to help with a paper drive. He probably couldn't even pick up a stack of papers. He probably couldn't even help pull the wagon.

I bet this is the happiest day of her life, I was thinking. I was lying in my treehouse watching her. She was sitting on the back steps putting liquid hose on her legs. She was waiting for the Episcopal minister to come by for a drink. He'd been coming by a lot since my daddy was overseas. That was just like my mother. To be best friends with a minister.

"She picked out a boy that's been sick to help her on the paper drive," I heard her tell him later. "I think it helped a lot to get her to lose weight. It was smart of you to see that was the problem."

"There isn't anything I wouldn't do for you, Ariane," he said. "You say the word and I'll be here to do it."

I got a few more cookies and went back up into the treehouse to finish my book. I could read all kinds of books. I could read Book-of-the-Month Club books. The one I was reading now was called *Cakes and Ale*. It wasn't coming along too well.

I settled down with my back against the tree, turning the pages, looking for the good parts. Inside the house my mother was bragging on me. Above my head a golden sun beat down out of a blue sky. All around the silver maple leaves moved in the breeze. I went back to my book. "She put her arms around my neck and pressed her lips against mine. I forgot my wrath. I only thought of her beauty and her enveloping kindness.

" 'You must take me as I am, you know,' she whispered.

" 'All right,' I said."

Saturday was not going to be a good day for a paper drive. The sky was gray and overcast. By the time we lined up on the Horace Mann playground with our wagons a light rain was falling.

"Our boys are fighting in rain and snow and whatever the heavens send," Mr. Harmon was saying. He was standing on the bleachers wearing an old baseball shirt and a cap. I had never seen him in anything but his gray suit. He looked more shell-shocked than ever in his cap.

"They're working over there. We're working over here. The Germans are defeated. Only the Japs left to go. There're canvas tarps from Gentilly's Hardware, so take one to cover your papers. All right now. One grade at a time. And remember, Mrs. Winchester's third grade is still ahead by seventy-eight pounds. So you're going to have to go some to beat that. Get to your stations now. Get ready, get set, go. Everybody working together . . ."

Billy and I started off. I was pulling the wagon, he was walking along beside me. I had meant to wait awhile before I started interviewing him but I started right in.

"Are you going to have to leave to go get it?" I said.

"Go get what?"

"You know. Your shot."

"I got it this morning. I already had it."

"Where do they put it in?"

"I don't know," he said. "I don't look."

"Well, you can feel it, can't you?" I said. "Like, do they stick it in your navel or what?"

"It's higher than that."

"How long does it take? To get it."

"I don't know," he said. "Till they get through."

"Well, at least you aren't going to get rabies. At least you won't be foaming at the mouth. I guess you're glad about that." I had stopped in front of a house and was looking up the path to the door. We had come to the end of Sycamore, where our territory began.

"Are you going to be the one to ask them?" he said.

"Sure," I said. "You want to come to the door with me?"

"I'll wait," he said. "I'll just wait."

We filled the wagon by the second block. We took that load back to the school and started out again. On the second trip we hit an attic with bundles of the *Kansas City Star* tied up with string. It took us all afternoon to haul that. Mrs. Jansma said she'd never seen anyone as lucky on a paper drive as Billy and I. Our whole class was having a good day. It looked like we might beat everybody, even the sixth grade.

"Let's go out one more time," Mrs. Jansma said. "One more trip before dark. Be sure and hit all the houses you missed."

Billy and I started back down Sycamore. It was growing dark. I untied my Brownie Scout sweater from around my waist and put it on and pulled the sleeves down over my wrists. "Let's try that brick house on the corner," I said. "They might be home by now." It was an old house set back on a high lawn. It looked like a house where old people lived. I had noticed old people were the ones who saved things. "Come on," I said. "You go to the door with me. I'm tired of doing it by myself."

He came along behind me and we walked up to the door and rang the bell. No one answered for a long time although I could hear footsteps and saw someone pass by a window. I rang the bell again.

A man came to the door. A thin man about my father's age.

"We're collecting papers for Horace Mann School," I said. "For the war effort."

"You got any papers we can have?" Billy said. It was the first time he had spoken to anyone but me all day. "For the war," he added.

"There're some things in the basement if you want to go down there and get them," the man said. He turned a light on in the hall and we followed him into a high-ceilinged foyer with a set of winding stairs going up to another floor. It smelled musty, like my grandmother's house in Clarksville. Billy was right beside me, sticking as close as a burr. We followed the man through the kitchen and down a flight of stairs to the basement.

"You can have whatever you find down here," he said. "There're papers and magazines in that corner. Take whatever you can carry."

There was a large stack of magazines. Magazines were the best thing you could find. They weighed three times as much as newspapers.

"Come on," I said to Billy. "Let's fill the wagon. This will put us over the top for sure." I picked up a bundle and started up the stairs. I went in and out several times carrying as many as I could at a time. On the third trip

Billy met me at the foot of the stairs. "Rhoda," he said. "Come here. Come look at this."

He took me to an old table in a corner of the basement. It was a walnut table with grapes carved on the side and feet like lion's feet. He laid one of the magazines down on the table and opened it. It was a photograph of a naked little girl, a girl smaller than I was. He turned the page. Two naked boys were standing together with their legs twined. He kept turning the pages. It was all the same. Naked children on every page. I had never seen a naked boy. Much less a photograph of one. Billy looked up at me. He turned another page. Five naked little girls were grouped together around a fountain.

"Let's get out of here," I said. "Come on. I'm getting out of here." I headed for the stairs with him right behind me. We didn't even close the basement door. We didn't even stop to say thank you.

The magazines we had collected were in bundles. About a block from the house we stopped on a corner, breathless from running. "Let's see if there're any more," I said. We tore open a bundle. The first magazine had pictures of naked grown people on every page.

"What are we going to do?" he said.

"We're going to throw them away," I answered, and started throwing them into the nandina bushes by the Hancock's vacant lot. We threw them into the nandina bushes and into the ditch that runs into Mills Creek. We threw the last ones into a culvert and then we took our wagon and got on out of there. At the corner of Sycamore and Wesley we went our separate ways.

"Well, at least you'll have something to think about tomorrow when you get your shot," I said.

"I guess so," he replied.

"Look here, Billy. I don't want you to tell anyone about those magazines. You understand?"

"I won't." His head was going down again.

"I mean it, Billy."

He raised his head and looked at me as if he had just remembered something he was thinking about. "I won't," he said. "Are you really going to write about me in the paper?"

"Of course I am. I said I was, didn't I? I'm going to do it tonight."

I walked on home. Past the corner where the Scout hikes met. Down the alley where I found the card shuffler and the Japanese fan. Past the yard where the violets grew. I was thinking about the boys with their legs twined. They looked like earthworms, all naked like that. They looked like something might fly down and eat them. It made me sick to think about it and I stopped by Mrs. Alford's and picked a few iris to take home to my mother.

Billy finished getting his shots. And I wrote the article and of course they put it on page one. BE ON THE LOOKOUT FOR MAD SQUIRREL, the headline read. By Rhoda Katherine Manning. Grade 3.

> We didn't even know it was mean, the person it bit said. That person is in the third grade at our school.

His name is William Monday. On April 23 he had his last shot. Mrs. Jansma's class had a cake and gave him a pencil set. Billy Monday is all right now and things are back to normal.

I think it should be against the law to keep dangerous pets or dogs where they can get out and get people. If you see a dog or squirrel acting funny go in the house and stay there.

I never did get around to telling my mother about those magazines. I kept meaning to but there never seemed to be anywhere to start. One day in August I tried to tell her. I had been to the swimming pool and I thought I saw the man from the brick house drive by in a car. I was pretty sure it was him. As he turned the corner he looked at me. *He looked right at my face.* I stood very still, my heart pounding inside my chest, my hands as cold and wet as a frog, the smell of swimming pool chlorine rising from my skin. What if he found out where I lived? What if he followed me home and killed me to keep me from telling on him? I was terrified. At any moment the car might return. He might grab me and put me in the car and take me off and kill me. I threw my bathing suit and towel down on the sidewalk and started running. I ran down Linden Street and turned into the alley behind Calvin Boulevard, running as fast as I could. I ran down the alley and into my yard and up my steps and into my house looking for my mother to tell her about it.

She was in the living room, with Father Kenniman and Mr. and Mrs. DuVal. They lived across the street and had a gold star in their window. Warrene, our cook, was there. And Connie Barksdale, our cousin who was visiting from the Delta. Her husband had been killed on Corregidor and she would come up and stay with my mother whenever she couldn't take it anymore. They were all in the living room gathered around the radio.

"Momma," I said. "I saw this man that gave me some magazines . . ."

"Be quite, Rhoda," she said. "We're listening to the news. Something's happened. We think maybe we've won the war." There were tears in her eyes. She gave me a little hug, then turned back to the radio. It was a wonderful radio with a magic eye that glowed in the dark. At night when we had blackouts Dudley and I would get into bed with my mother and we would listen to it together, the magic eye glowing in the dark like an emerald.

Now the radio was bringing important news to Seymour, Indiana. Strange, confused, hush-hush news that said we had a bomb bigger than any bomb ever made and we had already dropped it on Japan and half of Japan was sinking into the sea. Now the Japs had to surrender. Now they couldn't come to Indiana and stick bamboo up our fingernails. Now it would all be over and my father would come home.

The grown people kept on listening to the radio, getting up every now and then to get drinks or fix each other sandwiches. Dudley was sitting beside my mother in a white shirt acting like he was twenty years old. He always did that when company came. No one was paying any attention to me.

Finally I went upstairs and lay down on the bed to think things over. My father was coming home. I didn't know how to feel about that. He was always yelling at someone when he was home. He was always yelling at my mother to make me mind.

"What do you mean, you can't catch her," I could hear him yelling. "Hit her with a broom. Hit her with a table. Hit her with a chair. But, for God's sake, Ariane, don't let her talk to you that way."

Well, maybe it would take a while for him to get home. First they had to finish off Japan. First they had to sink the other half into the sea. I curled up in my soft old eiderdown comforter. I was feeling great. We had dropped the biggest bomb in the world on Japan and there were plenty more where that one came from.

I fell asleep in the hot sweaty silkiness of the comforter. I was dreaming I was at the wheel of an airplane carrying the bomb to Japan. Hit 'em, I was yelling. Hit 'em with a mountain. Hit 'em with a table. Hit 'em with a chair. Off we go into the wild blue yonder, climbing high into the sky. I dropped one on the brick house where the bad man lived, then took off for Japan. Down we dive, spouting a flame from under. Off with one hell of a roar. We live in flame. Buckle down in flame. For nothing can stop the Army Air Corps. Hit 'em with a table, I was yelling. Hit 'em with a broom. Hit 'em with a bomb. Hit 'em with a chair.

❧❧❧

Music

RHODA was fourteen years old the summer her father dragged her off to Clay County, Kentucky, to make her stop smoking and acting like a movie star. She was fourteen years old, a holy and terrible age, and her desire for beauty and romance drove her all day long and pursued her if she slept.

"Te amo," she whispered to herself in Latin class. "Te amo, Bob Rosen," sending the heat of her passions across the classroom and out through the window and across two states to a hospital room in Saint Louis, where a college boy lay recovering from a series of operations Rhoda had decided would be fatal.

"And you as well must die, beloved dust," she quoted to herself. "Oh, sleep forever in your Latmian cave, Mortal Endymion, darling of the moon," she whispered, and sometimes it was Bob Rosen's lanky body stretched out in the cave beside his saxophone that she envisioned and sometimes it was her own lush, apricot-colored skin growing cold against the rocks in the moonlight.

Rhoda was fourteen years old that spring and her true love had been cruelly taken from her and she had started smoking because there was nothing left to do now but be a writer.

She was fourteen years old and she would sit on the porch at night looking down the hill that led through the small town of Franklin, Kentucky, and think about the stars, wondering where heaven could be in all that vastness, feeling betrayed by her mother's pale Episcopalianism and the fate that had brought her to this small town right in the middle of her sophomore year in high school. She would sit on the porch stuffing chocolate chip cookies into her mouth, drinking endless homemade chocolate milkshakes, smoking endless Lucky Strike cigarettes, watching her mother's transplanted roses move steadily across the trellis, taking Bob Rosen's thin letters in and out of their envelopes, holding them against her face, then going up to the new bedroom, to the soft, blue sheets, stuffed with cookies and ice cream and cigarettes and rage.

"Is that you, Rhoda?" her father would call out as she passed his bedroom. "Is that you, sweetie? Come tell us goodnight." And she would go into their bedroom and lean over and kiss him.

"You just ought to smell yourself," he would say, sitting up, pushing her away. "You just ought to smell those nasty cigarettes." And as soon as she went into her room he would go downstairs and empty all the ashtrays to make sure the house wouldn't burn down while he was sleeping.

"I've got to make her stop that goddamn smoking," he would say, climbing back into the bed. "I'm goddamned if I'm going to put up with that."

"I'd like to know how you're going to stop it," Rhoda's mother said. "I'd like to see anyone make Rhoda do anything she doesn't want to do. Not to mention that you're hardly ever here."

"Goddammit, Ariane, don't start that this time of night." And he rolled over on his side of the bed and began to plot his campaign against Rhoda's cigarettes.

Dudley Manning wasn't afraid of Rhoda, even if she was as stubborn as a goat. Dudley Manning wasn't afraid of anything. He had gotten up at dawn every day for years and believed in himself and followed his luck wherever it led him, dragging his sweet southern wife and his children behind him, and now, in his fortieth year, he was about to become a millionaire.

He was about to become a millionaire and he was in love with a beautiful woman who was not his wife and it was the strangest spring he had ever known. When he added up the figures in his account books he was filled with awe at his own achievements, amazed at what he had made of himself, and to make up for it he talked a lot about luck and pretended to be humble but deep down inside he believed there was nothing he couldn't do, even love two women at once, even make Rhoda stop smoking.

Both Dudley and Rhoda were early risers. If he was in town he would be waiting in the kitchen when she came down to breakfast, dressed in his khakis, his pens in his pocket, his glasses on his nose, sitting at the table going over his papers, his head full of the clean new ideas of morning.

"How many more days of school do you have?" he said to her one morning, watching her light the first of her cigarettes without saying anything about it.

"Just this week," she said. "Just until Friday. I'm making A's, Daddy. This is the easiest school I've ever been to."

"Well, don't be smart-alecky about it, Rhoda," he said. "If you've got a good mind it's only because God gave it to you."

"God didn't give me anything," she said. "Because there isn't any God."

"Well, let's don't get into an argument about that this morning," Dudley said. "As soon as you finish school I want you to drive up to the mines with me for a few days."

"For how long?" she said.

"We won't be gone long," he said. "I just want to take you to the mines to look things over."

Rhoda french-inhaled, blowing the smoke out into the sunlight coming through the kitchen windows, imagining herself on a tour of her father's mines, the workers with their caps in their hands smiling at her as she walked politely among them. Rhoda liked that idea. She dropped two saccharin tablets into her coffee and sat down at the table, enjoying her fantasy.

"Is that what you're having for breakfast?" he said.

"I'm on a diet," Rhoda said. "I'm on a black coffee diet."

He looked down at his poached eggs, cutting into the yellow with his knife. I can wait, he said to himself. As God is my witness I can wait until Sunday.

Rhoda poured herself another cup of coffee and went upstairs to write Bob Rosen before she left for school.

Dear Bob [the letter began],

School is almost over. I made straight A's, of course, as per your instructions. This school is so easy it's crazy.

They read one of my newspaper columns on the radio in Nashville. Everyone in Franklin goes around saying my mother writes my columns. Can you believe that? Allison Hotchkiss, that's my editor, say she's going to write an editorial about it saying I really write them.

I turned my bedroom into an office and took out the tacky dressing table mother made me and got a desk and put my typewriter on it and made striped drapes, green and black and white. I think you would approve.

Sunday Daddy is taking me to Manchester, Kentucky, to look over the coal mines. He's going to let me drive. He lets me drive all the time. *I live for your letters.*

Te amo,
Rhoda

She put the letter in a pale blue envelope, sealed it, dripped some Toujours Moi lavishly onto it in several places and threw herself down on her bed.

She pressed her face deep down into her comforter pretending it was Bob Rosen's smooth cool skin. "Oh, Bob, Bob," she whispered to the comforter. "Oh, honey, don't die, don't die, please don't die." She could feel the tears coming. She reached out and caressed the seam of the comforter, pretending it was the scar on Bob Rosen's neck.

The last night she had been with him he had just come home from an operation for a mysterious tumor that he didn't want to talk about. It would be better soon, was all he would say about it. Before long he would be as good as new.

They had driven out of town and parked the old Pontiac underneath a tree beside a pasture. It was September and Rhoda had lain in his arms smelling the clean smell of his new sweater, touching the fresh red scars on his neck, looking out the window to memorize every detail of the scene, the black tree, the September pasture, the white horse leaning against the fence, the palms of his hands, the taste of their cigarettes, the night breeze, the exact temperature of the air, saying to herself over and over, I must remember everything. This will have to last me forever and ever and ever.

"I want you to do it to me," she said. "Whatever it is they do."

"I can't," he said. "I couldn't do that now. It's too much trouble to make love to a virgin." He was laughing. "Besides, it's hard to do it in a car."

"But I'm leaving," she said. "I might not ever see you again."

"Not tonight," he said. "I still don't feel very good, Rhoda."

"What if I come back and visit," she said. "Will you do it then? When you feel better."

"If you still want me to I will," he said. "If you come back to visit and we both want to, I will."

"Do you promise?" she said, hugging him fiercely.

"I promise," he said. "On my honor I promise to do it when you come to visit."

But Rhoda was not allowed to go to Saint Louis to visit. Either her mother guessed her intentions or else she seized the opportunity to do what she had been wanting to do all along and stop her daughter from seeing a boy with a Jewish last name.

There were weeks of pleadings and threats. It all ended one Sunday night when Mrs. Manning lost her temper and made the statement that Jews were little peddlers who went through the Delta selling needles and pins.

"You don't know what you're talking about," Rhoda screamed. "He's not a peddler, and I love him and I'm going to love him until I die." Rhoda pulled her arms away from her mother's hands.

"I'm going up there this weekend to see him," she screamed. "Daddy promised me I could and you're not going to stop me and if you try to stop me I'll kill you and I'll run away and I'll never come back."

"You are not going to Saint Louis and that's the end of this conversation and if you don't calm down I'll call a doctor and have you locked up. I think you're crazy, Rhoda. I really do."

"I'm not crazy," Rhoda screamed. "You're the one that's crazy."

"You and your father think you're so smart," her mother said. She was shaking but she held her ground, moving around behind a Queen Anne chair. "Well, I don't care how smart you are, you're not going to get on a train and go off to Saint Louis, Missouri to see a man when you're only fourteen years old, and that, Miss Rhoda K. Manning, is that."

"I'm going to kill you," Rhoda said. "I really am. I'm going to kill you," and she thought for a moment that she would kill her, but then she noticed her grandmother's Limoges hot chocolate pot sitting on top of the piano holding a spray of yellow jasmine, and she walked over to the piano and picked it up and threw it all the way across the room and smashed it into a wall beside a framed print of "The Blue Boy."

"I hate you," Rhoda said. "I wish you were dead." And while her mother stared in disbelief at the wreck of the sainted hot chocolate pot, Rhoda walked out of the house and got in the car and drove off down the steep driveway. I hate her guts, she said to herself. I hope she cries herself to death.

She shifted into second gear and drove off toward her father's office, quoting to herself from Edna Millay. "Now by this moon, before this moon shall wane, I shall be dead or I shall be with you."

But in the end Rhoda didn't die. Neither did she kill her mother. Neither did she go to Saint Louis to give her virginity to her reluctant lover.

The Sunday of the trip Rhoda woke at dawn feeling very excited and changed clothes four or five times trying to decide how she wanted to look for her inspection of the mines.

Rhoda had never even seen a picture of a strip mine. In her imagination she and her father would be riding an elevator down into the heart of a mountain where obsequious masked miners were lined up to shake her hand. Later that evening the captain of the football team would be coming over to the hotel to meet her and take her somewhere for a drive.

She pulled on a pair of pink pedal pushers and a long navy blue sweat shirt, threw every single thing she could possibly imagine wearing into a large suitcase, and started down the stairs to where her father was calling for her to hurry up.

Her mother followed her out of the house holding a buttered biscuit on a linen napkin. "Please eat something before you leave," she said. "There isn't a decent restaurant after you leave Bowling Green."

"I told you I don't want anything to eat," Rhoda said. "I'm on a diet." She stared at the biscuit as though it were a coral snake.

"One biscuit isn't going to hurt you," her mother said. "I made you a lunch, chicken and carrot sticks and apples."

"I don't want it," Rhoda said "Don't put any food in this car, Mother."

"Just because you never eat doesn't mean your father won't get hungry. You don't have to eat any of it unless you want to." Their eyes met. Then they sighed and looked away.

Her father appeared at the door and climbed in behind the wheel of the secondhand Cadillac.

"Let's go, Sweet Sister," he said, cruising down the driveway, turning onto the road leading to Bowling Green and due east into the hill country. Usually this was his favorite moment of the week, starting the long drive into the rich Kentucky hills where his energy and intelligence had created the long black rows of figures in the account books, figures that meant Rhoda would never know what it was to be really afraid or uncertain or powerless.

"How long will it take?" Rhoda asked.

"Don't worry about that," he said. "Just look out the window and enjoy the ride. This is beautiful country we're driving through."

"I can't right now," Rhoda said. "I want to read the new book Allison gave me. It's a book of poems."

She settled down into the seat and opened the book.

> *Oh, gallant was the first love, and glittering and fine;*
> *The second love was water, in a clear blue cup;*
> *The third love was his, and the fourth was mine.*
> *And after that, I always get them all mixed up.*

Oh, God, this is good, she thought. She sat up straighter, wanting to kiss the book. Oh, God, this is really good. She turned the book over to look at the picture of the author. It was a photograph of a small bright face in full profile staring off into the mysterious brightly lit world of a poet's life.

Dorothy Parker, she read. What a wonderful name. Maybe I'll change my name to Dorothy, Dorothy Louise Manning. Dot Manning. Dottie, Dottie Leigh, Dot.

Rhoda pulled a pack of Lucky Strikes out of her purse, tamped it on the dashboard, opened it, extracted a cigarette and lit it with a gold Ronson lighter. She inhaled deeply and went back to the book.

Her father gripped the wheel, trying to concentrate on the beauty of the morning, the green fields, the small, neat farmhouses, the red barns, the cattle and horses. He moved his eyes from all that order to his fourteen-year-old daughter slumped beside him with her nose buried in a book, her plump fingers languishing in the air, holding a cigarette. He slowed down, pulled the car onto the side of the road and killed the motor.

"What's wrong?" Rhoda said. "Why are you stopping?"

"Because you are going to put out that goddamn cigarette this very minute and you're going to give me the package and you're not going to smoke another cigarette around me as long as you live," he said.

"I will not do any such thing," Rhoda said. "It's a free country."

"Give me the cigarette, Rhoda," he said. "Hand it here."

"Give me one good reason why I should," she said. But her voice let her down. She knew there wasn't any use in arguing. This was not her soft little mother she was dealing with. This was Dudley Manning, who had been a famous baseball player until he quit when she was born. Who before that had gone to the Olympics on a relay team. There were scrapbooks full of his clippings in Rhoda's house. No matter where the Mannings went those scrapbooks sat on a table in the den. *Manning Hits One Over The Fence*, the headlines read. *Manning Saves The Day. Manning Does It Again.* And he was not the only one. His cousin, Philip Manning, down in Jackson, Mississippi, was famous too. Who was the father of the famous Crystal Manning, Rhoda's cousin who had a fur coat when she was ten. And Leland Manning, who was her cousin Lele's daddy. Leland had been the captain of the Tulane football team before he drank himself to death in the Delta.

Rhoda sighed, thinking of all that, and gave in for the moment. "Give me one good reason and I might," she repeated.

"I don't have to give you a reason for a goddamn thing," he said. "Give the cigarette here, Rhoda. Right this minute." He reached out and took it and she didn't resist. "Goddamn, these things smell awful," he said, crushing it in the ashtray. He reached in her pocketbook and got the package and threw it out the window.

"Only white trash throw things out on the road," Rhoda said. "You'd kill me if I did that."

"Well, let's just be quiet and get to where we're going." He started the motor and drove back out onto the highway. Rhoda crunched down lower in the seat, pretending to read her book. Who cares, she thought. I'll get some as soon as we stop for gas.

Getting cigarettes at filling stations was not as easy as Rhoda thought it was going to be. This was God's country they were driving into now, the hills rising up higher and higher, strange, silent little houses back off the road. Rhoda could feel the eyes looking out at her from behind the silent windows. Poor white trash, Rhoda's mother would have called them. The salt of the earth, her father would have said.

This was God's country and these people took things like children smoking cigarettes seriously. At both places where they stopped there was a sign by the cash register, *No Cigarettes Sold To Minors.*

Rhoda had moved to the back seat of the Cadillac and

was stretched out on the seat reading her book. She had found another poem she liked and she was memorizing it.

> *Four be the things I'd be better without,*
> *Love, curiosity, freckles and doubt.*
> *Three be the things I shall never attain,*
> *Envy, content and sufficient champagne.*

Oh, God, I love this book, she thought. *This Dorothy Parker is just like me*. Rhoda was remembering a night when she got drunk in Clarkesville, Mississippi with her cousin, Baby Gwen Barksdale. They got drunk on tequila LaGrande Conroy brought back from Mexico, and Rhoda had slept all night in the bathtub so she would be near the toilet when she vomited.

She put her head down on her arm and giggled, thinking about waking up in the bathtub. Then a plan occurred to her.

"Stop and let me go to the bathroom," she said to her father. "I think I'm going to throw up."

"Oh, Lord," he said. "I knew you shouldn't have gotten in the back seat. Well, hold on. I'll stop the first place I see." He pushed his hat back off his forehead and began looking for a place to stop, glancing back over his shoulder every now and then to see if she was all right. Rhoda had a long history of throwing up on car trips so he was taking this seriously. Finally he saw a combination store and filling station at a bend in the road and pulled up beside the front door.

"I'll be all right." Rhoda said, jumping out of the car. "You stay here. I'll be right back."

She walked dramatically up the wooden steps and pushed open the screen door. It was so quiet and dark inside she thought for a moment the store was closed. She looked around. She was in a rough, high-ceilinged room with saddles and pieces of farm equipment hanging from the rafters and a sparse array of canned goods on wooden shelves behind a counter. On the counter were five or six large glass jars filled with different kinds of Nabisco cookies. Rhoda stared at the cookie jars, wanting to stick her hand down inside and take out great fistfuls of Lorna Doones and Oreos. She fought off her hunger and raised her eyes to the display of chewing tobacco and cigarettes.

The smells of the store rose up to meet her, fecund and rich, moist and cool, as if the store was an extension of the earth outside. Rhoda looked down at the board floors. She felt she could have dropped a sunflower seed on the floor and it would instantly sprout and take bloom, growing quick, moving down into the earth and upwards toward the rafters.

"Is anybody here?" she said softly, then louder. "Is anybody here?"

A woman in a cotton dress appeared in a door, staring at Rhoda out of very intense, very blue eyes.

"Can I buy a pack of cigarettes from you?" Rhoda said. "My dad's in the car. He sent me to get them."

"What kind of cigarettes you looking for?" the woman said, moving to the space between the cash register and the cookie jars.

"Some Luckies if you have them," Rhoda said. "He said to just get anything you had if you didn't have that."

"They're a quarter," the woman said, reaching behind herself to take the package down and lay it on the counter, not smiling, but not being unkind either.

"Thank you," Rhoda said, laying the quarter down on the counter. "Do you have any matches?"

"Sure," the woman said, holding out a box of kitchen matches. Rhoda took a few, letting her eyes leave the woman's face and come to rest on the jars of Oreos. They looked wonderful and light, as though they had been there a long time and grown soft around the edges.

The woman was smiling now. "You want one of those cookies?" she said. "You want one, you go on and have one. It's free."

"Oh, no thank you," Rhoda said. "I'm on a diet. Look, do you have a ladies' room I can use?"

"It's out back," the woman said. "You can have one of them cookies if you want it. Like I said, it won't cost you nothing."

"I guess I'd better get going," Rhoda said. "My dad's in a hurry. But thank you anyway. And thanks for the matches." Rhoda hurried down the aisle, slipped out the back door and leaned up against the back of the store, tearing the paper off the cigarettes. She pulled one out, lit it, and inhaled deeply, blowing the smoke out in front of her, watching it rise up into thc air, casting a veil over the hills that rose up behind and to the left of her. She had never been in such a strange country. It looked as though no one ever did anything to their yards or roads or fences. It looked as though there might not be a clock for miles.

She inhaled again, feeling dizzy and full. She had just

taken the cigarette out of her mouth when her father came bursting out of the door and grabbed both of her wrists in his hands.

"Let go of me," she said. "Let go of me this minute." She struggled to free herself, ready to kick or claw or bite, ready for a real fight, but he held her off. "Drop the cigarette, Rhoda," he said. "Drop it on the ground."

"I'll kill you," she said. "As soon as I get away I'm running away to Florida. Let go of me, Daddy. Do you hear me?"

"I hear you," he said. The veins were standing out on his forehead. His face was so close Rhoda could see his freckles and the line where his false front tooth was joined to what was left of the real one. He had lost the tooth in a baseball game the day Rhoda was born. That was how he told the story. "I lost that tooth the day Rhoda was born," he would say. "I was playing left field against Memphis in the old Crump Stadium. I slid into second and the second baseman got me with his shoe."

"You can smoke all you want to when you get down to Florida," he was saying now. "But you're not smoking on this trip. So you might as well calm down before I drive off and leave you here."

"I don't care," she said. "Go on and leave. I'll just call up Mother and she'll come and get me." She was struggling to free her wrists but she could not move them inside his hands. "Let go of me, you big bully," she added.

"Will you calm down and give me the cigarettes?"

"All right," she said, but the minute he let go of her

hands she turned and began to hit him on the shoulders, pounding her fists up and down on his back, not daring to put any real force behind the blows. He pretended to cower under the assault. She caught his eye and saw that he was laughing at her and she had to fight the desire to laugh with him.

"I'm getting in the car," she said. "I'm sick of this place." She walked grandly around to the front of the store, got into the car, tore open the lunch and began to devour it, tearing the chicken off the bones with her teeth, swallowing great hunks without even bothering to chew them. "I'm never speaking to you again as long as I live," she said, her mouth full of chicken breast. "You are not my father."

"Suits me, Miss Smart-alecky Movie Star," he said, putting his hat back on his head. "Soon as we get home you can head on out for Florida. You just let me know when you're leaving so I can give you some money for the bus."

"I hate you," Rhoda mumbled to herself, starting in on the homemade raisin cookies. I hate your guts. I hope you go to hell forever, she thought, breaking a cookie into pieces so she could pick out the raisins.

It was late afternoon when the Cadillac picked its way up a rocky red clay driveway to a housetrailer nestled in the curve of a hill beside a stand of pine trees.

"Where are we going?" Rhoda said. "Would you just tell me that?"

"We're going to see Maud and Joe Samples," he said. "Joe's an old hand around here. He's my right-hand man in Clay County. Now you just be polite and try to learn something, Sister. These are real folks you're about to meet."

"Why are we going here first?" Rhoda said. "Aren't we going to a hotel?"

"There isn't any hotel," her father said. "Does this look like someplace they'd have hotels? Maud and Joe are going to put you up for me while I'm off working."

"I'm going to stay here?" Rhoda said. "In this trailer?"

"Just wait until you see the inside," her father said. "It's like the inside of a boat, everything all planned out and just the right amount of space for things. I wish your mother'd let me live in a trailer."

They were almost to the door now. A plump smiling woman came out onto the wooden platform and waited for them with her hands on her hips, smiling wider and wider as they got nearer.

"There's Maud," Dudley said. "She's the sweetest woman in the world and the best cook in Kentucky. Hey there, Miss Maud," he called out.

"Mr. D," she said, opening the car door for them. "Joe Samples' been waiting on you all day and here you show up bringing this beautiful girl just like you promised. I've made you some blackberry pies. Come on inside this trailer." Maud smiled deep into Rhoda's face. Her eyes were as blue as the ones on the woman in the store. Rhoda's mother had blue eyes, but not this brilliant and not this blue. These eyes were from another world, another century.

"Come on in and see Joe," Maud said. "He's been having a fit for you to get here."

They went inside and Dudley showed Rhoda all

around the trailer, priasing the design of trailers. Maud turned on the tiny oven and they had blackberry pie and bread and butter sandwiches and Rhoda abandoned her diet and ate two pieces of the pie, covering it with thick whipped cream.

The men went off to talk business and Maud took Rhoda to a small room at the back of the trailer decorated to match a handmade quilt of the sunrise.

There were yellow ruffled curtains at the windows and a tiny dressing table with a yellow ruffled skirt around the edges. Rhoda was enchanted by the smallness of everything and the way the windows looked out onto layers of green trees and bushes.

Lying on the dresser was a white leather Bible and a display of small white pamphlets, *Alcohol And You*, *When Jesus Reaches For A Drink*, *You Are Not Alone*, *Sorry Isn't Enough*, *Taking No For An Answer*.

It embarrassed Rhoda even to read the titles of anything as tacky as the pamphlets. but she didn't let on she thought it was tacky, not with Maud sitting on the bed telling her how pretty she was every other second and asking her questions about herself and saying how wonderful her father was.

"We love Mr. D to death," she said. "It's like he was one of our own."

He appeared in the door. "Rhoda, if you're settled in I'll be leaving now," he said. "I've got to drive to Knoxville to do some business but I'll be back here Tuesday morning to take you to the mines." He handed her three twenty-dollar bills. "Here," he said. "In case you need anything."

He left then and hurried out to the car, trying to figure

out how long it would take him to get to Knoxville, to where Valerie sat alone in a hotel room waiting for this night they had planned for so long. He felt the sweet hot guilt rise up in his face and the sweet hot longing in his legs and hands.

I'm sorry, Jesus, he thought, pulling out onto the highway. I know it's wrong and I know we're doing wrong. So go on and punish me if you have to but just let me make it there and back before you start in on me.

He set the cruising speed at exactly fifty-five miles an hour and began to sing to himself as he drove.

"*Oh, sure as the vine grows around the stump*
You're my darling sugar lump," he sang, and;

"*Froggy went a-courting and he did ride,*
Huhhrummp, Huhhrummp,
Froggy went a-courting and he did ride, Huhhrummp,

What you gonna have for the wedding supper?
Black-eyed peas and bread and butter, Huhhrummp,
huhhrummp . . ."

Rhoda was up and dressed when her father came to get her on Tuesday morning. It was still dark outside but a rooster had begun to crow in the distance. Maud bustled all about the little kitchen making much of them, filling their plates with biscuits and fried eggs and ham and gravy.

Then they got into the Cadillac and began to drive toward the mine. Dudley was driving slowly, pointing out everything to her as they rode along.

"Up on that knoll," he said, "that's where the Traylors live. Rooster Traylor's a man about my age. Last year his mother shot one of the Galtney women for breaking up Rooster's marriage and now the Galtneys have got to shoot someone in the Traylor family."

"That's terrible," Rhoda said.

"No it isn't, Sister," he said, warming into the argument. "These people take care of their own problems."

"They actually shoot each other?" she said. "And you think that's okay? You think that's funny?"

"I think it's just as good as waiting around for some judge and jury to do it for you."

"Then you're just crazy," Rhoda said. "You're as crazy as you can be."

"Well, let's don't argue about it this morning. Come on. I've got something to show you." He pulled the car off the road and they walked into the woods, following a set of bulldozer tracks that made a crude path into the trees. It was quiet in the woods and smelled of pine and sassafras. Rhoda watched her father's strong body moving in front of her, striding along, inspecting everything, noticing everything, commenting on everything.

"Look at this," he said. "Look at all this beauty, honey. Look at how beautiful all this is. This is the real world. Not those goddamn movies and beauty parlors and magazines. This is the world that God made. This is where people are really happy."

"There isn't any God," she said. "Nobody that knows anything believes in God, Daddy. That's just a lot of old stuff . . ."

"I'm telling you, Rhoda," he said. "It breaks my heart to see the way you're growing up." He stopped underneath a tree, took a seat on a log and turned his face to hers. Tears were forming in his eyes. He was famous in the family for being able to cry on cue. "You've just got to learn to listen to someone. You've got to get some common sense in your head. I swear to God, I worry about you all the time." The tears were falling now. "I just can't stand to see the way you're growing up. I don't know where you get all those crazy ideas you come up with."

Rhoda looked down, caught off guard by the tears. No matter how many times he pulled that with the tears she fell for it for a moment. The summer forest was all around them, soft deep earth beneath their feet, morning light falling through the leaves, and the things that passed between them were too hard to understand. Their brown eyes met and locked and after that they were bound to start an argument for no one can bear to be that happy or that close to another human being.

"Well, I'll tell you one thing," Rhoda said. "It's a free country and I can smoke if I want to and you can't keep me from doing it by locking me up in a trailer with some poor white trash."

"What did you say?" he said, getting a look on his face that would have scared a grown man to death. "What did you just say, Rhoda?"

"I said I'm sick and tired of being locked up in that damned old trailer with those corny people and nothing to read but religious magazines. I want to get some cigarettes and I want you to take me home so I can see my friends and get my column written for next week."

"Oh, God, Sister." he said. "Haven't I taught you anything? Maud Samples is the salt of the earth. That woman raised seven children. She knows things you and I will never know as long as we live."

"Well, no she doesn't," Rhoda said. "She's just an old white trash country woman and if Momma knew where I was she'd have a fit."

"Your momma is a very stupid person," he said. "And I'm sorry I ever let her raise you." He turned his back to her then and stalked on out of the woods to a road that ran like a red scar up the side of the mountain. "Come on," he said. "I'm going to take you up there and show you where coal comes from. Maybe you can learn one thing this week."

"I learn things all the time," she said. "I already know more than half the people I know . . . I know . . ."

"Please don't talk anymore this morning," he said. "I'm burned out talking to you."

He put her into a jeep and began driving up the steep unpaved road. In a minute he was feeling better, cheered up by the sight of the big Caterpillar tractors moving dirt. If there was one thing that always cheered him up it was the sight of a big shovel moving dirt. "This is Blue Gem coal," he said. "The hardest in the area. See the layers. Topsoil, then gravel and dirt or clay, then slate, then thirteen feet of pure coal. Some people think it was made by dinosaurs. Other people think God put it there."

"This is it?" she said. "This is the mine?" It looked like one of his road construction projects. Same yellow tractors, same disorderly activity. The only difference seemed to be the huge piles of coal and a conveyor belt going down the mountain to a train.

"This is it," he said. "This is where they stored the old dinosaurs."

"Well, it is made out of dinosaurs," she said. "There

were a lot of leaves and trees and dinosaurs and then they died and the coal and oil is made out of them."

"All right," he said. "Let's say I'll go along with the coal. But tell me this, who made the slate then? Who put the slate right on top of the coal everywhere it's found in the world? Who laid the slate down on top of the dinosaurs?"

"I don't know who put the slate there," she said. "We haven't got that far yet."

"You haven't got that far?" he said. "You mean the scientists haven't got as far as the slate yet? Well, Sister, that's the problem with you folks that evolved out of monkeys. You're still half-baked. You aren't finished like us old dumb ones that God made."

"I didn't say the scientists hadn't got that far," she said. "I just said I hadn't got that far."

"It's a funny thing to me how all those dinosaurs came up here to die in the mountains and none of them died in the farmland," he said. "It sure would have made it a lot easier on us miners if they'd died down there on the flat."

While she was groping around for an answer he went right on. "Tell me this, Sister," he said. "Are any of your monkey ancestors in there with the dinosaurs, or is it just plain dinosaurs? I'd like to know who all I'm digging up . . . I'd like to give credit . . ."

The jeep had come to a stop and Joe was coming towards them, hurrying out of the small tin-roofed office with a worried look on his face. "Mr. D, you better call up to Jellico. Beb's been looking everywhere for you. They had a run-in with a teamster organizer. You got to call him right away."

"What's wrong?" Rhoda said. "What happened?"

"Nothing you need to worry about, Sister," her father said. He turned to Joe. "Go find Preacher and tell him to drive Rhoda back to your house. You go on now, honey. I've got work to do." He gave her a kiss on the cheek and disappeared into the office. A small shriveled-looking man came limping out of a building and climbed into the driver's seat. "I'm Preacher," he said. "Mr. Joe tole me to drive you up to his place."

"All right," Rhoda said. "I guess that's okay with me." Preacher put the jeep in gear and drove it slowly down the winding rutted road. By the time they got to the bottom Rhoda had thought of a better plan. "I'll drive now," she said. "I'll drive myself to Maud's. It's all right with my father. He lets me drive all the time. You can walk back, can't you?" Preacher didn't know what to say to that. He was an old drunk that Dudley and Joe kept around to run errands. He was so used to taking orders that finally he climbed down out of the jeep and did as he was told. "Show me the way to town," Rhoda said. "Draw me a map. I have to go by town on my way to Maud's." Preacher scratched his head, then bent over and drew her a little map in the dust on the hood. Rhoda studied the map, put the jeep into the first forward gear she could find and drove off down the road to the little town of Manchester, Kentucky, studying the diagram on the gearshift as she drove.

She parked beside a boardwalk that led through the main street of town and started off looking for a store that sold cigarettes. One of the stores had dresses in the window. In the center was a red strapless sundress with a white jacket. $6.95, the price tag said. I hate the way

I look, she decided. I hate these tacky pants. I've got sixty dollars. I don't have to look like this if I don't want to. I can buy anything I want.

She went inside, asked the clerk to take the dress out of the window and in a few minutes she emerged from the store wearing the dress and a pair of leather sandals with two-inch heels. The jacket was thrown carelessly over her shoulder like Gene Tierney in *Leave Her to Heaven.* I look great in red, she was thinking, catching a glimpse of herself in a store window. It isn't true that redheaded people can't wear red. She walked on down the boardwalk, admiring herself in every window.

She walked for two blocks looking for a place to try her luck getting cigarettes. She was almost to the end of the boardwalk when she came to a pool hall. She stood in the door looking in, smelling the dark smell of tobacco and beer. The room was deserted except for a man leaning on a cue stick beside a table and a boy with black hair seated behind a cash register reading a book. The boy's name was Johnny Hazard and he was sixteen years old. The book he was reading was *U.S.A.* by John Dos Passos. A woman who came to Manchester to teach poetry writing had given him the book. She had made a dust jacket for it out of brown paper so he could read it in public. On the spine of the jacket she had written, *American History.*

"I'd like a package of Lucky Strikes," Rhoda said, holding out a twenty-dollar bill in his direction.

"We don't sell cigarettes to minors," he said. "It's against the law."

"I'm not a minor," Rhoda said. "I'm eighteen. I'm Rhoda Manning. My daddy owns the mine."

"Which mine?" he said. He was watching her breasts as she talked, getting caught up in the apricot skin against the soft red dress.

"The mine," she said. "The Manning mine. I just got here the other day. I haven't been downtown before."

"So, how do you like our town?"

"Please sell me some cigartttes," she said. "I'm about to have a fit for a Lucky."

"I can't sell you cigarettes," he said. "You're not any more eighteen years old than my dog."

"Yes, I am," she said. "I drove here in a jeep, doesn't that prove anything?" She was looking at his wide shoulders and the tough flat chest beneath his plaid shirt.

"Are you a football player?" she said.

"When I have time," he said. "When I don't have to work on the nights they have games."

"I'm a cheerleader where I live," Rhoda said. "I just got elected again for next year."

"What kind of a jeep?" he said.

"An old one," she said. "It's filthy dirty. They use it at the mine." She had just noticed the package of Camels in his breast pocket.

"If you won't sell me a whole package, how about selling me one," she said. "I'll give you a dollar for a cigarette." She raised the twenty-dollar bill and laid it down on the glass counter.

He ignored the twenty-dollar bill, opened the cash register, removed a quarter and walked over to the jukebox. He walked with a precise, balanced sort of cockiness, as if he knew he could walk any way he wanted but had carefully chosen this particular walk as his own. He walked across the room through the rectangle of light coming in the door, walking as though he were the first boy ever to be in the world, the first boy ever to walk across a room and put a quarter into a jukebox. He pushed a button and music filled the room.

Kaw-Liga was a wooden Indian a-standing by the door,
He fell in love with an Indian maid
Over in the antique store.

"My uncle wrote that song," he said, coming back to her. "But it got ripped off by some promoters in Nashville. I'll make you a deal," he said. "I'll give you a cigarette if you'll give me a ride somewhere I have to go." "All right," Rhoda said. "Where do you want to go?"

"Out to my cousin's," he said. "It isn't far."

"Fine," Rhoda said. Johnny told the lone pool player to keep an eye on things and the two of them walked out into the sunlight, walking together very formally down the street to where the jeep was parked.

"Why don't you let me drive," he said. "It might be easier." She agreed and he drove on up the mountain to a house that looked deserted. He went in and returned carrying a guitar in a case, a blanket, and a quart bottle with a piece of wax paper tied around the top with a rubber band.

"What's in the bottle?" Rhoda said.

"Lemonade, wtih a little sweetening in it."

"Like whiskey?"

"Yeah. Like whiskey. Do you ever drink it?"

"Sure," she said. "I drink a lot. In Saint Louis we had this club called The Four Roses that met every Monday at Donna Duston's house to get drunk. I thought it up, the club I mean."

"Well, here's your cigarette," he said. He took the package from his pocket and offered her one, holding it near his chest so she had to get in close to take it.

"Oh, God," she said. "Oh, thank you so much. I'm about to die for a ciggie. I haven't had one in days. Because my father dragged me up here to make me stop smoking. He's always trying to make me do something I don't want to do. But it never works. I'm very hardheaded, like him." She took the light Johnny offered her and blew out the smoke in a small controlled stream. "God, I love to smoke," she said.

"I'm glad I could help you out," he said. "Anytime you want one when you're here you just come on over. Look," he said. "I'm going somewhere you might want to see, if you're not in a hurry to get back. You got time to go and see something with me?"

"What is it?" she asked.

"Something worth seeing," he said. "The best thing in Clay County there is to see."

"Sure," she said. "I'll go. I never turn down an adventure. Why not, that's what my cousins in the Delta always say. Whyyyyyyy not." They drove up the mountain and parked and began to walk into the woods along a path. The woods were deeper here than where Rhoda had been that morning, dense and green and cool. She felt silly walking in the woods in the little high-heeled sandals, but she held on to Johnny's hand and followed him deeper and deeper into the trees, feeling grown up and brave and romantic. I'll bet he thinks I'm the bravest girl he ever met, she thought. I'll bet he thinks at last he's met a girl who's not afraid of anything. Rhoda was walking along imagining tearing off a piece of her dress for a tourniquet in case Johnny was bit by a poisonous snake. She was pulling the tourniquet tighter and tighter when the trees opened onto a small brilliant blue pond. The water was so blue Rhoda thought for a moment it must be some sort of trick. He stood there watching her while she took it in.

"What do you think?" he said at last.

"My God," she said. "What is it?"

"It's Blue Pond," he said. "People come from all over the world to see it."

"Who made it?" Rhoda said. "Where did it come from?"

"Springs. Rock springs. No one knows how deep down it goes, but more than a hundred feet because divers have been that far."

"I wish I could swim in it," Rhoda said. "I'd like to jump in there and swim all day."

"Come over here, cheerleader," he said. "Come sit over here by me and we'll watch the light on it. I brought this teacher from New York here last year. She said is was the best thing she'd ever seen in her life. She's a writer. Anyway, the thing she likes about Blue Pond is watching the light change on the water. She taught me a lot when she was here. About things like that."

Rhoda moved nearer to him, trying to hold in her stomach.

"My father really likes this part of the country," she said. "He says people up here are the salt of the earth. "He says all the people up here are direct descendants from England and Scotland and Wales. I think he wants us to move up here and stay, but my mother won't let us. It's all because the unions keep messing with his mine that he has to be up here all the time. If it wasn't for the unions everything would be going fine. You aren't for the unions, are you?"

"I'm for myself," Johnny said. "And for my kinfolks." He was tired of her talking then and reached for her and pulled her into his arms, paying no attention to her small resistances, until finally she was stretched out under him on the earth and he moved the dress from her breasts and held them in his hands. He could smell the wild smell of her craziness and after a while he took the dress off and the soft white cotton underpants and touched her over and over again. Then he entered her with the way he had of doing things, gently and with a good sense of the natural rhythms of the earth.

I'm doing it, Rhoda thought. I'm doing it. This is doing it. This is what it feels like to be doing it.

"This doesn't hurt a bit," she said out loud. "I think I love you, Johnny. I love, love, love you. I've been waiting all my life for you."

"Don't talk so much," he said. "It's better if you stop talking."

And Rhoda was quiet and he made love to her as the sun was leaving the earth and the afternoon breeze moved in the trees. Here was every possible tree, hickory and white oak and redwood and sumac and maple, all in thick foliage now, and he made love to her with great tenderness, forgetting he had set out to fuck the boss's daughter, and he kept on making love to her until she began to tighten around him, not knowing what she was doing, or where she was going, or even that there was anyplace to be going to.

Dudley was waiting outside the trailer when she drove up. There was a sky full of cold stars behind him, and he was pacing up and down and talking to himself like a crazy man. Maud was inside the trailer crying her heart out and only Joe had kept his head and was going back and forth from one to the other telling them everything would be all right.

Dudley was pacing up and down talking to Jesus. I know I had it coming, he was saying. I know goddamn well I had it coming. But not her. Where in the hell is she? You get her back in one piece and I'll call Valerie and break it off. I won't see Valerie ever again as long as I live. *But you've got to get me back my little girl. Goddammit, you get me back my girl.*

Then he was crying, his head thrown back and raised up to the stars as the jeep came banging up the hill in third gear. Rhoda parked it and got out and started walking toward him, all bravado and disdain.

Dudley smelled it on her before he even touched her. Smelled it all over her and began to shake her, screaming at her to tell him who it had been. Then Joe came running out from the trailer and threw his hundred and fifty pounds between them, and Maud was right behind him. She led Rhoda into the trailer and put her into bed and sat beside her, bathing her head with a damp towel until she fell asleep.

"I'll find out who it was," Dudley said, shaking his fist. "I'll find out who it was."

"You don't know it was anybody," Joe said. "You don't even know what happened, Mr. D. Now you got to calm down and in the morning we'll find out what happened. More than likely she's just been holed up somewhere trying to scare you."

"I know what happened," Dudley said. "I already know what happened."

"Well, you can find out who it was and you can kill him if you have to," Joe said. "If it's true and you still want to in the morning, you can kill him."

But there would be no killing. By the time the moon was high, Johnny Hazard was halfway between Lexington, Kentucky and Cincinnati, Ohio, with a bus ticket he bought with the fifty dollars he'd taken from Rhoda's pocket. He had called the poetry teacher and told her he was coming. Johnny had decided it was time to see the world. After all, that very afternoon a rich cheerleader had cried in his arms and given him her cherry. There was no telling what might happen next.

Much later that night Rhoda woke up in the small room, hearing the wind come up in the trees. The window was open and the moon, now low in the sky and covered with mist, poured a diffused light upon the bed. Rhoda sat up in the bed and shivered. Why did I do that with him? she thought. Why in the world did I do that? But I couldn't help it, she decided. He's so sophisticated and he's so good-looking and he's a wonderful driver and he plays a guitar. She moved her hands along her thighs, trying to remember exactly what it was they had done, trying to remember the details, wondering where she could find him in the morning.

But Dudley had other plans for Rhoda in the morning. By noon she was on her way home in a chartered plane. Rhoda had never been on an airplane of any kind before, but she didn't let on.

"I'm thinking of starting a diary," she was saying to the pilot, arranging her skirt so her knees would show. "A lot of unusual things have been happening to me lately. The boy I love is dying of cancer in Saint Louis. It's very sad, but I have to put up with it. He wants me to write a lot of books and dedicate them to his memory."

The pilot didn't seem to be paying much attention, so Rhoda gave up on him and went back into her own head.

In her head Bob Rosen was alive after all. He was walking along a street in Greenwich Village and passed a bookstore with a window full of her books, many copies stacked in a pyramid with her picture on every cover. He recognized the photograph, ran into the bookstore, grabbed a book, opened it and saw the dedication. *To Bob Rosen, Te Amo Forever, Rhoda.*

Then Bob Rosen, or maybe it was Johnny Hazard, or maybe this unfriendly pilot, stood there on that city street, looking up at the sky, holding the book against his chest, crying and broken-hearted because Rhoda was lost to him forever, this famous author, who could have been his, lost to him forever.

Thirty years later Rhoda woke up in a hotel room in New York City. There was a letter lying on the floor where she had thrown it when she went to bed. She picked it up and read it again. *Take my name off that book*, the letter said. *Imagine a girl with your advantages writing a book like that. You mother is so ashamed of you.*

Goddamn you, Rhoda thought. Goddamn you to hell. She climbed back into the bed and pulled the pillows over her head. She lay there for a while feeling sorry for herself. Then she got up and walked across the room and pulled a legal pad out of a briefcase and started writing.

Dear Father,

You take my *name off those checks you send those television preachers and those goddamn right-wing politicians. That name has come to me from a hundred generations of men and women . . . also, in the future let my mother speak for herself about my work.*

Love,
Rhoda

P.S. The slate was put there by the second law of thermodynamics. Some folks call it gravity. Other folks call it God.

I guess it was the second law, she thought. It was the second law or the third law or something like that. She leaned back in the chair, looking at the ceiling. Maybe I'd better find out before I mail it.

❧❧❧

The Lower Garden District Free Gravity Mule Blight or Rhoda, a Fable

RHODA woke up dreaming. In the dream she was crushing the skulls of Jody's sheepdogs. Or else she was crushing the skulls of Jody's sisters. Or else she was crushing Jody's skull. Jody was the husband she was leaving. Crunch, crunch, crunch went the skulls between her hands, beneath her heels.

As the dream ended her father was taking her to the police station so she could turn herself in. The family was all over the place, weeping and wringing their hands. Her mother's face was small and broken, peering down from the stairwell.

She woke from the dream feeling wonderful, feeling purged of evil. She pulled on Jody's old velour bathrobe and sat down at the dining room table to go over her lists. Getting a divorce was easy as pie. There was nothing to it. All you needed was money. All you needed for anything was money. Well, it was true. She went back to her lists.

Today the real estate agent was coming to see the house. Then she would sell it. Then she would get a cute little shotgun apartment in the Faubourg-Marigny. Then she would get a job. Then she would get a new boyfriend. Everything would fall into place. Jody would hang himself and the will would still be made out in her favor and she would quit her job and go live in New York. In the meantime she might have to be poorer than she was accustomed to being.

That's okay, she told herself. She took off her robe and went into the dressing room and stood in front of the mirror. Dolphins don't have anything, she told herself. A hawk possesses nothing. Albert Einstein wore tennis shoes. I am a dolphin, she decided. I am a hawk high in the Cascade Mountains. I am not a checkbook. I am not a table. I am not a chair.

She got into the bathtub and ran the water all the way to the top, pretending she was a dolphin in the summer seas somewhere off the coast of Martinique or Aruba. The morning sun was coming in the window, making long slanting lines on the walls and shutters and the water in the tub . . . now what about those tablecloths, she began thinking, imagining the contents of a closet she hadn't opened in years. What am I going to do about all those tablecloths? She saw them stacked in rows, tied with small blue ribbons, monogrammed with her initials and her mother's initials and her grandmother's initials. Oh, God, she thought, what will I do with all those goddamn tablecloths? There won't be room for them in a tiny house in the Faubourg-Marigny. She sat up in the tub and began cleaning the mortar between the tiles with a fingernail brush.

She had worked her way up to the hot water faucet when the phone rang. "Now what?" she said. She jumped out of the bathtub and padded into the bedroom and answered it. She grabbed the receiver and threw herself down on the unmade bed, letting the sheets dry her body.

"Mrs. Wells," the soft black voice said. "I hope I didn't wake you. I've been trying to get hold of you for days."

"Who is it?" she said. But she knew who it was. It was the insurance adjuster who was in charge of her claim for the diamond ring she had sold last month.

"It's Earl," he said. "Earl Treadway. Remember, we talked last week."

"Oh, Earl. I'm so glad you called. I talked to Father Ryan about getting your son into the summer arts program. He said he was sure it could be arranged. Are you still interested in that?" Five thousand dollars, she was thinking. She shivered, a wonderful shiver that went all the way from her scalp to her groin. Five thousand dollars. Easy as pie.

"I told my son about talking to you," the black voice said. "He was excited about it. But listen, before we start talking about that. I need to see you about your claim. I think we have it straightened out now."

"Oh, God," she said. "I'd almost forgotten about it. It's all so embarrassing. I can't believe I left that ring lying out when there were workmen in the house. I guess

I've just always been too trusting. I just couldn't believe it would happen to me."

"It happens to everyone sooner or later," he said. "That's what I'm for. Look, would it be possible for me to come by on my way to work? I have the check. I'd like to go on and deliver it."

"A check?"

"For four thousand, six hundred and forty-three dollars. Will that settle it?"

"Oh, well, yes. I mean, a check. I didn't know they did those things that fast. But, sure, come on by. I mean, I'm up and dressed. How long will it take you to get here? I mean, sure, that'll be fine. Then this afternoon I can go out and start shopping for a new diamond, can't I?"

"I'll be by in about thirty minutes then," he said. "I'm glad you were there. I'm glad it's all worked out. I'm looking forward to meeting you after all these nice talks we've had." Earl hung up the phone and leaned back against the refrigerator. The baby's bottle had spilled milk on the counter. He reached for a rag to wipe it up, then changed his mind and left it there. He straightened his tie and took his coat off the back of the highchair and put it on. It was too hot for his corduory suit but he was wearing it anyway. All those nice talks, he was thinking. All those nice long talks.

Rhoda rolled off the bed and started trying on clothes. She settled on a tennis skirt and a red sweater. They love red, she told herself. They love bright colors. Besides, what had she read about red? Wear red, red keeps you safe.

Well, I don't need anything to keep me safe, she thought. All I'm doing is cheating an insurance company. It's the first time I ever stole anything in my life except that one time in the fifth grade. Everybody gets to steal something sooner or later. I mean, that little Jew stole my ring, didn't he? And Jody stole five years of my life. And this black man's going to bring that check and I'm going to take it and I don't give a damn whether it's honest or not.

She sat down on a chair and pulled on her tennis shoes and tied the strings in double knots.

Cheating an insurance company hadn't been Rhoda's idea. All she had started out to do was sell her engagement ring. All she had done was get up one morning and take her engagement ring down to the French Quarter to sell it. A perfect stone, a two-carat baguette. A perfect stone for a perfect girl, Gabe Adler had said when he sold it to Jody. It was insured for five thousand dollars. Rhoda had thought all she had to do was go downtown and turn it in and collect the money.

She drove to the Quarter, parked the car in the Royal Orleans parking lot and proceeded to carry the ring from antique store to antique store. One after the other the owners held the diamond up to the light, admired it and handed it back. "There's a place down on the Avenue that's buying stones," the last dealer told her. "Near Melepomene, on the Avenue. A new place. I heard they were giving good prices. You might try there."

"Oh, I don't think I really want to sell it," she said, slipping it back on her finger. "I just wanted to see what it was worth. I'm a reporter, did you know that? It would be a real pity if all those people out there buying diamonds found out what it's like to try to sell one, wouldn't it? If they found out what a racket you guys have going? This ring's insured for seven thousand dollars. But no one will give me half of that. I ought to write an article about it. I ought to let the public in on this."

"There's no need to talk like that," the man said. He was a big, sad-looking man in baggy pants. He took the glass out of his eye; his big droopy face was the shape of one of his chandeliers. "There's no need for that." A group of tourists lifted their eyes from the cases and turned to watch.

"You antique dealers are just a bunch of robbers," Rhoda said as loudly as she could. "Selling all this goddamn junk to people. And the jewelry stores are worse. How can my ring be worth seven thousand dollars if no one will buy it when I want to sell it? You want to tell me that? You want to explain that to me?"

"Leave the store," the man said, coming around the counter. "You just go on now and leave the store." He was moving toward her, his stomach marching before him like a drum. Rhoda retreated

"Thanks for the diamond lesson," she said. "I'll be able to use that in my work."

The place at Melepomene and Saint Charles was a modern showroom in an old frame house. There were gardens in front and a shiny red enamel door. This looks more like it, Rhoda thought. She opened the door and went inside, pretending to be interested in the watches in a case. "Can I help you?" the boy behind the counter said. He was a very young boy dressed like an old man. "I don't know," she said. "I have some jewelry I'm thinking of selling. Some people I know said this was a good place. I'm thinking of selling some things I don't wear anymore and getting a Rolex instead. I see you sell them."

"What was it you wanted to sell? Did you bring it with you?"

"I might sell this," she said, taking off the ring and handing it to him. "If I could get a good enough price. I'm tired of it. I'm bored with wearing rings anyway. See what you think it's worth."

He took the ring between his chubby fingers and held it up above him. He looked at it a moment, then put a glass into his eye. "It's flawed," he said. "No one is buying diamonds now. The prime was twenty percent this morning."

"It is not flawed," she said. "It came from Adler's. It's a perfect stone. It's insured for six thousand dollars."

"I'll give you nine hundred," he said. "Take it or leave it."

"How old are you?" she said. "You don't look like you're old enough to be buying diamonds."

"I'm twenty-five," he said. "I run this place for my father. I've been running it since it opened. Do you want to sell this ring or not? That's my only offer."

"I don't know," she said. "It's insured for six thousand dollars. I only meant to sell it for a lark."

"Well, I guess it depends on how badly you need the money," he said. "Of course if you don't like the ring there's not much sense in keeping it."

"Oh, I don't need the money." She had drawn herself up so she could look at him on a slant. "My husband's a physician. I don't need money for a thing. I just wanted to get rid of some junk." She squared her shoulders. "On the other hand I might sell it just so I wouldn't have to bother with keeping it insured. There's a painting I want to buy, at the Bienville. I could sell the ring and buy that painting. It's all irrelevant anyway. I mean, it's all just junk. It's all just possessions."

"Well, make up your mind," he said. He held the ring out to her on a polishing cloth. "It's up to you."

"I'll just keep it," she said. "I wouldn't dream of selling a ring that valuable for nine hundred dollars."

It was almost a week before she went back to sell the ring. "Seven hundred and fifty," he said. "That's the best I can do."

"But you said nine hundred. You definitely said nine hundred."

"That was last week. You should have sold it then." Rhoda looked into his little myopic piggy eyes, hating him with all her clean white Anglo-Teutonic heart. "I'll take it," she said, and handed him the ring.

He left the room. She sat down in a chair beside his desk, feeling powerless and used. He came back into the room. She was trying not to look at his hands, which were holding a stack of bills.

"Here you are," he said. "We don't keep records of these things, you know. We don't give receipts."

"What do you mean?" she said.

"There isn't any record. In case you want to file a claim."

She took the money from him and stuffed it into her handbag without counting it. "My God," she said. Her power was returning. She felt it coursing up her veins. Her veins were charged with power. A thousand white horses of pure moral power pouring up and down her neck and face and legs and arms and hands. "I've never filed an insurance claim in my life," she said. "I probably wouldn't bother to file one if I actually lost something." She stood up. "You are really just the epitome of too goddamn much, are you aware of that?" Then she left, going out into the sweltering heat of the summer day, out onto the Avenue where a streetcar was chugging merrily by.

I'm going to turn them in, she thought. As soon as I get home I'll call the mayor's office and then I'll call the Better Business Bureau and then I'll write a letter to *Figaro* and the *Times-Picayune*. I'll get that little fat Jewish bastard. My God, it must be terrible to be a nice Jew and have to be responsible for people like that. That's the strangest thing, how they all get lumped together in our minds, a saint like Doctor Bernstein and a little bastard like that. No wonder they all want to move to Israel. Oh, well. She got into the car and opened her bag and counted the money. Seven hundred and fifty dollars. Well, it would pay the bills.

It was several days before she called the insurance company and filed the claim. "It was right there in the jewelry box on the dresser where I always leave it," she told the police when they came to make a report. "I can't imagine who would take it. My housekeeper is the most honest person in this city. My friends come in and out but none of them would touch it. I just don't know . . ."

"Have you had any work done on the house?" The

police officer was young. He was standing in the doorway to her bedroom getting a hard-on but he was trying to ignore it. She was very pretty. With a big ass. He liked that in a woman. It reminded him of his mother. He shifted his revolver to the front and cocked his head sideways, giving her his late night look.

"Oh," she was saying. "I forgot all about that. I had the bedrooms painted last month. I had a whole crew of painters here for three days. You don't think . . . I mean, they all work for Mr. Sanders. He's as honest as the day is long. He paints for everyone. Still, the ring is gone. It isn't here. It was here and now it isn't."

"I'd bet on the painters," the policeman said. "There's been a lot of that going on lately. This is the third claim like this I've had in a week. In this same neighborhood."

"But why would he only take the ring?" Rhoda said. "Why didn't he take anything else? There was other jewelry here. Expensive things."

"They're after diamonds. And flat silver. They don't mess with small stuff. No, I think we've got a pretty professional job here. Looks like he knew what he was looking for."

"I only want my ring back," she told Earl the first time he called. "Or one just like it to replace it. I'm so embarrassed about this. I've never filed an insurance claim of any kind. But everyone said I had to go on and report it. I didn't want to."

"There's a lot of unemployment right now," he said. "It makes things happen."

"I know," she said. "That's why I hate to report this. I don't want to get anyone in trouble, any poor person or someone that had to steal to eat or something like that."

"You sure sound like a nice lady. I'd sure like to meet you sometime."

"Well, sure," she said. "Before this is over we'll have to see about that."

That had been the beginning. He had called her several times, asking for details of the robbery, checking facts. The conversations had drifted into discussions of movies, city politics, civil rights, athletics, her divorce, his divorce, his little boy, her connections that could get his little boy into a summer painting program. Somewhere along the way she told him the rest of the robbery story and he filed the claim and the money had been sent on its way from the home office of the insurance company.

Then he was there, standing on her doorstep, all dressed up in a corduroy suit with an oxford cloth shirt and a striped tie, six feet three inches tall, soft brown eyes, kinky black hair.

"Come on in the kitchen," she said. "Come have a cup of coffee." She led him through a dining room filled with plants. Rhoda's whole house was filled with plants. There were plants of every kind in every room. Lush, cool, every color of green, overflowing their terra-cotta pots, spilling out onto the floor. It took the maid all day Tuesday to water them. Earl followed her into the kitchen and sat down on a maple captain's chair. He put his briefcase beside him and folded his hands on the breakfast room table. He smiled at her. She was trying not to look at the briefcase but her eyes kept going in that direction.

"Where are you from, Earl Treadway?" she said.

"Where in the Delta did you escape from with that accent? Or is it Georgia?"

"I escaped from Rosedale," he said. He was laughing. He wasn't backing off an inch. "My daddy was a sharecropper. How about you?"

"I escaped from Issaquena County," she said. "Sixty miles away. Well, I only lived there in the summers. In the winter I lived in Indiana. I lived up north a lot when I was young."

"Are you married? Oh, no, that's right. You told me you were getting a divorce. We talked so much I forgot half the things we said." He picked up a placemat from a stack of them at the end of the table. It was a blue and yellow laminated map of the British Virgin Islands, bright blue water, yellow islands. The names of the islands were in large block letters, Tortola, Beef Island, Virgin Gorda, Peter Island, Salt Island, The Indians. All the places Rhoda had been with her husband, Jody, summer after boring summer, arguing and being miserable on the big expensive sailboat. Dinner on board or in some polite resort. Long hungover mornings with whiskey bottles and ashtrays and cigarettes and cracker crumbs all over the deck. Anchored in some hot civilized little harbor. While somewhere ashore, down one of the dirt roads where Jody never let her go, oh, there Rhoda imagined real life was going on, a dark musky, musical real life, loud jump-ups she heard at night, hot black wildness going on and on into the night while she sat on the boat with her husband and people they brought along from New Orleans, gossiping about people they knew, planning their careful little diving trips for the morning, checking the equipment, laughing good-naturedly about their escapades in the water, wild adventures thirty feet below the dinghy with a native guide.

Earl picked up one of the placemats and held it in his hand. "What is this?" he said again. He was looking right at her. His face was so big, his mouth so red and full, his voice so deep and rich and kind. It was cool in the room. So early in the morning. I wonder what he smells like, she thought. I wonder what it would be like to touch his hair.

"My husband bought those," she said. "They're maps of the British Virgin Islands, where I have a sailboat. I used to go there every summer. I know that place like the back of my hand. I've been bored to death on every island in the Sir Francis Drake Channel. I guess I still own part of the sailboat. I forgot to ask. Well, anyway, that's what it is. On the other hand, it's a placemat."

"I like maps," he said. "I remember the first one I ever saw, a map of the world. I used to stay after school to look at it. I was trying to find the way out of Rosedale." She smiled and he went on. "Later, I had a job at a filling station and I could get all the maps I wanted. I was getting one of every state. I wanted to put them on a wall and make the whole United States.

"How old are you?" she said.

"I'm thirty-four. How old are you?"

"I'm thirty-four. Think of that. Our mothers could have passed each other on the street with us in their stomachs."

"You say the funniest things of anyone I ever talked to. I was thinking that when I'd talk to you on the phone. You think real deep, don't you?"

"Oh, I don't know. I read all the time. I read Albert Einstein a lot. Oh, not the part about the physics. I read his letters and about political systems and things like that. Yeah, I guess that's true. I guess I do think deep."

"You really own a sailboat in this place?" he said. He was still holding the placemat.

"I guess I do. I forgot to put it in the divorce." She laughed. His hand had let the placemat drop. His hand was very near to hers. "It isn't nearly as much fun as it looks in the pictures," she said. "It's really pretty crowded. There are boats all over the place there now, big power boats from Puerto Rico. It's all terribly middle class really. A lot of people pretending to have adventures." She was looking at the briefcase out of the corner of her eye. It was still there. Why don't you go on and give me the check, she wanted to say, and then I'll give you a piece of ass and we'll be square. She sighed. "What did you want to talk to me about? About settling the robbery I mean."

"Just to finalize everything. To give you the check they cut this morning."

"All right," she said. "Then go on and give it to me. Just think, Earl, in my whole life I never collected any insurance. It makes me feel like a criminal. Well, you're an insurance salesman. Make me believe in insurance."

He picked up the briefcase and set it down in front of him on the table. "Will this hurt the finish on your table? It's such a pretty table. I wouldn't want to scratch it up."

"Oh, no," she said. "It's all right. It's an old table. It's got scratches all over it."

He opened the briefcase and moved papers and took out the check. He held it out very formally to her. "I'm sorry about the ring," he said. "I hope this will help you get another one."

She took it from him. Then she laid it carelessly down behind her on a counter. She laid it down a few inches away from a puddle of water that had condensed around a green watering can. Once she had put it there she would not touch it again while he was watching. "Thanks for bringing it by. You could have mailed it."

"I wanted to meet you. I wanted to get to know you."

"So did I," she said. Her eyes dug into his skin, thick black skin. real black skin. Something she had never had. It was cool in the room. Three thousand dollars' worth of brand-new air-conditioning was purring away outside the window. Inside everything was white and green. White woodwork, green plants, baskets of plants in every window, ferns and philodendrons and bromeliads, gloxinia and tillansias and cordatum. Leaves and shadows of leaves and wallpaper that looked like leaves. "What are you doing tonight?" she said. "What are you doing for dinner?"

"I'll be putting napkins in your lap and cutting up your steak if you'll go out with me," he said. "We'll go someplace nice. Anywhere you want."

"What time?"

"I have to go to a meeting first. A community meeting where I live. I'm chairman of my neighborhood association. It might be eight or nine before I can get away. Is that too late?" He had closed his briefcase and was standing up.

"I'll be waiting," she said. He locked the briefcase and came out from beside the table. "Don't lose that check," he said. It was still sitting on the edge of the counter.

The circle of water was closing in. "Don't get it wet. It would be a lot of trouble to get them to make another one."

When he was gone Rhoda straightend up the house and made the bed. She put all the dishes in the dishwasher and watered the plants. She cleaned off the counters one by one. She moved the watering can and wiped up the ring of water. Then she picked up the check and read the amount. Four thousand six hundred and forty-three dollars. Eight months of freedom at five hundred dollars a month. And forty-three dollars to waste. I'll waste it today, she decided. She picked up the phone and called the beauty parlor.

Six o'clock is the time of day in New Orleans when the light cools down, coming in at angles around the tombs in the cemeteries, between the branches of the live oak trees along the avenues, casting shadows across the yards, penetrating the glass of a million windows.

Rhoda always left the drapes open in the afternoons so she could watch the light travel around the house. She would turn on "The World of Jazz" and dress for dinner while the light moved around the rooms. Two hours, she thought, dropping her clothes on the floor of her bedroom. Two hours to make myself into a goddess. She shaved her legs and gave herself a manicure and rubbed perfumed lotion all over her body and started trying on clothes. Rhoda had five closets full of clothes. She had thousands of dollars' worth of skirts and jackets and blouses and dresses and shoes and scarves and handbags.

She opened a closet in the hall. She took out a white

lace dress she had worn one night to have dinner with a senator. She put the soft silk-lined dress on top of her skin. Then, one by one, she buttoned up every one of the fifty-seven tiny pearl buttons of the bodice and sleeves. The dress had a blue silk belt. Rhoda dropped it on the closet floor. She opened a drawer and found a red scarf and tied it around the waist of the dress. She looked in the mirror. It was almost right. But not quite right. She took one of Jody's old ties off a tie rack and tied that around the waist. There, that was perfect. "A Brooks Brothers' tie," she said out loud. "The one true tie of power."

She went into the kitchen and took a bottle of wine out of the refrigerator and poured herself a glass and began to walk around the house. She stopped in the den and put a Scott Joplin record on the stereo and then she began to dance, waving the wineglass in the air, waiting for Earl to come. She danced into the bedroom and took the check out of a drawer where she had hidden it and held it up and kissed it lavishly all over. Jesus loves the little children, she was singing. All the children of the world. Red and yellow, black and white, all are precious, precious, precious. Four thousand, six hundred and forty-three dollars and thirty-seven cents. A day's work. At last, a real day's work.

The doorbell was ringing. She set the wineglass down on the table and walked wildly down the hall to the door. "I'm coming," she called out. "I'll be right there."

"Now what I'd really like to do with you," Earl was saying, "is to go fishing." They were at Dante's by the River, a restaurant down at the end of Carrollton Avenue. They had stuffed themselves on Crab Thibodeaux and Shrimp Mousse and Softshell Crabs Richard and were starting in on the roast quail. It was a recipe with a secret sauce perfected in Drew, Mississippi, where Earl's grandfather had been horsewhipped on the street for smarting off to a white man. But that was long ago and the sauce tasted wonderful to Rhoda and Earl.

"I'm stuffed," she said. "How can I eat all this? I won't be able to move, much less make love to you. I am going to make love to you, you know that, don't you?"

"If you say so," he said. "Now, listen, Miss Rhoda, did you hear what I said about going fishing?"

"What about it?"

"I want to take you fishing. I'm famous for my fishing. I won a fishing rodeo one time."

"We don't have to do it tonight, do we? I mean, I have other plans for tonight as I just told you."

"We'll pretend we're fishing," he said. "How about that?" He was laughing at her but she didn't care. Black people had laughed at Rhoda all her life. All her life she had been making black people laugh.

"What are you thinking of?" he said.

"I was thinking about when I was little and my mother would take me to Mississippi for the summer and if I wanted attention I would take off my underpants and the black people would all die laughing and the white people would grab me up and make me put them back on. Well, I guess that's a racist thing to say, isn't it?"

"You want to see if it makes me laugh?"

"Yeah, I do. So hurry up and finish eating. When I think of something I like to go right on and do it. In case they blow the world up while I'm waiting." Earl took a piece of French toast and buttered it and laid it on her plate. "Are you sure you aren't married, Earl? I made a vow not to mess around with married men. I've had enough of that stuff. That's why I'm getting a divorce. Because I kept having these affairs and I'd have to go home and eat dinner and there the other person would be. With no one to eat dinner with. That doesn't seem right, does it? After they'd made love to me all afternoon? So I'm getting a divorce. Now I'll have to be poor for a while but I don't care. It's better than being an adultress, don't you think so?" She picked up the bread and put it back on his plate.

"Why don't you stop talking and finish your quail?"

"I can't stop talking when I'm nervous. It's how I protect myself." She pulled her hand back into her lap. Rhoda hated to be reminded that she talked too much.

"I'm not married," he said. "I told you that on the phone. I've got a little boy and I keep him part of the time. Remember, we talked about that before. It's all right. There isn't anything to be afraid of." He felt like he did when he coached his Little League baseball team. That's the way she made him feel. One minute she reminded him of a movie star. The next minute she reminded him of a little boy on his team who sucked his glove all the time. "We've got plenty of time to get to know each other. We don't have to hurry to do anything."

"Tell me about yourself," she said. "Tell me all the good parts first. You can work in the bad parts later."

"Well, I'm the oldest one of thirteen children. I worked my way through Mississippi Southern playing football.

Then I spent three years in the Marines and now I'm in insurance. Last year I ran for office. I ran for councilman in my district and I lost but I'm going to run again. This time I'll win." He squared his shoulders. "What else? I love my family. I helped put my brothers and sisters through school. I'm proud of that." He stopped a moment and looked at her. "I've never known anyone like you. I changed shirts three times trying to get ready to come and get you."

"That's enough," she said. "Pay for this food and let's get out of here."

"My grandmother was a free woman from Natchez," he continued. They were in the car driving along the Avenue. "A light-skinned woman, what you'd call an octoroon. She lived until last year. She was so old she lost count of the years. Her father was a man who fought with Morrell's army. I have pictures of many of my ancestors. They were never slaves . . . you sure you want to hear all this?"

"Yeah, I want to know who I'm going to bed with."

"You talk some. You have a turn."

"I have two sons. They go to school in Virginia. They're real wild. Everyone in my family's wild. It's a huge family, a network over five states. I love them but they don't have any power over me anymore. Not that they ever did. I think I'm the first person in my family to ever really escape from it. It's taken me a long time to do it. Now I'm free. I might learn to fly. I might teach in a grade school. I might be a waitress. I might move to Europe. I might learn to sew and take up hems. I don't know what I'm going to do next. But right now I'm going to go home and fuck you. I'm tired of waiting to do it. I've been waiting all day."

"So have I," he said and pulled her closer to him.

"Another thing," she said. "I stole that money from you. I sold that diamond ring you paid me for. I sold it to this fat piggy little Jewish boy on Melepomene. He paid me in cash and told me I could file a claim. I'm thinking of reporting him to the Jewish temple. Well, he thought it up. But I'm the one that did it."

"Did you see that mule?" Earl said. "That mule flying by. That's the damndest thing. A gray mule with black ears."

"I stole the money from you," she said. "The money for the diamond. Don't you care? Don't you even care?" She moved his hand from around her waist and put it between her legs.

"That's the damndest thing about those mules when they get to town," he said, turning down the street to her house. "You can't keep them on the ground. They'll take off every time. Also, I am married. I guess we might as well go on and get that on the table."

"What mule," Rhoda said. "I don't see any mules. They don't allow mules on Saint Charles Avenue."

Crazy, Crazy, Now Showing Everywhere

❧❧❧

Looking Over Jordan

LADY Margaret Sarpie felt terrible. The city of New Orleans was covered by a mile of clouds. The bathroom scales said 134. Her cousin. Devoie, had decided to stay another week. And the phone kept ringing. It had been ringing all morning. First it would ring. Then Lady Margaret would answer it. Then nothing.

"Hello," Lady Margaret would say. "Hello. Hello. Who's there? Who is it? Why are you calling me? Why are you doing this to me?"

Lady Margaret's father had been a brigadier general in the army. People weren't supposed to call Lady Margaret and hang up. They weren't even supposed to look at her unless she told them to.

She got a dial tone and called her mother to see if she could borrow the house in Mandeville for a few days. "It's that Anna Hand that's doing it. Or some of her friends. Her friends could be anybody. She could know gangsters."

"Then what did you write about her for? If you lie down with dogs you get up with fleas, Lady Margaret. I've told you that. Those people at the newspaper only want to use your name. They don't care what happens next."

"I didn't write about her. I reviewed her book. It could be the beginning of big things for me, Momma. When they called and asked me to do it I was bowled over. You could have knocked me over with a broomstick."

"And now these gangsters are calling you up and you have to go and hide in Mandeville? Well, we reap what we sow."

"Can I have the house or not? Devoie's here. She's going with me."

"Armand's there. You can't go until he leaves."

"Why did you let Armand go? He sold his half. Every time I want to go Armand's there. I mean, what's wrong with Armand getting his own summer house now that he sold out of ours. Every single time I want to go Armand's there. You might remember I'm your daughter. You might give that some thought . . . you might act like . . ." But Mrs. Sarpie had hung up. That was how the Sarpies ended their conversations with each other. Whoever got fed up, hung up.

Lady Margaret put the phone down on its receiver and began to pace up and down the living room, feeling the grainy surface of the oriental rug beneath her feet. The rug was very old and wrinkled in the center. The texture of the rug came up through the soles of Lady Margaret's feet, moved into her bloodstream, arrived at her tongue.

Her mouth felt dry, grainy and dry. Some terrible memory of the desert assailed her. The desert, and captive women weaving in the sun, spitting out the threads, weaving and spitting, spitting and weaving.

I could catch anything from this rug, she thought. God knows where this rug's been.

It was hot in the room. The air pressed against her arms. A ceiling fan turned slowly above her head. The air was thick and close, thick and tight. Lady Margaret could hardly breathe. She lay her fingers against her throat, searching for the pulse. She closed her eyes and imagined air-conditioning. Being poor wasn't working out. Being poor and living in a shotgun apartment wasn't working out. It was terrible. It wasn't working out. Nothing was working out.

I need some Homer, she decided. I'll listen to Homer. Homer'll fix me up. She took a Homer Davis album out of its cover and set it down on the turntable. She looked down at the cover, at the black face with the wild teeth and the terrible patch over one eye. The patch was black with a star in the center where the eye used to be. One night when she was drunk Lady Margaret had sat beside Homer on a piano bench at Tipitina's. She had put a twenty-dollar bill into the tip jar and sat beside him while he played, her hip almost touching his hip. He had gone on playing as if she wasn't even there. The song was called "Parchman Farm." When it was over he lifted his hands from the keys and turned to her. He reached up and removed the patch from his eye. Lady Margaret had stared into the darkness of the scar. She could not stop looking. She could not pull her eyes away.

"What you want to hear now, white lady?" Homer had said. "What you want Homer Davis to play for you?"

The music started. The strange deadly voice filled the room. "Am I getting through to you . . . that's what I want to know . . . am I getting through to you . . . that's what I'm wondering about. . . ." Lady Margaret moved through the house, swaying to the music. Through the dining room and into the bedroom where her cousin, Devoie Denery, was passed out on the bed, the pale blue sheets wrapped around her legs, her blond crotch wild and exposed, her breasts fallen against her arm. Devoie was an actress. Even in sleep she posed. What is she dreaming? Lady Margaret wondered. What outrageous performance is she watching on the screen of her mind? Devoie sighed and pursed out her lips, sinking further into the pillow. "Wake up," Lady Margaret said. "It's eleven o'clock in the morning. I promised Settle we'd go with him to the races. Don't you remember, Devoie? You said you'd go."

"I thought we were going to Mandeville. You said you were getting the house."

"We are going. After the races. Armand's over there. Mother gave Armand the house. First she buys his half for God knows how much, then she lets him go over all the time. Well, we'll just crowd in on top of him."

"Who's he got with him?"

"I don't know. Someone to fuck, I imagine. He always has someone to fuck."

☙ ☙ ☙

"Oh, your love washes on me like moonlight on the Lacassine." Homer was singing. "Oh, your love washes on me like rain on a dead man's shoes. . . ." Lady Margaret moved on into the kitchen, humming along with the music. "Oh, your love washes on me . . . your love make my car run funny . . . like sugar in the gas tank make my carburetor skip. . . ." She opened a cabinet, took down a box of vanilla wafers and began to stuff them into her mouth. She put water on to boil for tea. She opened the door of the old refrigerator and surveyed its contents. She pulled a piece of yellow ice off the coils of the freezer and stuck it into her mouth shivering at the forbidden gaseous taste. When she was a child Lady Margaret had longed for the ice on the coils of her grandmother's refrigerator but the maid always caught her and took it away. "Why you want to go and do yourself that way," Maeleen would say. "That ice all full of poison gas. That ice gonna make a hole in your stomach. You the craziest little girl in the world, Lady Margaret. You the craziest child I ever did see."

Lady Margaret took a carton of yogurt down from a shelf and tasted it, hoping to diffuse the poison gas. She walked over to the kitchen table carrying the yogurt and set it down beside the newspaper, which was opened to her review.

"Writer Attacks Crescent City," the headline said.

The Assumption, by Anna Hand

Ms. Hand's new book abounds in clichés, crude language, and uses real names of places in New Orleans in a way that can only be called name-dropping. Her sketchy characterizations leave the reader wondering if a woman like Lelia Clark can be called a heroine. Lelia thinks only of herself as we see her living a debauched life in New Orleans, then running away to join a bunch of hippies in Montana. There, Ms. Hand would have us believe, she finds love and a sense of social consciousness by working with delinquent boys.

The cover, a copy of a painting by El Greco, is a tasteless use of a religious painter's work to decorate what can only be called a book written by an atheist.

Last year Ms. Hand shocked the city by publishing a book of stories based on real-life tragedies in the Crescent City. Many people went out and bought the book anyway. Well, this time New Orleans is not going to pay to be attacked. Especially by a heroine who is supposed to be good at languages (she is teaching French to the delinquents) but can only express herself in the sort of expressions better left in late night bars.

The back cover of the book is a photograph of Ms. Hand wearing a big grin and a plantation hat with long streamers. The picture is doubly shocking considering the things inside.

Margaret Lanier Sarpie

Lady Margaret dropped the newspaper on the floor and picked up the box of papers beside it. She thumbed through the pages, pulled one out, began to read. It was a novel she had been writing for several years. "When Sherry got home from her luncheon with her aunt there was a note on a silver salver by the door. The salver, in a pattern called Fleur-de-lis, was part of a set of silver left to Sherry by her great-grandmother. The note was from Doug Hamilton again. Would he never leave her alone? This time he was more persistent than ever. 'We simply can't do without you. No one else in the state has the voice and personality to sing that part. We know you are in mourning and we honor your sorrow. But we beg you to join us in saving the opera house. That opera house is important, Miss Claverie. It is the heart of the city's cultural life. Won't you reconsider your decision? Won't you give it your deepest, truest thought?'

"Sherry looked up the long curving marble stairway made of pink Georgia marble to the landing where John had stood the last time she ever saw him. She had been wearing a floor-length silver and blue gown of satinade worked with lace insets at the hem and sleeves. Every time she walked up the stairs he was still there. Would they never understand she would never sing again?"

"Oh, your love washes on me, like heroin on a drunk man," Homer was singing. "Oh, your love washes on me, like cocaine on the schoolground." Lady Margaret dropped the page into the box. She let her fingers wander across her stomach and on down to her secret garden. Her fingernails found the little pump. moving it softly from side to side. A line of sweat rolled down her breast and landed on her leg. A bluejay called outside the window, then called again. Richard Gere walked down the garden path between the oleanders and the poppies. He came to rest on a marble bench beside the roses. He held out his hands to her. Come to me, he whispered. I always wanted to know a woman who was smarter than me. Come here. Don't be afraid. What a beautiful place you live in, Lady Margaret. What a wonderful, wonderful place to be.

"All right," Devoie said. "I'm up." She was standing in the door of the kitchen with the sheet wrapped around her. "But I'm not staying up unless I get some coffee. Goddamn Settle for getting us drunk. He's such a barbarian. I ought to know better than to get mixed up with him. What are you doing, Lady Margaret? Are you asleep in the chair?"

"No, I'm just thinking about something. Are we going to the races or not?"

"I'm not going anywhere with Settle Westfelt today. That's that. I'll go to Mandeville with you and lie on the beach. Armand's there? You said Armand's there?"

"He took his boat."

"Well, make some coffee and let's go on over. It's too hot in this house to live. Let's go lie on the beach. If we feel better we'll get Armand to take us out in his boat."

"Go turn that Homer Davis album over, will you? Play the other side."

Across the lake in Mandeville, in a bedroom painted the color of cream, Anna Hand knelt beside a man she was trying without much success to like. She had been in New Orleans for five days, a publicity tour for a new book, a tedious, wearing experience. At the very last autograph party a man she remembered from when she lived in the city, but barely knew, didn't really know at all, had hung around for hours while she wrote on books. He had been helpful and smiling, attentive and kind, bringing her glasses of water, standing by her side. "Come with me to the country," he wrote on a piece of paper and handed to her. "Let me take you away. You will sleep like a baby. You will eat like a queen."

The strange lassitude of New Orleans in summer, the wine at the party, the tiredness in her bones. Why not, she thought. I'll be gone tomorrow. Get drunk, eat sugar, get laid by a native, *be here.*

When the last book was signed she took him up on his offer. "As long as I'm on that plane tomorrow afternoon," she said. "You have to see to that."

Now she smiled down into his silly spoiled face, trying not to blame him for anything at all. She reached down and touched his hair. After all, he had kept his promise. He had made her sleep. "I'm starving, Armand," she said. "You promised to make waffles for breakfast."

"Let's do it some more. Let's do it one more time."

"After we eat. I'm tired of it now. You're too wild for me. I can't keep up with you."

"It was great in the swing. All my life I dreamed of doing it in a swing."

"The swing broke. Don't you remember? We barely escaped with our lives."

"I'll have to fix it today. Aunt Helen will never forgive me if I leave it like that."

"First breakfast. First that waffle you promised me. I have to leave by one. I have to go by the hotel and get the rest of my things."

"I know," he said. "Don't worry. I'll take care of it. I'll get you there."

Lady Margaret and Devoie threw their beach bags into the back of Lady Margaret's Audi and headed on out for Mandeville. The sun was beginning to shine.

The front that had covered the city for days was breaking up. They rolled up the windows of the car, turned on the air-conditioner and found a Sunday morning radio station that was playing classical music. "Pavane for a Dead Princess" filled the car.

"I love that piece," Devoie said. "It always reminds me of playing bridge at the Myersons' down in Rolling Fork. Gee Myerson used to love it so much. He would play it over and over. That and Yma Sumac. He worshipped Yma Sumac."

"It really isn't about a dead princess. Did you know that? He named it that a long time after he wrote it. Look, you want to stop at the Morning Call and get some beignets? It's by the causeway now. They had to move."

"Sure. I'll stop if you want to." They turned off the highway into a shopping mall and came to a stop before the Morning Call, a famous old French Quarter coffee-house that had been run off Chartres Street by rising rents. It had moved, lock, stock, and barrel, including its mirrored walls and old-fashioned stools, right out to Metairie. It was doing great business. A line of customers was all the way out the door and waiting on the sidewalk. A middle-aged couple greeted them as they joined the line. They were people who had moved to New Orleans from the North. Lady Margaret couldn't stand them. They were the very worst of Yankees who moved to New Orleans and started trying to get right into everything. They had even bought an antebellum house and restored it.

"We saw your little piece in the paper this morning," the woman said.

"Good for you," the man added. "That Hand woman is really just too much. You gave her what she deserved,

Lady Margaret. You really nailed the bitch. You did us all a favor."

"I only reviewed the book. Why, have you read it?"

"I sort of liked it," the woman said. "It made me want to move out to Montana. She made it sound so nice out there."

"Allenne," the man said. "I don't believe you said that."

"Well, it did. She made it sound so civilized."

"Let's don't talk about it here," he said. "Lady Margaret, how's your mother? I haven't seen her around lately. Has she been out of town?"

Lady Margaret was saved a reply. They had arrived at the takeout window where a white-coated Vietnamese waiter was dispensing beignets and café au lait. Through the window Lady Margaret could see the bakers rolling out the dough, cutting and frying and dipping the hot sweet little squares of flour. The room was covered with flour. White walls, white tables, white uniforms, white baker's hats, all dusted with flour. Near the window were pitchers of hot sweet milk, piles of golden doughnuts, cartons of chocolate milk. It was all just as it had been when Lady Margaret was a child and her father would take her to the Quarter on summer nights to pick up the last edition of the paper and sit beside the levee dipping beignets into coffee while he discussed the state of the world with friends he met there. If she asked, he would hold her up so she could see into the kitchen to watch the bakers. A foghorn would sound on the river, mosquitoes would buzz. It was all as it had been. Except the General was dead and the Morning Call had moved to Metairie and the bakers were not black anymore. Now the bakers were yellow. Still, the beignets were the same. Plaisir, plaisir, she thought. Joy to the world, sugar is come. Sugar, sugar, sugar. Pale green cane blowing in the fields near Lafayette. It had made her family rich and her mother fat. Win some, lose some, she thought. Her mouth watered as she watched the Vietnamese shake powdered sugar over the beignets in her little white sack.

"Come by for a drink sometime," the doctor said. Lady Margaret shrugged him off with a mumbled excuse and she and Devoie took their beignets and made their escape. They started back on their way. "You're getting famous," Devoie said. "Getting your name in the paper."

"Oh, shut up," Lady Margaret said. She lifted a beignet from the sack and sank her teeth into its sweetness. "I adore these goddamn things. I just have to have them."

"Yeah, beignets. The heart of the swamp. When I get lonesome for New Orleans I just go down to the grocery and get a box of powdered sugar and pour it on my hands and lick it off."

"It's not that bad."

"Highest cancer rate in the country, give or take New Jersey. Our friends lost a total of seven breasts last year. That ought to tell you something."

"Why do you keep coming down here to visit if you don't like it?"

"I didn't say I didn't like it. I'm just telling the truth. Telling the truth isn't disliking anything. It's just telling the truth."

"Well, a lot of people don't understand things you say. You really hurt Church's feelings last night. Do you know that? She was almost in tears."

"Which one was Church? The crazy girl that threw the butter plate at me?"

"She can't help it if she's crazy. Her chemistry's mixed up."

"Chemistry my ass. That girl adores being crazy. She's a crazy specialist. She threw the plate at me because I wouldn't act like it was interesting that she's crazy. Crazy doesn't fool me, Lady Margaret. Not after living in this family. Do you want another beignet or not?"

"Half of one. Break one in two. Look, Devoie, out on the lake. There's a regatta. Can you see what flags they're flying? Oh, damn, it's too far away." They were on the causeway now, the long concrete bridge that connects New Orleans with the little fishing villages across the lake. Mandeville, old live oaks along the seawall, old houses mildewing in the moist thick air. Evangeline, the moss-covered trees seem to call. Tragedies, mosquitoes, malaria, yellow fever, priests and nuns and crazy people.

The Audi was moving cheerfully along the bridge, its tires bumping against the span connectors. Small neat signs marked off the miles. Ten, eleven, twelve, thirteen, until they reached twenty-five and the car moved out onto the highway.

"Whatever happened to Redmond, that sailor you were going with?" Devoie was saying. "The one that was trying to get on an Olympic team."

"He went back to his wife. I didn't like him much anyway. He was always reading the labels on wine out loud. It drove me crazy."

"I wish Armand would have some interesting men with him."

"He won't have. Armand never has men. I don't think he has a single male friend."

"What is this?" Anna Hand said. She had picked up a photograph that was facedown on a dresser. She dusted it off on her sleeve. It was a photograph of two men standing together by a rock wall with the Swiss Alps in the background. They had their arms around each other's waists and they were smiling.

"That's Uncle Robert. He's the black sheep. He used to stay here when he had to be in town. That's Switzerland. It's the only place he liked to be."

"Who's that with him? He looks familiar."

"That's Stravinsky. They were friends. They used to meet in Vienna to hear music."

"How wonderful. If this was mine it would be hanging on a wall. Why don't you hang it on the wall?"

"Oh, Aunt Helen wouldn't want to be reminded of him. He disappeared. No one in the family's seen or heard from him in years. Well, never mind our skeletons. Come have the waffles."

"What was his name? Your uncle's name?"

"His name was Robert. I told you that. Now, please come on. The waffles are getting cold." Anna replaced the photograph on the dresser, laying it down beside a catalog and a bill for repairing the screens. She opened a dresser drawer. A Scrabble set was there, a half-finished double-crostic, a jar of suppositories, a silver doubloon, a comb. The mysterious drawers of summer houses, she thought, secrets no real house would hoard or remember.

"Come on," Armand called. "Or I'm throwing your waffles to the birds."

"I want to get a paper on the way to the airport," she said, going into the breakfast room. "I want to see if the paper reviewed my book. God only knows who they'll give it to. They gave the last one to a Jesuit. Can you believe it? He said I made unjustified attacks on the Church. Unjustified. Isn't that wonderful?"

Lady Margaret and Devoie came off the highway and down a narrow road between pine trees. The trees looked wet. The earth looked wet. The buzzards circling the trees looked wet. Even the modern road could not make the swamp look like anything but a swamp. On the outskirts of the town small businesses and restaurants began to appear, grimy and tacky, wet and forlorn. Fried Chicken, a sign said. Fried Catfish, said another. Thibodeaux Insures You, Lakefront Rentals, Golden Acres, Lots.

At a corner Cajun women were selling shrimp from a truck. Beside a fruit stand piles of melons rotted in the sun. It was getting hotter. A high wind had chased the clouds away without stirring a single leaf on the ground.

"We'll be able to sunbathe," Lady Margaret said. "Thank God for that." They crossed a bridge, turned at a light, entered a driveway, and came to a stop before the house. It was set in the middle of a yard lush with live oaks and catalpa and eucalyptus and pine. A beautiful yard leading down to the largest private beach on the river. The yard was a park, was everything a yard should be.

But there was something wrong with the house. It disturbed the eye. From any angle it disturbed the eye. There was something wrong, something badly wrong, something disproportionate and Procrustean and wrong.

Once the house had been a proud resort hotel. It had been three stories high. Couples came over on the ferry from New Orleans to spend the weekend and dance in the bathhouse and play in the small brown river. That was when the property had been a public beach. During the Depression the city of Mandeville had sold all its public beaches. Lady Margaret's grandfather had bought the place for a song and left it to his children.

As soon as Lady Margaret's mother inherited it she bought out her sisters and went to work to improve the property. She conceived the idea of lowering the house a floor to save on electricity. All one summer she labored with carpenters and a house-moving man. Every day she drove across the old railroad bridge to oversee the modernization project. Then she called in the painters.

The result was a squat green hulk surrounded by porches. It looked like a fat lady seated on a stool with her skirts spread out around her. "Crayfish," the house seemed to say. "Come and get your crayfish. Crayfish for sale. Fresh crayfish waiting for the pot."

"Here's the house," Lady Margaret said. "And there's Armand's car. So he's still here."

"We should have called. There's no telling what's going on in there."

"Oh, my God, Devoie. It's a big house. He can't be doing it in every room. Well, I'm going in and put on my suit. I'm white as snow. I haven't been in the sun in days."

"You go in. I'm changing in the beach house. I'll wait for you down there." Devoie started down the path to the river. Lady Margaret pulled her bag out of the back seat and walked up the steps and onto the porch.

The swing was lying on the floor with a wineglass beside it. A hat was sitting on the arm of the swing. An outrageous hat with long yellow streamers. I know that hat, Lady Margaret thought. I've seen that hat somewhere. She picked it up. The streamers fell across her arms. They made goosebumps on her arms. She laid the hat back down on the swing and walked over to the door and took hold of the handle. Through the glass panels she could see a woman coming down the hall carrying a cup of coffee. Lady Margaret opened the door and stepped into the hall. "I'm Margaret Sarpie," she said. "I'm Armand's cousin. I own this house."

"Well, it's a very nice house. I'm Anna Hand, from Washington. We came over last night. Your cousin's been trying to get me fat." She smiled a wonderful smile at Lady Margaret, standing very still with the cup in her hands. Steam was rising from the cup. It was only a few feet away.

"What did you say? What did you say your name was?"

"Anna Hand. I'm a visitor. Only at the moment I'm trying to catch a plane. Is something wrong? Are you all right?"

"I didn't know anyone was going to be here. Is Armand around? I mean, where is he?" She didn't hear me, Lady Margaret thought. She didn't hear my name.

"He's gone to get chain for the swing. Tell me your name again. I'm getting so bad about names. I think I must be going deaf. Heather, is that it? Was it Heather?"

"I don't know," Lady Margaret said. "I don't know what to say."

"I'm sorry about your swing. Armand was singing spirituals. He was singing 'Swing Low, Sweet Chariot.' Then the swing fell. It's a wonder we weren't killed. You should have seen our faces. Oh, God, it really was very funny." She was laughing. "Anyway, I am sorry about the swing."

"Oh, the swing is nothing. The swing doesn't matter." Lady Margaret was stepping back, moving away from the cup of coffee. But the woman was following her. Lady Margaret would step back. Each time the woman followed. She will throw it on me now, Lady Margaret thought. She will throw it in my face. It will all be over, two thousand years of history, two thousand years of law. "What was he singing?" she said. "What was Armand singing?"

" 'Swing Low, Sweet Chariot.' You know, that old spiritual. Coming for to carry me home. Then the swing broke. It scared us to death. Well, I wish he'd get back. I'm frantic about catching this plane. There won't be another one until late tonight." She laid the cup of coffee down on the hall table.

She knows, Lady Margaret thought, I think she knows. This is some joke of Armand's. Maybe it isn't even true. Maybe it's just a joke he's playing on me.

Armand came hurrying up the stairs, carrying a

package of swing chain. "Oh, hello, Lady Margaret. I thought that was your car. Did you see who was here? Did you introduce yourself? This is Anna Hand, the writer. This famous lady spent the night in your house, sitting at your table, sleeping in your bed."

"Drinking your wine," the woman said. "Breaking your swing. Armand, we really need to be leaving. I'm getting worried about the time. I have to go by the hotel."

"The traffic's heavy on the bridge," Lady Margaret said. "You had better go on and leave if you're in a hurry." Armand disappeared down the hall for their bags and left the women alone again. "I'm sorry I don't have time to thank you properly for letting me visit," the woman said. "I seem to be spending my life lately apologizing for not having time to be polite."

"I know about your work," Lady Margaret said. "I've read about it."

"Well, now you know me instead. And I know you. The world is really quite astonishing, all the people you can meet. Don't you find it so?"

"I don't know," Lady Margaret said. "I don't think I do. Not really. Well, maybe I do. I don't know if I do or not." Armand reappeared. He was hurrying now. Lady Margaret walked them outside and stood watching as Armand's Triumph disappeared into the trees.

A moon was in the sky, a frazzled, gibbous moon, a bad moon, a bad luck moon. Lady Margaret watched a cloud go past the moon. The world is full of danger, she thought. Anything can happen to anyone at anytime. Anything at all. She turned toward the beach. Devoie was coming up the path with a towel wrapped around her head like a turban. "Who was that with Armand?" she said. "I saw him spiriting her away. Was it someone married? Someone we know?"

"It wasn't anything like that. It was someone from out of town. She had to catch a plane. They were in a hurry."

"Well, who was it then? What was her name?"

"I don't know. I don't remember."

"Are you all right? You look funny."

"Yes, I'm all right. I'm perfectly all right."

"Are we going to sunbathe then? Are you coming down?"

"In a minute. As soon as I change."

"I want to go to the Station and eat lunch in a while."

"Fine. Whatever you want to do." Devoie shook her head and started back down to the beach. Lady Margaret walked up the stairs and across the porch and into the house. It was quiet in the hall, musty and dark and cool. Light was coming in the open door, cutting the hall into diagonal halves. Half of it is light, Lady Margaret thought. And half is dark, like Homer's patch. Does the dark cover the light? Or the light invade the dark? Maybe both things are true. Yes, that's it. Everything is true. Or nothing. Maybe nothing really happens. Maybe I just make it all up.

The cup of coffee was still on the table. Lady Margaret lifted it from its saucer and held it out in front of her, raising it like a chalice. Then, very slowly, as if in a pantomine, she lowered it to her lips and drank, slowly at first, in tiny sips, then in larger sips. *I looked over Jordan and what did I see, coming for to carry me home. A band of angels coming after me*. She shivered. It was cold in the hall. The air conditioner was running full blast. *They must have used up twenty dollars' worth of electricity*. Lady Margaret set the cup back down on the table. *Well, to hell with it*, she decided. *I didn't do anything wrong. I just wrote what I thought.* She pushed the thermostat up to eighty-five, slammed out of the house and started down the flagstone path to the beach, her sandals slapping against the stones, her hands curled into fists and pushing against the pockets of her shorts. She walked by a garter snake curled up in the roots of a tree, past a pair of grasshoppers mating on a leaf, beneath a mourning dove and the nest of a sleeping owl. *What difference does it make? She won't even see it until she gets on the plane and if Armand tells anyone about it I'll tell Momma never to let him have the house again. To hell with it. To hell with all of them. Swing low, sweet chariot. I'm going to quit thinking about it. I'm going to put it out of my mind and get to work on my tan. Oh, God, what a Sunday.*

Oh, your love washes on me like waiting for the paint to dry. Oh, your love washes on me like the muffler falling off. Coming for to carry me home. Hello, little old dried up white lady, what you want Homer Davis to play for you?

Shut up. I can't. Try. I'm trying.

❧❧❧

The Gauzy Edge of Paradise

THE only reason Lanier and I went to the coast to begin with was to lose weight. We didn't know we were going to have a ménage à trois with Sandor. We didn't even know Sandor was coming down there.

Lanier and I are best friends. We've been going on diets together since we were thirteen years old. We dieted together through high school and Ole Miss and when we went to Jackson to be secretaries to the legislature. That's what we do now. Lanier's secretary to Senator Huddleston from Bovina and I'm secretary to Senator Ladd from Aberdeen. It's good work but you're sitting down all day. The fat settles. I'm not giving in to that. "It's natural," my mother says. "You're too hard on yourself, Diane. Let nature have some say."

"Not on my hips," I tell her. "I'll die before I'll get fat. I'll jump off a bridge. You forget, Mother, I'm not married yet."

"Whose fault is that?" she says. "Certainly not the young men you've left crying in the living room. The rings you've returned. Not to mention Fanny Claiborne's son." It's true. I've broken three engagements. Something just comes over me. Suddenly I look at them and they look so pitiful, the way their hands start to look like paws.

Meanwhile the problem is to keep my body going uphill. I'm twenty-nine this August. I've got to watch it. Well, I've got Lanier. And she's got me or she would have given in long ago. She'd be the size of a house if I didn't keep after her.

This trip to the coast was a Major Diet. We'd been at it five days, taking Escatrol, reading poetry out loud to keep ourselves in a spiritual frame of mind, exercising morning, night and noon. I was down to 126 and Lanier was down to 129 when Mother called and asked us to pick up Sandor in Pensacola. "Try to keep him from drinking," she said. "Aunt Treena and Uncle Lamar are worried sick about him drinking. And be on time, Diane. There's nothing worse than getting off a plane and no one's there. Are you listening? Diane, are you listening to me?"

I was listening. I was leaning against the portable dishwasher wondering what effect Sandor's coming would have on our diet. A diet's a very delicate thing. You have to keep your momentum going. You have to stick to your routine. Well, it was Mother's beach house, and if she told Sandor he could come there was nothing I could do but meet the plane.

"Who's coming?" Lanier said. "Who's on their way?"

"My cousin, this gorgeous cousin of mine that had a nervous breakdown trying to be a movie star. He used to be a football player before he took up acting. Then he went to California. He's got these beautiful shoulders and he plays a saxophone. Haven't you ever been here when he was here?"

She was pulling on her leotards. We wear them even in the heat. To make us sweat. There are several schools of thought about that. Lanier and I are of the school that says the hotter you get the better. "Let's don't take a pill today if we're going to Pensacola," she said. "I'm sick of taking them. They make me nervous. They make me talk too much."

"We have to take them. Ten days. Ten pills. We swore we'd do it. Besides, I'd take cyanide to get this fat off my stomach." I handed her a pill and a glass of water. "Come on. Just four more days. Go on. Take it. Then we'll do leg raises, then stomach crunches, then we'll run down to the beach and take a swim. You have to look on this as a religious experience, Lanier. Pretend you're the Buddha going on a fast. Or Jesus in the wilderness or something."

She took it and put it in her mouth and swallowed it. We had gone to a lot of trouble to get that Escatrol. We had begged a young surgeon for weeks, convincing him we wouldn't tell where we got it. Or drink on top of it.

She put down the water glass and heaved a sigh. Lanier's got a lot of guilt. She can even feel guilty about going on a fast. I work on her and work on her but she's still that way. "Okay," she said. "I want to try standing in the waves for an hour again. I could tell a big difference in my thighs today. I think they look a lot better."

She took the aerobic dance record out of its cover and put it on the turntable. "What's he like, this Sandor?"

"He's sad," I said. "Beautiful and sad. Even when he plays his saxophone it's always sad music, songs he writes. If you ask him to play anything you know he puts it back in the case. Anyway, he's gorgeous. If worse comes to worse we can always look at him."

"Let's start on the exercises. I think the pill's taking effect. I'm starting to feel it. I'm going to try to get in my pink denim skirt to wear to Pensacola." She dropped the needle down on the record and we went into our routine.

"GET THOSE BODIES WORKING," a woman named Joanie demanded. "LET'S SEE SOME ACTION IF YOU WANT ATTRACTION. HE'S NOT GOING TO LOVE YOU IF HE HAS THAT FAT STOMACH TO CONTEND WITH. YOU CAN'T HIDE BENEATH AN OVERBLOUSE FOREVER. COME ON," she was getting mean now. "YOU GREW IT. YOU LIFT IT. SQUEEZE IT. SQUEEZE IT LIKE YOU MEAN IT. SQUEEZE IT LIKE YOU OWN IT. . . ."

We bent and stretched, jumped and pulled, turned and squeezed, panted and breathed, groaned and creaked. "STRETCH THOSE OLD TRAPS," Joanie demanded. "HOW LONG SINCE YOU FELT A GOOD STRETCH IN THE OLD PECS? CRUNCH IT. CRUNCH IT LIKE YOU MEAN IT. FEEL THAT STUFF MELTING. THE FAT'S ON THE FIRE. . . ." We finished up with a hundred jumping jacks and fell back on the floor exhausted.

"Your midriff looks a lot better," Lanier said. "I swear I can see your ribs."

"You think so?" I walked over to Momma's gilt picture frame mirror and surveyed my ribs. "Oh, God, if they would only show from the back. If only once more before I died I could see the ribs in my back. The last time was that year I was engaged to Saint-John Royals. Remember that year? I weighed 114 for five straight months." I gazed off into a découpage umbrella stand, glorying in the memory. "Maybe I should have married him."

"I think it's time for us to marry someone," Lanier said. "I think we're going to have to lower our standards, Diane. He's really gorgeous, your cousin Sandor?"

"Like a god. I don't know why he didn't go over in Hollywood. I guess the sadness showed up on the screen test."

"What's he sad about?"

"I don't know. It's just how he is. He's always been that way."

"Maybe we can fix him up," she said, and laughed her old skit night laugh. Lanier's a riot when she wants to be. "Maybe we can cheer old Sandor up." She settled her hands on her hips and gazed out the window at the water.

We were in my mother's beach house, a frame house up on stilts, looking out on the Gulf of Mexico at the exact point where the state of Alabama meets the state of Florida. A dark green house with white shutters. White sand stretching as far as the eye can see, clean white dunes and deep green sea and always a breeze even on the hottest day. The Redneck Riviera people call that part of the country now, rednecks and power boats and waterfront developments growing up beside every little stagnant bayou. Baldwin County, Alabama. Black man, don't let the sun go down on you. The natives used to boast there wasn't a black man in the county limits. The white people have these opaque blue eyes. Churches on every corner. A man who boasts he can kill, pluck, cook and eat a chicken in eighty seconds.

Still, I loved it. I'd been going down there all my life. From a time when it was so desolate you had to stop in Mobile for groceries. When we hauled drinking water from behind the Orange Beach post office. When the dolphins still swam by the pier in the mornings, lifting their heads to look at us, rolling and playing, touching and caressing, nudging each other with their snouts. "Why would you need to read a book about dolphins to know how smart they are?" my mother said to me one day. "Anybody that ever saw one would figure that out."

Lanier and I finished up our morning routine and dressed and got into the car. We had a cooler with some Tabs and carrot sticks and shredded cabbage and one small apple apiece. Not that we were hungry. Escatrol takes care of being hungry.

We were feeling good. Lanier had made it into the pink skirt and I was wearing a yellow playsuit, *with a belt*. We stopped at a gift shop in Gulf Shores and found some cards to send to Jackson and had our picture taken together in a three-for-a-dollar photograph machine. We always did that when we came to the coast. It was part of our history. Then we went into the Gulf Shores doughnut shop to look at the buckets of lemon filling that were always sitting on the floor with flies all over them and the tops half off. Aversion therapy. Lanier's the one that thought that up. It still worked. They hadn't changed management and cleaned it up.

At the drugstore Lanier bought a book about Anita Bryant's private life and read it out loud to me all the way to Pensacola, putting in the stuff the writer left out. "Anita Bryant was always very close to her father, Big Jack Bryant," the book would say. "Oh, Big Jack, show me again that big black secret thing of yours," Lanier would add. We thought it was hilarious. We laughed all the way to Pensacola. Escatrol, queen of prescription drugs.

Sandor looked wonderful getting off the plane. He didn't look like he'd had a nervous breakdown. He didn't even look as sad as usual. He had on a beige shirt with epaulets, made of some soft material. And tan slacks with no belt. This Greek god kind of blond hair, with natural streaks. I couldn't believe I'd been sorry a minute that he was coming. Lanier went crazy when she saw him. You could hear her pull her stomach in.

She moved right in. "You want an Escatrol," she said. We were waiting for the luggage. She'd forgotten I was there. "Diane and I have some Escatrol. We got it from a doctor. You want one? You can have one if you want it." "Sure," he said. "Where are they?" She took the bottle out of her purse. We'd been taking turns keeping them. She undid the safety cap, took out a green and white capsule and held it out to him. "Happy landings," she said. They laughed like old buddies. Sandor took the pill from her and walked off toward the water fountain.

"Let's have a party," he said when he got back. "Where do you want to start?"

We started at this place called the Quarter, modeled on the French Quarter in New Orleans. Six different bars under one roof. Every bar has a different kind of music, juke boxes in the daytime, live bands at night. Country music in one place, jazz guitar in the next, rock and roll, new wave. One even has old fifties stuff, for old people, so they can hear their old songs.

It was four in the afternoon when we got there. Everything just getting started for the night. The bartenders changing shifts, people wiping off the tables, straightening chairs, dusting glasses. We started in a part called the Seven Sailors. Fishnets on the wall and stuffed monkeys and parrots hanging from the nets and a juke box with Greek music. Sandor ordered a double gin martini and Lanier ordered wine and somehow or other I decided on a Salty Dog. Tequila on top of dexadrine is sort of like you took sunlight and squeezed it through a cylinder so what comes out the other end is the size of a thread. The thread is how you feel for about thirty minutes. After that, well, there's good and bad in everything. You have to take your chances, make your choices. Not that we were making the right ones that day. Only I'm not going to start feeling guilty about it. Even with what happened next . Even if I'll see him standing in that door holding a gun forever. Even if I'll feel his hands on my arms till the day I die.

☙ ☙ ☙

We settled down at a table with our drinks. "I heard you had a nervous breakdown," I said, moving my chair over close to Sandor's.

"Who told you that?" he said.

"Momma said Aunt Treena said so. Well, did you have one or not?"

"No, I didn't have a nervous breakdown. I checked into a hospital because Hollywood was driving me crazy. I needed to think things over. It was a good rest. I decided the best thing to do was come on home and settle down and get a regular job. So here I am." He smiled that gorgeous smile and took a big drink of his martini. "That's dynamite speed. Where did you get it? You can't get stuff like that even on the Coast."

"It's for a diet," I said. "We had to take the prescription to five drugstores to get it filled. They don't even stock it anymore. Lanier and I are going to be so thin when we get back to Jackson no one will even know us. What kind of job are you going to get?"

"I don't know. Whatever they'll let me do. Selling cars or construction work. Maybe real estate. I'm not worried. I'll think of something. Something'll turn up."

"Of course you're worried," I said. "You're worried sick. You've wasted your youth trying to be a movie star and now you haven't got a profession. Don't try to pretend you aren't worried about that, Sandor."

"I guess you're right," he said. "I guess I'm more worried than I realize."

"Come up to Jackson where we are," Lanier said. "There's always work around the legislature. Senator Huddleston will find you something."

"That's an idea," he said. "Maybe I'll drive up with

you when you leave." He signaled the waiter and we had another round of drinks. Then I got an idea. "Let's rent a hotel room and park the car and take taxis and go on and get good and drunk," I said. "Let's celebrate Sandor returning to Dixie. Back in the fold. No Tails. That's what we called Sandor when he was little, Lanier. One summer we were all at the beach house and he discovered he didn't have a tail. He was just a little boy. He'd go around all summer pointing out his back end to people. No tails, he'd say. No tails."

"That's the trouble with getting drunk with your cousins," Sandor said. "They tell everything you did. We called Diane the Duchess because she always tried to boss everyone around."

"She's still that way," Lanier said. Now they had that in common. I had tried to boss them both around. She leaned against his arm. Sandor was leaning back. They were leaning on each other. But what about me? Who was I supposed to lean on?

We found a taxi and went over to the old Piedmont Hotel and got a room and took a shower and put our clothes back on and went out and got drunker. On the way out of the room I took one of the Escatrol capsules and opened it up on a piece of hotel stationery and we took turns licking up the little green and yellow balls with our tongues. "Why not," I said to Sandor. It was an old thing my cousins and I like to say when we're really going to get in trouble. "Whyyyyyyy not," he answered.

Around ten that night we ended up at a gay bar called the Monkey's Paw listening to a female impersonator named Lady Aurelius. She was singing Barbra Streisand when we came in. People, people who need people. Songs like that. It made me feel like crying. I sat there watching Lady Aurelius mouthing the words of a Barbra Streisand album, missing all my old boyfriends and fiancés. Some day he'll come along, Lady Aurelius was singing now, switching styles. THE MAN I LOVE.

I don't know what came over me. I'm not an exhibitionist. Maybe I was sick of watching Sandor and Lanier lean on each other. Maybe I was under the influence of the Monkey's Paw. All those smiling faces. I got up and walked up on the stage and went over to Lady Aurelius and put my arm around her waist and started helping her sing. I'VE GOT TO BE ME, I was singing. I'VE GOT TO BE ME. I was into it. I moved out in front of her. I took the stage. She didn't seem to mind. She was a very strong looking female impersonator. As tall as my father. I started screaming out new words to the songs. *I've got to be me. No matter what happens. Or how much it hurts anybody. Or whether they like it or not. To hell with it. I've got to be me. I've got to be me.* I was right up to the edge of the stage yelling my head off. Then I started doing my exercise routine. Rolling my arms around in the air, bending from side to side so the audience could see how supple I was. Twisting and shaking and doing the boogie. I looked back at Lady Aurelius. She had stopped smiling. She was standing very still.

Someone in the audience started throwing money. A handful of change hit the stage. Some dollar bills. A wad of paper. More change. A paper cup. I was yelling out more words. Anything I thought up. Now I wasn't even bothering with the music. *Anybody that wants to stop me has got another think coming*, I sang. *Diane doesn't stop for no man. No man calls my name. No man's got the drop on me. No one's got my number*. About like that.

I could see it all so clearly. I had missed my calling. I was a singer who had never gotten to sing. A singer who forgot to sing. I had been denied my destiny. I meant to stay up there all night and make up for lost time but a bouncer came up on the stage and dragged me off and delivered me to Sandor.

After that the heart went out of the evening. The bars were closing. The streets looking wet and deserted. We wandered back to the Quarter to see if we could recapture the night but the night was gone. The parrots were falling from the nets, someone had turned a pitcher of beer over on a table. It was dripping slowly down off the black leather edges. My mind kept going away. I kept thinking about fields of wheat I had seen once in Kansas. Fields of barley. Malt growing somewhere I had never visited. Rain falling. All of that to end up beer. A surly, embarrassing fat sort of drink.

We piled into a taxi and told the driver to take us home. It was some off-brand taxi company. The driver was a hard-looking black man without much to say. He didn't turn his head until we got to the hotel. Then Sandor pulled a wad of money out of his pocket to pay him and half of it fell on the floor and we had to pick it up. We were too drunk to tell the ones from the tens. Finally Sandor handed the driver a handful and we got out and went on up to our room.

☙ ☙ ☙

It was Lanier who thought up the ménage à trois. I guess she didn't want me to feel left out. I was so depressed by then I'd have gone along with anything. We took off our clothes and got in bed and started trying to decide what to do. I couldn't find anything I really wanted to do. Finally I ended up with my mouth on Sandor's arm, sort of sucking on his arm. Sandor and Lanier kept kissing each other, stopping every now and then to try to kiss me or pat me here or there. "Stop it, Lanier," I said finally. "I may be crazy but so far I'm not queer."

"This isn't queer," she said. "It's a ménage à trois. Everyone in Paris used to do this. I read about it in a book by Simone, what's her name. You're the one that always wants to be so free, Diane."

I sighed. Sandor rubbed his hand across my head. I patted him on the back and tried to roll over to the unused part of the bed. I knew we should have gotten two rooms, I was thinking. But I can't sleep by myself in a hotel. I never sleep a wink.

"Come on, Diane," Sandor said in his sweetest voice. "Let me make you feel good too. Come back over here by me." I was going to do it but I heard a sound, like breathing underwater. I looked toward the door. The black man was standing in the door with a gun in his hand. He moved into the room and closed the door. He had a face like a shell. We were all very still. We had been waiting all our lives for this to happen. Now it was here.

"One of you get out of bed and collect the money for me," he said. "Come on. I'm sick of all this shit. I'd just as soon shoot all three of you in the face as look at you.

Come on. Come on. And if you turn me in to the police I'll track you down and have your asses. So think it over before you file a report."

Lanier got out of the bed. She was trying to tie the sheet around her but it was still attached at the bottom of the bed. She picked up her pants to put them on then thought better of that and started sort of skipping or hopping around the room getting our billfolds. She laid everything she could find on the untouched bed. Sandor and I were very still. I don't know what we were doing. "That's it," the man said. "Now take the driver's licenses and credit cards out of the billfolds and the money and any jewelry you have. Come over here. Put them on the floor. About a foot from me. That's it. That's a good girl. You sure are a big girl to have such little tiny teats. That's it. Now then, go tie your buddies up. Tear off part of the sheet and tie their hands behind them. On the bed. Come on. Hurry up. I'm sick of all this shit. I'd just as soon kill all three of you. Save tying you up."

"I'll tie them up as fast as I can," Lanier said. "I used to be a Girl Scout. I know how to tie things." I couldn't believe how cool she was being. Like she had forgotten she was naked. "We have some Escatrol," she said. "It's a prescription drug. It's very hard to get. Would you like that too? It's in my pocketbook. Should I get that and put it by the money?"

"Yeah," he said. "I'll take it. Put it there, pancake teats, then get on that bed. I'll do the tying." He was wearing a dark jacket with a white shirt. That's all I remember. Except his face, like an oyster shell. There was a design on the shirt, calligraphy. In black and red. Lanier walked right over to him and laid the stuff on the floor. I thought he would hit her with the gun but he let her go away. Then he tied her to the other bed and cut the phone wires and tied our hands together. I closed my eyes when he touched me. His hands were so cold. I will feel them until I die. He turned off all the lights and left the room.

Everything was very quite when we got back to Momma's house the next afternoon. The beaches were deserted as far as I could see. Hardly a seagull was in sight. I went into the kitchen and started making chocolate milkshakes with some old moldy ice cream I found in the freezer. I made them so thick you had to eat them with a spoon. I ate half a pound of ice cream while I was getting them ready. I took one and gave it to Sandor. He was lying on the living room floor watching TV. I took one to Lanier. She was on the sleeping porch reading a magazine. I took mine and a bag of chocolate mint cookies and went into my mother's bedroom and lay down on the bed and started nibbling on the cookies. It was six o'clock. Before long it would be seven o'clock. Then it would be night. The old heron by the pier would snuggle down into his nest. All my life I had wondered where he put his feet. I pulled my knees up against my soft full stomach. I would never weigh 114 again as long as I lived. Nothing would change. Good girls would press their elegant rib cages against their beautiful rich athletic husbands. Passionate embraces would ensue. I would be lying on a bed drinking chocolate milkshakes. Eating cookies. Wishing Lanier hadn't given the Escatrol away.

❧❧❧

Defender of the Little Falaya

LENNY Weiss had been sweeping sand for an hour. Was that any way to treat asthma? He stopped for a moment, leaning on his broom. He looked out across the picnic tables to the cool brown river, the Little Falaya. How many small brown fish had his poles pulled from its waters? How many times had he waded out and let the river take him, legs, thighs, everywhere?

It was his river. It was his beach. It was his beach house. It was his property. It was his No Trespassing sign and goddamn them they had been there again. Their footprints were everywhere. How could he be expected to run the store and protect the beach house and keep people from stealing ties and belts and keep vandals off the beach and take care of Mother and have money left to buy tanks for Israel? It was too much. It was just too goddamn much. Well, at least I'm not married to Crystal, he consoled himself. No matter what else Manny got, he got Crystal along with it. It was fair. There was always justice in the end. Wasn't there? Wasn't there?

Crystal was Lenny's sister-in-law. She was the only enemy he had in the world. She knew it and he knew it and Manny knew it and her crazy son, King, knew it, and Mother knew it. It was not a secret. It was war. Like this summer house business. Who kept the screens repaired? Who replaced the trash cans? Who got the calls from the sheriff? Who always came over, *all by himself*, and cleaned the messes up? Lenny Weiss, Leonard Sidney Weiss, that's who.

He sneezed again. Perhaps it was the cape jasmine covered with dusty blooms. Perhaps the oleander. He fished the vaporizer out of his pocket and sprayed his good nostril. He sprayed his bad nostril, wondering what it would be like to have a good nose, a nose that worked, a nose that could be depended upon.

He replaced the vaporizer in his pocket and went back to work on the sand. He swept the flagstones leading to the bridge over the lagoon. He swept the dance floor beside the pavilion. He swept the playroom and under the canoes and picked up the empty bottles and potato chip bags.

Now all he had left was the ladies' room. He hated to go in there. It seemed a place so sacrosanct, so holy with Mother's flowered suit hanging on its peg, so radiant with her hand creme, her bathing cap, her comb. All his life Lenny had watched her disappear through that door, then reappear, shy and sweet in her little suit, ready for the sun, ready for the river.

Well, someone had to clean it up. Manny wasn't coming to help. And Zale had run off to Detroit and Witherspoon was dead, God rest her beautiful black soul. Lenny sighed and wiped his hands on his khaki shorts. Why should today be different from any other day?

He squared his shoulders and went on into the ladies' dressing room. It wasn't too bad. At least they hadn't written on the walls this time. He straightened up the dressers and the benches and picked up the beer cans and a pair of red bikini underpants someone had dropped in the shower. He swept the trash into a pile, and picked it up with a dustpan.

He had just replaced the top on the last of the trash cans when Ernest appeared, walking down the path through the cypress trees, looking sober and good-natured, looking like a man who knew what he was about. Ernest was the Weisses' poacher. The Weisses let Ernest poach and in return Ernest guarded the beach from trespassers.

Ernest was especially zealous about tubers coming down the Little Falaya from Red Rock. He would lie in wait for them by the lagoon, then storm down out of the catalpa trees, waving his hands in the air, shouting, "ALLIGATORS, ALLIGATORS, ALLIGATORS! NO TRESPASSING. PRIVATE PROPERTY! KEEP OFF! KEEP OFF!"

"So they got you again," Ernest said. "I'll be damned. I'll just be damned."

"Where were you? I thought you were guarding the place."

"I was gone to Boutee to a funeral. I can't be everywhere at once. Well, it's the best beach on the river. That last flood really left some sand."

"What will we do?" Lenny said. "That's three times since March. It upsets Mother. She wants it stopped."

"Who told her? You ought to keep her out of it."

"The sheriff called. They hit the Arnolds too, and the Savoies. It looks like a gang this time. Who's been here? Who's been around that could have seen them?"

"Your sister-in-law and some of her buddies were here. They made a fire, right out on the beach. In the middle of the beach. You can still see the ashes. Your mother isn't going to like that one bit."

"Did they stay the night?"

"They were on the beach with no clothes on. So I left. I stay clear when she comes over. I don't want nothing to do with that."

"I'm sorry," Lenny said. "I apologize for that."

"Not your fault. It's nothing to me. It's none of you, Mr. Lenny. I know it's none of you."

"The vandals have been so bad this year. It's because they closed the public beaches. That's been bad for everybody."

"Had to. The water's poisoned. Well, it's poisoned everywhere. Price you pay for civilization I suppose. Always a price to pay."

"Did anyone spend the night?"

"Her boy did. The one they call the King. He stayed. He's still here. He lives here now."

"King is here? In Livingston? In the house?"

"He's right up there living in the house. Him and some girl he's with. Some Yankee girl."

"Excuse me," Lenny said. He laid his broom against a cypress tree. He wiped his hand across his brow. He got out his vaporizer and sprayed his nose. "Excuse me,

Ernest. I really have to go and see about this. Watch the beach a minute, will you?" Without waiting for an answer he strode up the hill to the house. Beneath his feet the thick roots of the trees made a pattern in the washed-out ground. Above his head a jay rattled the cottonwood leaves. In the distance a motorboat tore down the river.

"It was different when your black woman was alive," Ernest called after him. "It was different then. Everything was different then."

The house was at the top of the path, a sprawling dust-covered antique of a house. On top was a widow's walk, the kind they build in New England for sailors' wives to watch the sea. Idleweiss, the Weiss's called the old house. Lenny's uncle had taken it for a bad debt thirty years before. The Weisses could not remember a time when it belonged to someone else. It was their summer house. It gave them an added dimension, a sort of moss-covered dusty aristocracy. "This is our beach," the little Weiss children loved to call out to people who came in boats. "You can't stop here. This is a private beach. This is private property."

Paint was chipping off the sides, palings missing from the porch railings, the inside smelled like an old closet, but Lenny loved it. When he opened the front door he expected Witherspoon to be calling out to him from the kitchen, offering him cream puffs or meringue tarts, asking about his fishing, praising his little fish, running her moist black hand across his shoulders, sticking his vaporizer up his little nose.

Witherspoon had lived in the attic of the house, standing guard over its treasures, spreading its floors with layers of wax, sweeping the paths to the beach, keeping the beachfront spotless. Not a leaf that fell, not a twig blown in by rain, not a carton washed up on the shore had escaped her eyes until the day she died, fallen dead on the path to the bridge, with her head on the steps and her feet curled up beside a cypress root. Some boys had found the body the next morning, the broom still in her hand, the straw hat Manny and Crystal brought back from Little Dix Bay tied firmly under her chin. Witherspoon might have worn the hat, Lenny decided. But she had seen through Crystal. She had seen through Crystal from the start.

"She's bad business," Witherspoon had said when Manny first started bringing her around. "She's bad business. And that boy of hers is worse than that. King, what kind of a name is that to call a boy?"

Lenny turned the lock on the door with a trembling hand. Don't let it be true, he prayed. Please don't let King be here. He sneezed, then sneezed again. His hand went for the vaporizer. No, he mustn't use it this soon again. He'd be back in bed acting like that. King Mallison! Lenny stood in the doorway remembering Manny's wedding day. Inside Momma's house the wedding was going on. Outside King was destroying Momma's roses. The Marechal Neil had never grown again. Eight years ago, could it be eight years that King had plagued his life. Except for Uncle Ted's suicide there had never been a breath of scandal in the Weiss family. Before Crystal their lives had moved along with only sickness to trouble them. Then Crystal, the King. King Mallison! "They said he was in Texas," Lenny said out loud. "They told me he was in school in Texas."

Lenny opened the door and looked down the hall. Everything looked all right. The library table was a bit askew. He made his way down the hall and through the dining room and into the kitchen. The kitchen was littered with pots and pans. There was flour all over a counter, as if someone had been making bread. A walnut cutting board that retailed for $46.50 was sitting on the table filled with marijuana. *He was using Momma's cutting board to clean marijuana.* "That's it," Lenny said "That's the last straw. That broke the camel's back."

"Hey, Uncle Lenny," King said, coming in behind him. He had his arm around a tall dark-haired girl wearing a blouse with little chess figures printed on it, queens and rooks and castles. Underneath the figures were breasts like the ones in magazines, so full and perfect it was impossible not to look at them. A very small button seemed to hold the blouse together. The breasts moved as she laughed. "Meet Roxanne Rothschild from New York," King said. "I told her I had a Jewish family and she wouldn't believe me. Tell her I'm okay, Uncle Lenny. Tell her I know the rabbi."

"What happened at the beach, King? What was going on down there?"

"I don't know what happened. I locked up good for the night, didn't I, Roxanne? We locked everything. It was that way when the sheriff woke us up this morning. I'll lend you a hand cleaning up. Is that what you came over for?"

"Are you living here? In the house?"

"Just temporarily. I'm going to move into town next week. I'm going back to Tulane. Well, how's it going? How's business? You doing okay?"

"Does Momma know you're living over here?"

"I guess so. How's she doing? Is her back okay?"

"She's better. She's walking most of the time."

"It's nice to know you," the black-haired girl said. She was moving closer. "Your nephew said I'd like you. He said you were the sweetest one in the family." She smiled deep into his face. She was very good at this. She had survived three stepmothers. She could charm her way out of a snakepit if she had to. "Have dinner with us, won't you? I'm a great cook. Wait till you taste my paella. Will you stay? We'd like it so much if you would."

"I guess so," he said. "I guess I will. If you have enough. I mean, that's kind of you. It's nice of you to ask." He was embarrassed. For a moment he had forgotten it was his house.

"Well, you just take King on down to the beach and about the time the sun goes down we're going to have some paella." She started moving pans out of her way and took an apron down from a hook and tied it around the blouse. "Go on, King, you two get out of my way."

"Her old man's a congressman," King said. "Would you believe it?"

When they came back up from the beach Roxanne had spread the table with a linen tablecloth and found wineglasses and opened a bottle of Margaux and left it on the table to breathe. It was out of Lenny's wine cabinet. She had taken off the blouse. In its place was a pink silk kimono that was so small it barely came to her knees. She was sticking candles into holders when Lenny came in the dining room. The back of the kimono was embroidered with a great white heron. Where had he seen that before?

"Look at this old thing I found in the attic," she said. "It must be fifty years old. King said nothing around here really belonged to anybody. He said it was okay to wear it."

"It was Sarah Louise's," he said. "She died when she was young. She was my cousin."

"What did she die of?"

"I don't know. Something was wrong with her heart. Her heart gave out."

"Do you mind me wearing it? Does it bother you?"

"Oh, no," he said. "It was a long time ago."

"Well, go wash up for supper and tell King. I'm almost ready. This is going to be a feast. I'm so glad you could stay." She smiled at him again, a long slow smile.

"Come here to me, you wild woman," King said, coming into the room and pulling her into his arms. "Quit turning all that stuff on Uncle Lenny. He's a bachelor." They laughed and pressed their bodies so close together Lenny thought they would melt as he watched. "Excuse me," he said. "I'll go and change my shirt."

He went into his room and stood by the bookcase. He pulled out his vaporizer and cleared his passages. He felt better. Maybe fall was coming. Perhaps this would be a good season.

He looked around his room. Everything was just where he left it. His autographed picture of Leonard Bernstein, his speed-reading course, his toolkit, his flash-light, his scaling knife. He touched a book on his desk. *Tropic of Cancer*, it said on the dustjacket. Inside was a dictionary. He turned the pages, letting them flip through his fingers. *Love*, he stopped at the word. "To feel affection for, hold dear, CHERISH."

He closed the book and went into the bathroom and took a shower and pulled on some clean slacks and a white shirt. He put on his socks and some tennis shoes and went out the door and in to dinner. The hall was full of the smell of bread baking.

The bread was hot, soft in the middle, crisp on the outside. They ate it with a salad. Drinking the wine. Then Roxanne served the paella, the steam rising from it. Lenny was hungry. He hadn't eaten all day. He forgot himself in the wine and food. Then he remembered something. A memory of some trouble King had been in assailed him. He took his fork and picked a small black thing out of the paella and put it on the side of his plate. "Are these mushrooms?" he said. "Sometimes I'm al-lergic to them. Certain kinds. I mean, the paella is very good. I don't think I've ever had any that was better. But I shouldn't eat mushrooms. You don't mind if I pick them out, do you?"

King and Roxanne looked at each other, then smiled. "I bought them at the store," she said. "They came from Piggly-Wiggly."

"We could get some of the other kind," King said. "If you'd like to try them."

"Oh, no," he said. "I mean, do you, ah, ever do that now? I mean, anymore?"

"Not very often," King said. "I'm cleaning up my act. I'm coming into town to get my cows."

"Your cows."

"I'm joining the tribe. Never mind, Uncle Lenny, it's just a figure of speech. Don't worry about it. We wouldn't feed you funny mushrooms without telling you about it."

"What's it like?" Lenny said. He took another bite of paella and poured himself more wine. "What's it like to do that?"

"Just pretty," she said. "Real funny and real beautiful. Sort of scary."

"Let's have another bottle of that wine," he said. "Go get it, King. You know where I keep the key."

A few of the mushrooms in the paella had not come from the store. A few of them were mushrooms King and Roxanne had picked in a field near the house, beautiful mushrooms with wide full lips like Roxanne's vagina. They had taken them home and baked them in the oven to take the bitter taste away and chopped them and mixed them with green onions and tamari sauce and chives and parsley and thyme and Roxanne added them to the paella just before she stuck it in the oven. It was a recipe Roxanne had learned in a commune in Minnesota. At King's commune in Texas they just fried them with eggs and bacon.

"I'm sorry," Lenny said finally. "I can't eat another

bite. That was perfect. They should make you a Chevalier, Roxanne." He started to pick up his plate but King took it from his hand.

"You just sit right there and enjoy your wine and let Roxanne and me clean this up. We'll have it done before you know it. Then we'll go for a walk down to the water. The moon's full. I love to watch it on the water, don't you?"

The night was very still. Not a leaf stirring in all those trees. They walked down the cobblestone path to the beach. The path led down between cypress and catalpa. The moon was like a spotlight. Lenny had never seen it so bright. An August moon, he thought, the biggest kind. When they reached the bridge over the lagoon Lenny felt Roxanne's hand. She had taken him by the arm as if to lead him. He felt her fingers going into his flesh, into his bones. A piece of moonlight took off and climbed a tree. The moon was all over the water. It was many colors, as many colors as a rainbow. Fish were swimming through the colors, a circle of light was opening up and taking everything. It took the lagoon, then the trees, then the beach. It was taking everything. It was on his legs, then his waist, coming up to take his eyes. It was on Roxanne's hand holding him. It was on his arm. His bones would melt from the colors. He would slide into the colored water and bubble away into nothing. Then singing. All that singing. What was all that singing? There could not be that many crickets in the world, din, din, din, an unimaginable din. Now the water was singing too. Even the water was singing.

"Come over here and sit down," Roxanne said. "Come

with me. You're safe with me, Lenny-Wenny. Come on, come on over here." She led him across the bridge. It took many hours to cross the bridge. It took a long time to lift his foot and put it down. It took forever to shift his weight from one foot to the other foot. Then they went through a forest of catalpa trees.

She led him down the sandy beach. King laid out a blanket and they sat down on each side of him and began to talk to him about the stars. They told him things he had never known about the stars. "They can't believe we are so well-behaved," King said. "They can't believe we are so cruel."

The moon was so bright. Lenny could see every ripple on the water. The ripples started far away on the other shore. Lenny watched each one until it reached the Weisses' shore. He must not take his eyes away. He must follow every ripple. He was growing weary. It was very tiring. It was wearing him out to watch the water like this. It was too much. He could feel the sand beneath him working, shaping him with its hands. "Oh, my God," he said. "Why am I here?" "Hush," Roxanne said. "It's just a trip. You'll get used to it. Give in, Lenny, enjoy yourself, let it take you. There you are, see, it's not so bad, now is it?"

A lion was making its way across the water. It was riding on a piece of deadwood. There were people behind it. Many of them, the color of fallen leaves, naked like the leaves. They were the leaf people, coming to take the beach. And the lion, golden in the moonlight. It was a moon lion. It was coming for him. He could not move. He would never get away.

"We're going to leave you now," King said. He towered over the place where Lenny lay. "For a little while. We're going to swim to the swing."

"We'll be back soon," Roxanne said. "You wait for us here." Then they were gone, moving away like tall black trees. They were going to swim. They would be eaten by the moon. He would never see them again.

"Come back," he cried out, sitting up on his elbows. "Come back to me. Don't leave me here alone." He turned over and put his face down into the blanket. His chin sank down into the sand. Around him the leaf people danced. The lion walked among them swinging his tail. A band began to play. Free beach, a man was calling through a megaphone. Free cookies, free beach, room for everyone. *It was Ernest.* Ernest had turned on him. Witherspoon was beside Ernest wearing her Little Dix Bay hat. *She was not dead!* People were coming from all directions, hordes of people with their children. They were drinking all the water from the river. They were filling cups and buckets and pitchers. They were trampling the sand, touching the cypress knees. Down the river came more tubers. They were naked. *They had taken off their clothes.* They were brown people with soft faces. The leaf people. The people of the leaf. They were coming from all directions, down from the trees, across the bridge, over the roof. They were picking the cape jasmine. Tying it in their hair. "Stay on the paths," Lenny was calling. "Please stay on the paths. Don't touch the cypress knees. Don't pick the jasmine. Dandaddy planted that," he cried out. "Oh, no, oh, please don't touch it. Stop it!" he screamed. "Stop it! Stop it! Stop it!"

"Come on in," a voice was calling from the water. One of the leaf girls had stood up on her leaf and was calling him. The moonlight was all around her like a halo. "Come on, chicken. Come on into the water."

"Come on," Roxanne called from the opposite shore. She and King were sitting on a swing that hung out over the water. A rope swing with a board for a seat. Lenny had played on that swing a thousand afternoons when he was a child, pretending he was at a great auction buying things. He would sit on the swing and call out bids for chifferobes and paintings and oriental rugs and chandeliers. Diamond tiaras which the owners thought were worthless would fall into his hands from the trees.

Lenny got up from the sand and walked across the beach toward the water. "Come on, Lenny," King called. "There's room for one more. Come on over." Lenny stepped into the water, it covered his ankles, it covered his knees. His feet were sinking down into the sand. It was quicksand. He fell forward into the water. He sank to the bottom of the little shallow river. He took hold of a root with his hand. He was a fish. He, Lenny Weiss, could turn himself into a fish. He could breathe in water.

"He's gone," Roxanne said. "He hasn't come up. He's disappeared." She dove from the swing and pulled through the water until she found him. She tore his hands loose from the plant and dragged him to the surface. King was beside her. Between them they dragged Lenny back to the beach and began to work on him. "There weren't enough mushrooms in that stuff to get a robin off," Roxanne said. "And now we're going to jail for murder."

"Hold his legs," King said. "Hold his legs up. God-damn you, Lenny, start breathing. Lenny, don't you dare die on me. Goddammit, start breathing, do you hear me. Breathe." Then King grabbed him around the chest and pushed and manhandled Lenny's skinny body until a little river of water ran out of his mouth and the lungs filled back up with air. King took him in his arms, cradling him into his body like a child. "Oh, Lenny, you baby, you angel, you old trooper you, good old Lenny, good old Uncle Lenny."

"Stop them, King," he said. "You've got to stop them. Call the sheriff, will you. Get the sheriff down here. Can't you make them stop. They're sitting on the cypress knees. They let the lion peepee on the beach. Stop them, you've got to stop them, King. It's up to you."

"They're leaving now," King said. "They're all going home to go to bed."

"That's right," Roxanne said. "It's bedtime. They're all going home."

"Why did you do it to me?" Lenny said. "Why did you give it to me, King? What did I do to deserve it? What did I ever do to you?"

"Nothing, baby. You didn't do a thing and we didn't give you anything. It's just the moon and the wine. It's just the way it is."

"What did you do to me?" Lenny said. "What did you put in that paella?"

"There's nothing in the paella, Lenny," Roxanne said. "And there's no one on the beach. They've all gone home to bed like good little dreams."

"What's going on?" Ernest said. He'd been hauling

in his trot line around the bend and heard the commotion. He pulled his skiff up on the beach and came walking over. He was half drunk on Dixie beer. His shoulders had rounded down into his chest. He was into his night-time mode. "What's happening?"

"Oh, nothing," King said. "Lenny had too much wine and fell in the river. Come on, take his other side. Help me get him up to the house. We've got to put him to bed."

They pulled Lenny along between them. Up onto the porch and into his room. They tucked him into bed and left a small light burning on the dresser.

"Can't ever tell what's going to happen next," Ernest said. "Well, all's well that ends well, as my granddaddy always said."

"Are you hungry?" Roxanne said. "We've got some homemade bread and some paella. Come on in the kitchen and have a bite to eat."

"Ernest is the poacher," King said, taking her by the arm. "We don't invite Ernest in for food, do we Ernest? Come on, let's be hanging it up for the night. I want to get some sleep."

"Well, I wouldn't mind a bite if you've got enough," Ernest said.

"Not tonight," King said. He took Ernest by the arm and led him out onto the porch and down the steps to the yard. "Good night, old buddy," he said. "See you in the morning. Guard the beach."

Lenny rolled his legs up against his chest. His head sank down into the soft down pillow. He picked up his broom and began to sweep. The beach went on forever. It was going to take all night. If he worked all night as hard as he could he could erase the footsteps before Mother came. He made a little pattern, starting at the tree line each time, sweeping smooth paths down to the water. By morning it would all be clean again. By morning it would be like new.

❧❧❧

Crazy, Crazy, Now Showing Everywhere

IT is fall again, or what passes for fall in Alexandria. Sultry October days that drift into a brief wet winter without even changing the leaves on the trees.

I sit here two blocks from Fanny's house, gazing out my window. I sit here nearly every afternoon, listening to jazz on the radio, waiting for Duncan to come home and ruin my day. And two blocks away his revered ideal idol, Fanny's husband, Gabe, Gabe Yellin, the gorgeous ageless archconservative, by which means he means with Duncan's help to conserve whatever made and keeps him a millionaire, Greedy Gabe, as Fanny calls him, her stormtrooper, lugs his briefcase up her stairs and hands her the pills.

And no one knows and no one wants to know and no one wants to talk about it anymore. There is nothing anyone can do, they say. No one can help her unless she helps herself. It's nice of you to be concerned, Lilly. It's nice of you to care. It's nice of you to visit her.

"Twin beds," Fanny is saying. "Twin beds all over the house. Darling, when I first met those people, when Gabe took me to visit them, I thought they must be real old. I didn't know married people slept in twin beds. I thought to myself, what is the matter with these people?"

She is talking about my in-laws. That's what Fanny and I do when I visit. We say terrible things about my in-laws and her in-laws and my husband and her husband and Yellin-Kase, the water heater factory that makes us all that dough. Yellin-Kase, The World's Largest Manufacturer Of Water Heaters.

At the moment Fanny and I are working over my mother-in-law. "I kept looking around the house for evidence of life," she is saying. "For something that wasn't put away. It was all put away. It was all in cabinets. Even the pillows had these plastic covers. We spent the night, and I said, Gabe, can I take the cover off the pillow while I sleep? Of course, that was the beginning, when they had just begun the factory. When it was all a dream. But she had money, your mother-in-law. Even then. But it was put away. Everything was put away."

"Look at her sons," I say. "Donny has ulcers, Jerry has asthma and Duncan's practically impotent. The perfect mother. They kiss without touching. I swear they do. I never saw such armor."

"Hush," Fanny says. "You know this room is bugged." She laughs her wonderful laugh, wishing it really were.

"I forgot," I say in a whisper, laughing back into her

beautiful ruined face, hypnotized by her great black eyes, her musical voice, forgetting she is crazy, forgetting I am crazy to be there.

I am seated on a soft flowered chair, my feet propped up on her bed. I have been for a walk in the park and stopped by for a cup of chicory coffee and cookies from the tall glass jars on the nightstand. Who else but Fanny keeps Oreos and Lorna Doones and Hershey's Kisses out in the open for anyone to see? Usually I do not sit in the chair. Usually I get my cookies and jump right into bed, kiss her soft welcoming cheeks, hold her in my arms. But today the bed is full of dogs. There are six or seven of them, spaniels and terriers and Irish setters.

"Goddamn these dogs," I say. One of them is licking me.

"Bribe them," she says. "They can be bribed." I take dog biscuits from the package she hands me and lead them out into the hall.

"Go for a walk with me," I say, returning to the room. "It's a glorious day. You can't afford to miss this day."

"I can see it," she says. "It's outside the windows. I've been watching it."

"Aren't you ever going to leave the room again?"

"Oh, I go down to dinner. I go nearly every evening. It's the new game. We have dinner. Then we have dessert."

"Who cooks now?"

"Gabe does. Since his cook died." Everything is his with Fanny. His house, his children, his dogs, his factory, his game. Only the room is hers. "Or we send out for things. It doesn't matter. It's all right, Lilly. I know what I'm doing."

"You don't know what you're doing." I stand up, starting to walk around the room. "You can't take those pills without seeing a psychiatrist."

"He goes for me. I told you all about it. I told Treadway that if he liked me so much he could just come over here and see me. I was tired of going over there. Get dressed. Get in the car. Go see Treadway. Come back home." She laughed, falling back against the pillows. "Now Gabe goes. They're crazy about each other. They give each other things. Gabe gives him money and he gives Gabe pills." She looked away.

"I'm sorry. I don't mean to make you unhappy. I know what you're afraid of. I just don't like the idea of you staying here forever taking those pills. . . ."

"They'll lock me up again if I don't take them."

"They can't lock you up unless you let them. There's a new law. Oh, God, Fanny, why won't you believe me? Or go to a good psychiatrist and believe him. There are good psychiatrists. They aren't all like Treadway. They don't lock people up anymore."

"You don't understand," she says. "You just don't understand."

I am staring at the open drawer of the nightstand. The drawer is always open, the bottles are always there for us to see, Elavil and Stelazine and lithium. Her little maids, she calls them. They travel day and night around her bloodstream, destroying the muscles, doing God knows what to the liver and kidney and spleen, to the will and desire and ambition and rage. Not the intelligence. Her intelligence is beyond the reach of chemicals. Who knows? Perhaps she is right to believe this bed, these pills, this childlike life are her only refuge.

"Oh, Fanny, I love you," I say, knocking the dogs off the bed, for they have come back in, cuddling up in her arms. This morning light is pouring in the tall windows of the famous room.

"I will save you," she says. "I will save you if I can. I cannot bear it if they have you too."

It is Friday, the worst day of my week. On Friday nights we dine with Duncan's family. Two black women cook all afternoon in the Kases' kitchen, making stuffed artichokes and oyster soup and rack of lamb and au gratin potatoes and creamed spinach, setting the long table with finger bowls and heavy silver and crystal wineglasses.

At six-thirty we assemble in the den, all the Kase sons and their wives. We talk about taxes and crime and corruption and society people who are deadbeats or hippies or drunks. I do not speak of Mrs. Kase's sister's suicide. They do not speak of my childlessness.

At seven one of the black women calls us to dinner and we file into the dining room and light the Sabbath candles.

"I saw Fanny today," I say. "She looks wonderful. She's the wisest person I've ever known."

"I'm glad to hear that," my father-in-law says. "That's nice."

"It's criminal what Gabe is doing to her," I say. "I think all the time about reporting him to the police."

"It's such a shame," my mother-in-law says, not daring to tell me to shut up.

My father-in-law sighs and attends to the lamb. Gabe is his business partner in the factory. My husband,

Duncan, is third in command, the golden boy, the one they hope can hold it all together. They think of themselves as being in a state of siege, from the government and its meddling, from the labor unions' constant attempts to unionize the plant, from competitors in other states and foreign countries. It is hard staying rich. At any moment it could all fall apart. Meanwhile, their alliance is all that holds it together.

"She must have been beautiful when she was young," I say. "The paintings De Laureal did of her are wonderful. She put them back up. Did I tell you that?"

"That's nice," Mrs. Kase says. "It's such a shame what Gabe's been through."

"She's the one to pity," I say. "She might have been a great artist. She's the one to feel sorry for."

Duncan coughs, gets up, and starts pouring the Bordeaux. His mother and father exchange a long look.

"What in the world does Fanny say to Lilly?" the Yellins ask each other.

"What on earth is Lilly telling Fanny?" the Kases sigh.

"*You are next*," Fanny said to me the night we met. "Come to see me. Come right away. *I will save you if I can. You have to come to see me.*"

That was the night I met her, a New Year's Eve, the year I married Duncan for his money and came to live in Alexandria. I am from Monroe. My parents are schoolteachers. I thought I would have a more exotic life. I was raised to worship money. I was raised to get money any way I could. I met Duncan at Tulane. He couldn't even ask me to marry him without asking his parents' permission. I married him in spite of that. I married him to have his money. Now I have to pay for that. I have to pay and pay and pay. I am a cliché. Except for Fanny. She makes my life different from the lives around me.

That New Year's Eve I was wearing a black and white satin evening suit I ordered from a magazine. My hair was long and loose and shiny. I was Duncan's dream girl that winter, his bride, and he was taking me around to pay New Year's duty calls.

Fanny still went downstairs back then. She was seated on a loveseat before the fireplace watching her youngest son roast chestnuts. She was wearing a wrinkled red silk dress and her legs were folded under her. No stockings, no shoes. She loooked up at me, smiling a wonderful mysterious smile. She was the most interesting person I had ever met. I sat down beside her and told her anything she wanted to know, drinking martinis as fast as Gabe could bring them from the kitchen.

"I've just come home from Mandeville," she said. She was laughing, holding my hand. "You know, the Loony Bin."

"Oh, sure," I said. Of course I had not known. I had never known anyone who had been locked up for being crazy.

"It's wonderful," she said. "I never wanted to leave. I made a lot of friends."

"We have to be going, Lilly," Duncan said. "Mother wants us to go to the Durnings' with them."

"Come back," Fanny said, still holding on to my hand. "Promise you'll come. Promise you'll visit me *every* New Year's Eve of your life."

I promised. How could I stay away?

That was the year she painted the room, the famous, much talked about room, her "madness museum," as she called it.

"Crazy, Crazy, Now Showing Everywhere," it said on the door in two-inch letters.

Below that, in God forgive me, *my* handwriting, "Lilly says, spit in one hand and worry in the other and see which one fills up the fastest." She *made* me write it there. At that time, the first year I knew her, the year she was painting the room, you had to be very careful what you said around her as she might seize on *anything* and make you write it on the wall.

From the door the mural spread inward onto the four walls of the high-ceilinged, rectangular room. Water colors, crayons, oils, acrylics, long sections marked "Conspiracies" and "Swindles," names and dates and anecdotes from her fifty years' war with the wealthy Jewish world into which she was born.

There were crossword puzzles made of jargon cut from newspapers. WHOSE LIFE IS IT ANYWAY was glued to a chair. There were quotations from thick books on psychiatry. The east wall was devoted to R. D. Laing. The floor was littered with paintbrushes and jars of paint and hundreds of Marks-A-Lot pens.

All this frightened me, but I could not stay away. Fanny's room was the most exciting place in Alexandria.

Anyone was likely to be there, a museum director, a painter, a journalist, a poet, one of her former inmates from Mandeville, visitors from New Orleans.

Sometimes I would not see her for weeks. Then, suddenly, there would be her voice on the phone, soft, conspiratorial. "Hurry," she would say. "Come as soon as he leaves for work. I have a present for you. Please come. I need you."

I would go. It was impossible to stay away. She would be waiting, propped up in bed cutting words and slogans from magazines and newspapers. "My work," she called it. "I have to find the words, when I find the right words I will expose them. You'll see. I will have it all out in the open where everyone can see. Then they will not be able to deny it. Then everyone will know."

She would be working away, a music box playing her favorite song over and over. "Raindrops Keep Falling on My Head," that was the one she liked that year.

"Look," she said one morning, taking a jeweler's box out from underneath a pillow, putting it into my hand. "Keep this. In case you need to call me."

I opened it and found a beautiful pearl and diamond earring, just one. She showed me how to twist the pearl that hung like a drop from a diamond stem. "Just turn it," she said. "Like this. I'll hear you. No matter where I am I'll hear you."

"Sure," I said, going along with the joke.

"Tell me what's going on," she said. "What are those Kase people doing to you?"

"Oh, nothing. Everything's fine. I'm going to take some classes this fall, maybe go into the real estate business with Duncan's cousin. I'm fine. I'm getting used to being here. It's fine. I'm starting to like it here."

"You're going to be the scapegoat," she said. "They are going to use you for the scapegoat. They can't forgive you for being pretty. You know that, don't you?"

"Oh, it's not like that. I knew what I was getting into. I met them before I married him. I knew what it was going to be like."

"Be careful, Lilly, they are going to eat you alive."

"It's not like that. It isn't that bad. When I get worried I just go to the park and run as fast as I can."

"Write it down," she said, handing me a pen. "Here, take this. Write it on the wall."

"Oh, no, I don't want to write it."

"Write, 'When I worry I run as fast as I can.' Please write it. Please write it down for me." I took the pen and wrote it on the wall beside the door. It seemed like a perfectly reasonable thing to say until she made me write it down.

That spring, that April, that May, were bad times in both our lives. I played tennis all day long. She worked on the room.

"The black apes are on their way," she told me one morning on the phone. "They leave messages on my easel. I have put my paints away. Now it must all be in words. You have to help me, Lilly. You have to bring me words."

"Are you spitting out the pills?" I said. At that time I believed they were good for her. "Don't spit out the pills. Please don't spit out the pills."

"I have to," she said. "Gabe is after me to sign papers

again. They are bringing me papers to sign. Will you come to me? Will you come this morning?"

"I don't know. I have to play tennis. I have to play tennis every day this week."

"Please come," she said. "And bring me words. I need more words. I need all the words I can get."

She was too crazy for me that summer. I stayed away. I was trying to make my marriage work. I decorated the house, studied recipe books, had dinner parties, worked on my body. I had recurrent dreams about Fanny. I dreamed we were on a sailboat in the islands, sailing through clear blue Caribbean waters. I was at the tiller and Fanny was tied to the mast so she couldn't fall overboard. We sailed and sailed, laughing and talking, drinking endless cups of coffee. The journey was pleasant and I was happy at the tiller, but *I did not know where we were going.*

There was a destination, someplace I was supposed to deliver her to but she could not tell me where it was. I sailed to port after port but no one was waiting on the piers or they would not let us disembark. At the end of the dream I thought I saw our harbor in the distance and I set the sails and started for it through an open sea.

Then slowly, terribly, great whales began to surface before the prow. Great, brown whales rising up like uncharted shoals all around us. They wore harnesses around their bellies. They had riders. The black apes of Fanny's terrors were riding them. I would wake covered with sweat, shaking and terrified, determined to stay away from her.

☙ ☙ ☙

Duncan and I went off to the real Caribbean in July. While I was gone Fanny finished the room and moved out into the hall and bathroom.

"Oh, did you ever see the bathroom?" she said to me later. "Oh, I could never make it again. I painted on the bathtub, on the toilet, on the washstand, on the floor. 'Oh, dear, we have to lock Mother up again,' I heard Gloria saying.

"You should have seen the tub. They could not deny it now. Now they knew what they were doing. I had dumped the whole thing in their laps. They bought off Clark. They bought off Treadway. But I showed them. They had no way of not knowing anymore. 'Oh, dear, we have to lock poor old Mother up again,' Gloria said. 'Oh, dear, oh dear.' "

The day before they came to get her she wrote MURDER over the bed in three-foot letters.

"Gibberish," Doctor Treadway said when he saw it.

"Generalities," Gabe added. And as soon as Fanny was safely back in Mandeville he called the painters. They painted the room light blue with white trim. How could I have stopped them? I was sailing from Petit Saint Vincent to Mustique, locked up on a fifty-foot sailboat watching Duncan drink beer and brood over the unions and the government coming to take his money away.

"Oh, I could never make the room again," she said the other day, safe at home once more, safe in the arms of her wonderful keepers, Stelazine and lithium and Elavil. The little bottles standing guard beside her bed, the little maids. The room is so clean and cheerful, there is a blue silk quilt on the bed, a clean rug on the floor.

The paintings are hanging on the wall, the dresser drawers are shut, the books are on the shelves.

"I would have photographed it. If I had been here I would have stopped him. I can't believe he let them paint it all away."

"Here," she said, taking a sketch pad from a drawer beside the bed. "This is what I'm doing now. I'm going to play their game. I'm going to put them on paper and have them framed and nail nails into the wall and hang them up. That's what they told me at the Loony Bin. You have to play their game. That's the new idea. So I played their game. And now I'm home. Here, look at what I'm doing." She opened the pad. It was a scale drawing of her house, everything very precise like an architect's sketch. In front of the house were seven garbage cans, all in a row with the tops down nice and tight. "I'm going to do a series of these drawings," she said. "Won't they love it when they see it? Won't Gabe be surprised?"

"Oh, God, you're so subtle," I said. I gave her a kiss. "I have to get home now. I have to go cook dinner. I'll see you soon. I'll talk to you later."

"Bring me a present," she said. "Bring me words. I need some words. I want you to bring me words every day this week."

What words would I take her? What words could set her free? Could words undo the words that put her there? *Love is all you need.* I could tell her what the Beatles say. *Hey, Jude, don't be afraid. I want to hold your hand. Remember to let it out of your head.*

I could tear in there some morning and drag her out of bed and put her into the car and start driving. I would drive northwest into the mountains. I would drive all night. I would go up into the mountains until we were at fourteen thousand feet. I would make her get out and look at where she was. *Think how far she would see. How far I would see.*

"You're crazy," Duncan says. "You're as crazy as she is to even go over there, Lilly. There's nothing anyone can do. She's a pain in the ass, that's what she is. A terrible embarrassment. No one makes her stay in that room. No one makes her take those pills. Now quit worrying about it. Quit talking about it all the time."

"You're wrong," I say. "It's Gabe. It's his fault. He gives her the pills. He hands them to her. He's the one that does it."

"They do it together, Lilly. It's their life. It's what they do. It's what they like to do. Mind your own business, would you? Stop driving me crazy with this nonsense."

I go out and sit on the front steps. It's a beautiful old neighborhood, especially this time of year, in early fall. It's almost dark now, first dark, dusk some people call it. I like to sit here this time of day, watching the jays and nightjars fight above the city roofs, turning and swooping and diving, calling, caw, caw, caw, calling good news, good news, good news, calling hunger, hunger, hunger.

Nora Jane

AUTHOR'S NOTE

This is not the first time I have written about Nora Jane Whittington. In 1978 I wrote a story about her called "The Famous Poll at Jody's Bar." Here is how I introduced her in that story. "Nora Jane was nineteen years old, a self-taught anarchist and a quick change artist. She owned six Dynel wigs in different hair colors, a make-up kit she stole from Le Petit Theatre du Vieux Carré while working as a volunteer stagehand and a small but versatile wardrobe. She could turn her graceful body into any character she saw in a movie or on TV. . . . She could also do wonderful tricks with her voice, which had a range of almost two octaves."

All these attributes came in handy later in the story when Nora Jane, disguised as a Dominican nun, set out to rob a bar in the Irish Channel section of New Orleans. It was the quickest way she could think of to get enough money to go to California to join her young lover, Sandy Halter.

When the story ended Nora Jane had successfully completed the robbery and was on her way to California. I wish I could say that Sandy was waiting at the airport when she got there, sleepless and excited and true. I wish that dreams came true, that courage and tenderness were rewarded in the world as they should be. I wish I could tell you that Nora Jane and Sandy lived happily ever after in Sunny California. Alas, that is not the way it happened.

☙☙☙

Jade Buddhas, Red Bridges, Fruits of Love

SHE had written to him, since neither of them had a phone.

> *I'll be there Sunday morning at four. It's called the Night Owl flight in case you forget the number. The number's 349. If you can't come get me I'll get a taxi and come on over. I saw Johnny Vidocovitch last night. He's got a new bass player. He told Ron he could afford to get married now that he'd found his bass player. Doesn't that sound just like him. I want to go to that chocolate place in San Francisco the minute I get there. And lie down with you in the dark for a million years. Or in the daylight. I love you. Nora Jane*

He wasn't there. He wasn't at the gate. Then he wasn't in the terminal. Then he wasn't at the baggage carousel. Nora Jane stood by the carousel taking her hat on and off, watching a boy in cowboy boots kiss his girlfriend in front of everyone at the airport. He would run his hands down her flowered skirt and then kiss her again.

Finally the bags came. Nora Jane got her flat shoes out of her backpack and went on out to find a taxi. It's because I was too cheap to get a phone, she told herself. I knew I should have had a phone.

She found a taxi and was driven off into the hazy early morning light of San Jose. The five hundred and forty dollars she got from the robbery was rolled up in her bag. The hundred and twenty she saved from her job was in her bra. She had been awake all night. And something was wrong. Something had gone wrong.

"You been out here before?" the driver said.

"It's the first time I've been farther west than Alexandria," she said. "I've hardly ever been anywhere."

"How old are you?" he said. He was in a good mood. He had just gotten a $100 tip from a drunk movie star. Besides, the little black-haired girl in the back seat had the kind of face you can't help being nice to.

"I'll be twenty this month," she said. "I'm a Moonchild. They used to call it Cancer but they changed. Do you believe in that stuff?"

"I don't know," the driver said. "Some days I believe in anything. Look over there. Sun's coming up behind the mountains."

"Oh, my," she said. "I forgot there would be mountains."

"On a clear day you can see Mount Diablo. You ought to go while you're out here. You can see eighty percent of California from it. You came out to visit someone?"

"My boyfriend. Well, he's my fiancé. Sometimes he has to work at night. He wasn't sure he could meet me.

Is it far? To where I'm going?" They were in a neighborhood now, driving past rows of stucco cottages, built close together like houses in the Irish Channel. The yards looked brown and bare as if they needed rain.

"Couple of blocks. These are nice old neighborhoods. My sister used to live out here. It's called the Lewis tract." He turned a corner and came to a stop before a small pink house with an overgrown yard.

"Four fifty-one. Is that right?"

"That's right."

"You want me to wait till you see if anyone's here?"

"No, I'll just get out."

"You sure?"

"I'm sure." She watched as he backed and turned and went on off down the road, little clouds of dust rising behind the wheels. She stood looking up the path to the door. A red tree peeling like a sunburn shaded the yard. Here and there a few scraggly petunias bloomed in boxes. *Get your ass out here and see where the USA is headed*, Sandy had written her. *I've got lots of plans. No phone as yet. Bring some French bread. Everything out here is sourdough. Yours forever, Sandy.* He's here, she thought. I know he's here.

She walked on up the path. There was a spider's web across the screen door. They can make one overnight, she told herself. It's nothing to make one overnight.

She rang the door bell and waited. Then she walked around to the back and looked in the window. It was a large room with a modern-looking stove and a tile floor. I'm going in, she decided. I'm worn out. I'm going in.

She picked up a rock and broke a pane of glass in the

door, then carefully picked out all the broken pieces and put them in a pile under the steps. She reached her hand in the opening, undid the latch and went on in. It was Sandy's house all right. His old Jazzfest poster of Dr. John and the Mardi Gras Indians was hanging on a wall. A few clothes were in the closets. Not many. Still, Sandy traveled light. He'll be back, she thought. He's just gone somewhere.

She walked around the house looking for clues. She found only a map of San Francisco with some circles drawn on it, and a list, on an envelope, from something called the Paris Hotel. Willets, it said. Berkeley, Sebastopol, Ukiah, Petaluma, Occidental.

She walked back into the kitchen looking for something to eat. The refrigerator was propped open with a blue tile. Maybe he's in jail, she thought. Maybe I got here just in time.

She reached up a fingernail and flipped open a greeting card that was tacked up over the stove. It was a photograph of a snow-covered mountain with purple fields below and blue skies above. A hawk, or perhaps it was a buzzard, was flying over the mountain. FREEDOM IS THE GREATEST GIFT THAT ONE CAN GIVE ANOTHER, the card said. IT IS A GIFT BORN OF LOVE, TRUST, AND UNDERSTANDING. Nora Jane pulled out the pushpin and read the message inside.

Dear Sandy,
I am glad I am going to be away from you during our two weeks of abstinence. You were so supportive once you realized I was freaking out. I want to thank you for being there for me. We have climbed the mountain

together now and also the valley. I hope the valley wasn't too low for you.

I know this has been hard on you. You have had to deal with a lot of new feelings and need time to adjust to them. We will both hopefully grow from this experience. I want us to have many more meaningful experiences together. I love you more than words can say. In deepest friendship.

Pam

I'm hungry, Nora Jane thought. I'm starving. She walked over to a bed in a corner. She guessed it was a bed. It was a mattress on top of a platform made of some kind of green stone. It looked more like a place to sacrifice someone than a place to sleep.

She put her pack up on the bed and began riffling through the pockets for the candy bar she had saved from a snack on the plane. When she found it she tore open the cardboard box and began to eat it, slowly at first, then faster. *I don't know*, she thought. *I just don't know.* She leaned up against the green stone platform eating the chocolate, watching the light coming in the window through the leaves of the red tree making patches on the mattress. That's all we are, she decided. Patches of light and darkness. Things that cast shadows.

She ate the rest of the candy, stopping every now and then to lick her fingers. When she was finished she folded the candy box and put it carefully away in her pack. Nora Jane never littered anything. So far in her life she had not thrown down a single gum wrapper.

During the next week there were four earthquakes in the Bay Area. A five point, then a four point, then a two, then a three. The first one woke her in the middle of the night. She was asleep in a room she had rented near the Berkeley campus. At first she thought a cat had walked across the bed. Then she thought the world had come to an end. Then the lights went on. Everyone in the house gathered in the upstairs hall. When the excitement wore down a Chinese mathematician and his wife fixed tea in their room. "Very lucky to be here for that one," Tam Suyin assured Nora Jane. "Sometimes have to wait long time to experience big one."

"I was in a hurricane once," Nora Jane said. "I had to get evacuated when Camille came."

"Oh," Tam said to her husband. "Did you hear that? Miss Whittington have to be evacuated during hurricane. Which one you find most interesting experience, Miss Whittington, earthquake or hurricane?"

"I don't know," Nora Jane said. She was admiring the room, which was as bare as a nun's cell. "I guess the hurricane. It lasted longer."

The next morning she felt better than she had in a week. She was almost glad to be alive. She bought croissants from a little shop on Tamalpais Street, then spent some time decorating her room to look like a nun's cell. She put everything she owned in the closet. She covered the bed with a white sheet. She took down the drapes. She put the rug away and cleaned the floor. She bought flowers and put them on the dresser.

That afternoon she found a theatrical supply store on Shattuck Avenue and bought a stage pistol. It was time to get to work.

"What are you doing?" the proprietor said.

"Happy Birthday, Nora Jane. Have you ever seen it?"

"The Vonnegut play? The one with the animal heads?"

"No, this is an original script. It's a new group on the campus."

"Bring a poster by when you get them ready. We like to advertise our customers."

"I'll do that," she said. "As soon as we get some printed."

"When's it scheduled for?"

"Oh, right away. As soon as we can whip it together."

Freddy Harwood walked down Telegraph Avenue thinking about everyone who adored him. He had just run into Buiji. She had let him buy her a café mocca at the Met. She had let him hold her hand. She had told him all about the horrible time she was having with Dudley. She told him about the au pair girl and the night he threatened her with a gun and the time he choked her and what he said about her friends. It was Freddy she loved, she said. Freddy she adored. Freddy she worshipped. Freddy's hairy stomach and strong arms and level head she longed for. She was counting the days until she was free.

I ought to run for office, he was thinking. And just to think, I could have thrown it all away. I could have been a wastrel like Augustine. But no, I chose another way. The prince's way. Noblesse oblige. Ah, duty, sweet mistress.

Freddy Harwood was the founder and owner of the biggest and least profitable bookstore in northern California. He had one each of every book worth reading in the English language. He had everything that was still in print and a lot that was out of print. He knew dozens of writers. Writers adored him. He gave them autograph parties and unlimited credit and kept their books in stock. He even read their books. He went that far. He actually read their books.

In return they were making him famous. Already he was the hero of three short stories and a science fiction film. Last month *California Magazine* had named him one of the Bay Area's ten most eligible bachelors. Not that he needed the publicity. He already had more women than he knew what to do with. He had Aline and Rita and Janey and Lila and Barbara Hunnicutt, when she was in between tournaments. Not to mention Buiji. Well, he was thinking about settling down. *There are limits*, he said to himself. *Even to Grandmother's money. There are perimeters and prices to pay.*

He wandered across Blake Street against the light, trying to choose among his women. A man in a baseball cap took him by the arm and led him back to the sidewalk.

"Nieman," he said. "What are you doing in town?"

"Looking for you. I've got to see three films between now and twelve o'clock. Go with me. I'll let you help write the reviews."

"I can't. I'm up to my ass in the IRS. I'll be working all night."

"Tomorrow then. I'm at Gautier's. Call me for breakfast."

"If I get through. If I can."

"Holy shit," Nieman said. "Did you see that?" Nora Jane had just passed them going six miles an hour down the sidewalk. She was wearing black and white striped running shorts and a pair of canvas wedgies with black ankle straps, her hair curling all over her head like a dark cloud.

"This city will kill me," Freddy said. "I'm moving back to Gualala."

"Let's catch her," Nieman said. "Let's take her to the movies."

"I can't," Freddy said. "I have to work."

An hour later his computer broke. He rapped it across the desk several times, then beat it against the chair. Still no light. He laid it down on a pile of papers and decided to take a break. An accountant, he was thinking. They've turned me into an accountant.

Nora Jane was sitting by a window of the Atelier reading *The Bridge of San Luis Rey*. She was deep into a description of Uncle Pio. "He possessed the six attributes of an adventurer, a memory for names and faces, with the aptitude for altering his own, the gift of tongues; inexhaustible invention; secrecy, the talent for falling into conversation with strangers, and that freedom from conscience that springs from a contempt for the dozing rich he preyed upon." That's just like me, Nora Jane was thinking. She felt in her bag for the gun. It was still there.

Freddy sat down at a table near hers. Your legs are proof of the existence of God. No, not that. What if she's an atheist? If I could decipher the Rosetta Stone of your anklestraps. My best friend just died. My grandmother owns Sears Roebuck.

"I haven't seen one of those old Time-Life editions of that book in years," he said. "I own a bookstore. May I look at that a minute?"

"Sure you can," she said. "It's a great book. I bought it in New Orleans. That's where I'm from."

"Ah, the crescent city. I know it well. Where did you live? In what part of town?"

"Near the park. Near Tulane."

"On Exposition?"

"No, on Story Street. Near Calhoun." She handed him the book. He took it from her and sat down at the table.

"Oh, this is very interesting, finding this," he said. "This series was so well designed. Look at this cover. You don't see them like this now."

"I've been looking for a bookstore to go to," she said. "I haven't been here long. I don't know my way around yet."

"Well, the best bookstore in the world is right down the street. Finish your coffee and I'll take you there. Clara, I call it. Clara, for light. You know, the patron saint of light."

"Oh, sure," she said. The stranger, she thought. This is the stranger.

They made their way out of the café through a sea of ice cream chairs and out onto the sidewalk. It was in between semesters at Berkeley, and Telegraph Avenue was quiet, almost deserted. When they got to the store Freddy turned the key in the lock and held the door open for her. "Sorry it's so dark," he said. "It's on an automatic switch."

"Is anyone here?" she asked.

"Only us."

"Good," she said. She took the pistol out of her purse and stepped back and pointed it at him. "Where is the office?" she said. "I am robbing you. I came to get money."

"Oh, come on," he said. "You've got to be kidding. Put that gun down."

"I mean it," she said. "This is not a joke. I have killed. I will kill again." He put his hands over his head as he had seen prisoners do in films and led the way to his office through a field of books, a bright meadow of books, one hundred and nineteen library tables piled high with books.

"Listen, Betty," he began, for Nora Jane had told him her name was Betty.

"I came to get money," she said. "Where is the money? Don't talk to me. Just tell me where you put the money."

"Some of it's in my pocket," he said. "The rest is locked up. We don't keep much here. It's mostly charge accounts."

"Where's the safe? Come on. Don't make me mad."

"It's behind that painting. Listen, I'll have to help you take that down. That's a Helen Watermeir. She's my aunt. She'll kill me if anything happens to that painting."

Nora Jane had moved behind his desk. "Try not to mess up those papers," he said. "I gave up a chance to canoe the Eel River to work on those papers."

"What's it a painting of?" she said.

"It's A.E."

"A.E.?"

"Abstract Expressionism."

"Oh, I know about that. Sister Celestine said it was from painters riding in airplanes all the time. She said that's what things look like to them from planes. You know, I was thinking about that flying up here. We flew over all these salt ponds. They were these beautiful colors. I was thinking about those painters."

"I'll have to let you tell Aunt Helen that. She's really defensive about A.E. right now. That might cheer her up. Now, listen here, Betty, hasn't this gone far enough? Can't you put that gun down? They put people in Alcatraz for that." She was weakening. She was looking away. He pressed his luck. "Nobody with legs like yours should be in Alcatraz."

"This is what I do," she said. "I'm an anarchist. I don't know what else to do." The gun was pointing to the floor.

"Oh," he said. "There are lots of better things to do in San Francisco than rob a bookstore."

"Name one," she said.

"You could go with me," he said. He decided to pull out all the stops. He decided to go for his old standby. "We could go together 'while the evening is spread out against the sky, like a patient etherized upon a table. Oh, do not ask what is it. Let us go and make our visit.' "

"I know that poem," she said. "We had it in English." She wasn't pointing the gun and she was listening. Of course he had never known the "Love Song" to fail. He had seen hardhearted graduate students pull off their sweaters by the third line.

He kept on going. Hitting the high spots. Watching

for signs of boredom. By the time he got to "tea and cakes and ices," she had begun to cry. When he got to the line about Prince Hamlet she laid the gun down on top of the computer and dissolved in tears. "My name isn't Betty," she said. "I hate the name of Betty. My name is Nora Jane Whittington and tomorrow is my birthday. Oh, goddamn it all to hell. Oh, goddamn everything in the whole world to hell."

He came around the desk and put his arms around her. She felt wonderful. She felt as good as she looked. "I'm going home and turn myself in," she was sobbing. "They've got my fingerprints. They've got my handwriting. I'm going to have to go live in Mexico."

"No, you aren't," he said. "Come along. Let's go eat dinner. I've been dreaming all day about the prawns at Narsai's."

"I don't want any prawns," she said. "I don't even know what prawns are. I want to go to that chocolate store. I want to go to that store Sandy told me about."

Many hours later they were sitting in the middle of a eucalyptus grove on the campus, watching the stars through the trees. The fog had lifted. It was a nice night with many stars.

"The woods decay, the woods decay and fall," Freddy was saying, but she interrupted him.

"Do you think birds live up there?" she said. "That far up."

"I don't know," he said. "I never thought about it."

"It doesn't look like they would want to nest that high up. I watch birds a lot. I mean, I'm not a birdwatcher or anything like that. But I used to go out on the seawall and watch them all the time. The seagulls, I mean. Feed them bread and watch them fly. Did you ever think how soft flying seems? How soft they look, like they don't have any edges."

"I took some glider lessons once. But I couldn't get into it. I don't care how safe they say it is."

"I don't mean people flying. I mean birds."

"Well, look, how about coming home with me tonight. I want you to spend the night. You can start off your birthday in my hot tub."

"You've got a hot tub in your house?"

"And a redwood deck and a vegetable garden, corn, okra, squash, beans, skylights, silk kimonos, foton, orange trees. If you come over you won't have to go any place else the whole time you're in California. And movies. I just got *Chariots of Fire*. I haven't even had time to see it yet."

"All right," she said. "I guess I'll go."

Much later, sitting in his hot tub she told him all about it. "Then there was this card tacked up over the stove from this girl. You wouldn't believe that card. I wouldn't send anyone one of those cards for a million dollars. We used to have those cards at the Mushroom Cloud. Anyway, now I don't know what to do. I guess I'll go on home and turn myself in. They've got my fingerprints. I left them all over everything."

"We could have your fingers sanded. Did you ever see that movie? With Bette Davis as twin sisters? And Karl Malden. I *think* it was Karl Malden."

"I can't stay out here," she said. "I don't know how to take care of myself out here."

"I'll take care of you," he said. "Listen, N.J., you want me to tell you the rest of that quote I was telling you or not?"

"The one about the trees dying?"

"No, the one about the lice."

"All right," she said. "Go on. Tell the whole thing. I forgot the first part." She had already figured out there wasn't any stopping him once he decided to quote something.

"It's from Heraclitus. Now, listen, this is really good. 'All men are deceived by the appearances of things, even Homer himself, who was the wisest man in Greece; for he was deceived by boys catching lice; they said to him, 'What we have caught and what we have killed we have left behind, but what has escaped us we bring with us.' "

"Am I supposed to say something?" she said.

"Not unless you want to, come on, let's get to bed. Tomorrow we begin the F. Slazenger Harwood memorial tour of the Bay Area. The last girl who got it was runner-up for Miss America. It was wasted on her, however. She didn't even shiver when she put her finger in the passion fruit."

"What all do we have to do?" Nora Jane said.

"We have to see your chocolate store and the seismograph and the Campanile and the Pacific Ocean and the redwood trees. And a movie. At least one movie. There's this great documentary about Werner Herzog playing. He kills all these people trying to move a boat across a forest in Brazil. At the end he says, I don't know if it was worth it. Sometimes I don't know if movies are worth all this."

☙ ☙ ☙

The tour moved from the Cyclotron to Chez Panisse, from Muir Woods to Toroya's, from the Chinese cemetery to Bolinas Reef.

It began with the seismograph. "That needle is connected to a drum deep in the earth," Freddy quoted from a high-school science lecture. "You could say that needle has its finger on the earth's heart. When the plates shift, when the mantle buckles, it tells us just how much and where."

"What good does that do," Nora Jane said, "if the building you're in is falling down?"

"Come on," he said. "We're late to the concert at the Campanile."

They drove all over town in Freddy's new DeLorean. "Why does this car have fingerprints all over it?" Nora Jane asked. "If I had a car this nice I'd keep it waxed."

"It's made of stainless steel. It's the only stainless steel DeLorean in town. You can't wax stainless steel."

"If I got a car I'd get a baby blue convertible," she said. "This girl at home, Dany Nasser, that went to Sacred Heart with me, had one. She kept promising to let me drive it but she never did."

"You can drive my car," he said. "You can drive it all day long. You can drive it anyplace you want to drive it to."

"Except over bridges," she said. "I don't drive over bridges."

"Why not?"

"I don't know. It always seems like there's nothing underneath them. Like there's nothing there."

☙ ☙ ☙

He asked her to move in with him but she turned him down. "I couldn't do that," she said. "I wouldn't want to live with anyone just now."

"Then let's go steady. Or get matching tattoos. Or have a baby. Or buy a dog. Or call up everyone we know and tell them we can't see them anymore."

"There isn't anyone for me to call," she said. "You're the only one I know."

In August Sandy found her. Nora Jane was getting ready to go to work. She was putting in her coral earrings when Tam Suyin called her to the phone.

"I was in Colorado," he said. "I didn't get your letter until a week ago. I've been looking all over the place for you. Finally I got Ron and he told me where you were."

"Who's Pam," she said. "Tell me about Pam."

"So you're the one that broke my window."

"I'll pay for your window. Tell me about Pam."

"Pam was a mistake. She took advantage of me. Look, Nora Jane, I've got big plans for us. I've got something planned that only you and I could do. I mean, this is big money. Where are you? I want to see you right away."

"Well, you can't come now. I'm on my way to work. I've got a job, Sandy."

"A job?"

"In an art gallery. A friend got it for me."

"What time do you get off? I'll come wait for you."

"No, don't do that. Come over here. I'll meet you here at five. It's 1512 Arch Street. In Berkeley. Can you find the way?"

"I'll find the way. I'll be counting the minutes."

☙ ☙ ☙

She called Freddy and broke a date to go to the movies. "I have to talk to him," she said. "I have to give him a chance to explain."

"Oh, sure," he said. "Do whatever you have to do."

"Don't sound like that."

"What do you want me to do? Pretend like I don't care? Your old boyfriend shows up at eight o'clock in the morning . . . the robber baron shows up, and I'm supposed to act like I think it's great."

"I'll call you tomorrow."

"Don't bother. I won't be here. I'm going out of town."

He worked all morning and half the afternoon without giving in to his desire to call her. By two-thirty his sinus headache was so bad he could hardly breathe. He stood on his head for twenty minutes reciting "The Four Quartets." Nothing helped. At three he stormed out of the store. I'm sitting on her steps till she gets home from work, he told himself. I can't make myself sick just to be a nice guy. Unless that bastard picks her up at work. What if he picks her up at work. He'll drag her into drugs. She'll end up in the state pen. He'll put his mouth on her mouth. He'll put his mouth on her legs. He'll touch her hands. He'll touch her hair.

Freddy trudged up Arch Street with his chin on his chest, ignoring the flowers and the smell of hawthorn and bay, ignoring the pines, ignoring the sun, the clear light, the cool clean air.

At the corner of Arch and Brainard he started having second thoughts. He stood on the corner with his hands stuck deep in the pockets of his pants. A white Lincoln with Colorado plates pulled up in front of Nora Jane's house. A tall boy in chinos got out and walked up on the porch. He inspected the row of mailboxes. He had an envelope in his hand. He put it into one of the boxes and hurried back down the steps. A woman was waiting in the car. They talked a moment, then drove off down the street.

That's him, Freddy thought. That's the little son-of-a-bitch. The Suyins' Pomeranian met him in the yard. He knocked it out of his way with the side of his foot and opened Nora Jane's mailbox. The envelope was there, in between an advertisement and a letter from a politician. He stuck it into his pocket and walked up the hill toward the campus. He stopped in a playground and read the note.

> *Angel, I have to go to Petaluma on business. I'll call tonight. After eight. Maybe you can come up and spend the weekend. I'm really sorry about tonight. I'll make it up to you. Yours forever.*
>
> *Sandy*

When he finished reading it he wadded it up and stuck into a trash container shaped like a pelican. "All right," he said to the pelican. "I'll show him anarchy. I'll show him business. I'll show him war."

He walked back down to Shattuck Avenue and hailed a taxi. "Where's the nearest Ford place?" he asked the driver. "Where's the nearest Ford dealer?"

"There's Moak's over in Oakland. Unless you want to go downtown. You want me to take you to Moak's?"

"That's fine," Freddy said. "Moak's is fine with me."

"I wouldn't have a Ford," the driver said. "You

couldn't give me a Ford. I wouldn't have a thing but a Toyota."

Moak Ford had just what he was looking for. A pint-sized baby blue convertible sitting in the display window with the sunlight gleaming off its chrome and glass. The interior was an even lighter blue with leather seats and a soft blue carpet. "I'll need a tape deck," he said to the salesman. "How long does it take to install a tape deck?"

At six-thirty he called her from a pay phone near her house. "I don't want to bother you," he said. "I just want to apologize for this morning. I just wanted to make sure you're okay."

"I'm not okay," she said. "I'm terrible. I'm just terrible."

"Could I come over? I've got a present for you."

"A present?"

"It's blue. I bought you something blue."

She was waiting on the porch when he drove up. She walked down the steps trying not to look at it. It was so blue. So very blue. He got out and handed her the keys.

"People don't give other people cars," she said. "They don't just give someone a car."

"I do whatever I need to do," he said. "It's my charm. My fabled charisma."

"Why are you doing this, Freddy?"

"So you'll like me better than old Louisiana Joe. Where is he, by the way? I thought you had a big date with him."

"I broke the date. I didn't feel like seeing him right now. Did you really buy me that car?"

"Yes, I really did. Get in. See how good it smells. I got a tape deck but they can't put it in until Thursday. You want the top down or not?"

She opened the car door and settled her body into the driver's seat. She turned on the key. "I better not put it down just yet. I'll put it down in a minute. I'll stop somewhere and put it down later."

She drove off down Arch Street wondering if she was going crazy. "You don't have to stop to put it down," he said. He reached across her and pushed a button and the blue accordion top folded down like a wing, then back up, then back down again.

"Stop doing that," she said. "You'll make me have a wreck. Where should I go, Freddy? I don't know where to go."

"We could go by the Komatsu showroom and watch ourselves driving by in their glass walls. When I first got the DeLorean I used to do that all the time. Don't look like that, N.J. It's okay to have a car. Cars are all right. They satisfy our need for strong emotions."

"Just tell me where to go."

"I want to take you to the park and show you the Brundage collection but I'm afraid they're closed this time of day. They have this jade Buddha. It's like nothing you've ever seen in your life. I know, let's give it a try. Go down University. We'll drive across a couple of bridges. You need to learn the bridges."

"I can't drive across a bridge. I told you that."

"Of course you can. We'll do the Oakland first, then

the Golden Gate. You can't live here if you can't go across the bridges. You won't be able to go anywhere."

"I can't do it, Freddy. I can't even drive across the Huey P. Long, and it's only over the Mississippi."

"Listen to me a minute," he said. "I want to tell you about these bridges. People like us didn't build these bridges, N.J. People like Teddy Roosevelt and Albert Einstein and Aristotle built those bridges. People like my father. The Golden Gate is so overbuilt you could stack cars two deep on it and it wouldn't fall."

"Go on," she said. "I'm listening." She was making straight for the Oakland Bridge, *with the top down.* In the distance the red girders of the Golden Gate gleamed in the sun. She gripped the wheel and turned onto University Avenue leading to the bay.

"All right," he continued, "about these bridge builders. They get up every morning and put on a clean shirt and fill their pockets with pencils. They go out and add and subtract and read blueprints and put pilings all the way down to the bedrock. Then they build a bridge so strong their great-grandchildren can ride across it without getting hurt. My father helped raise money for the Golden Gate. That's how strong it is."

Nora Jane had driven right by the sign pointing to the Oakland Bridge. The little car hummed beneath her fingers. She straightened her shoulders. She kept on going. "All right," she said. "I'll try it. I'll give it a try."

"I wish to hell the Brundage was open. You've got to see this Buddha. It's unbelievable. It's only ten inches high. You can see every wrinkle. You can see every rib. The jade's the color of celadon. Oh, lighter than that. It's translucent. It just floats there."

"Don't talk so much until I get through the gate," she said. She almost sideswiped a black Mazda station wagon. There was a little boy in the back seat wearing a crown. He put his face to the window and waved.

"Did you see that?" Nora Jane said. "Did you see what he's wearing?" She drove through the toll gate and out onto the bridge. She was into it now. She was doing it.

"Loosen up," Freddy said. "Loosen up on the wheel. This Buddha I was telling you about, N.J. It's more the color of seafoam. You've never seen jade like this. It's indescribable. It's got a light of its own. Well, we'll never make it today. I know what, we'll stop in Chinatown and have dinner. I want you to have some Dim Sum. And tomorrow, tomorrow we're going to Mendocino. The hills there are like yellow velvet this time of year. You'll want to put them on and wear them."

I haven't been to confession in two years, Nora Jane was thinking. What am I doing in this car?

The Mazda passed them again. The boy with the crown was at the back window now. Looking out the open window of the tailgate, eating a package of Nacho Cheese Flavored Doritos and drinking a Coke. He held up a dorito to Nora Jane. He waved it out the window in the air. The Mazda moved on. A metallic green Buick took its place. In the front seat was a young Chinese businessman wearing a suit. In the back seat, a Chinese gentleman wearing a pigtail.

A plane flew over, trailing a banner. HAPPY 40TH, ED AND DEB, the banner said. Things were happening too fast. "I just saw an airplane fly by trailing breadcrumbs," she said.

"*What did you say,*" he said. "*What did you just say?*"

"I said . . . oh, never mind. I was thinking too many things at once. I'm going over there, Freddy, in the lane by the water." She put the turn signal on and moved over into the right-hand lane. "Now don't talk to me anymore," she said, squeezing the steering wheel, leaning into it, trying to concentrate on the girders and forget the water. "Don't say any more until I get this car across this bridge."

❧❧❧

The Double Happiness Bun

NORA Jane Whittington was going to have a baby. There was no getting around that. First Freddy Harwood talked her into taking out her Lippes Loop. "I don't like the idea of a piece of copper stuck up your vagina," he said. "I think you ought to get it out."

"It's not in my vagina. It's in my womb. And it's real small. I saw it before they put it in."

"How small?" he said. "Let me see." Nora Jane held up a thumb and forefinger and made a circle. "Like this," she said. "About like this."

"Hmmmmmmmm . . ." he said, and let it go at that. But the idea was planted. She kept thinking about the little piece of copper. How it resembled a mosquito coil. Like shrapnel, she thought. Like having some kind of weapon in me. Nora Jane had a very good imagination for things like that. Finally imagination won out over science and she called the obstetrician and made an appointment. There was really not much to it. She lay down on the table and squeezed her eyes shut and the doctor reached up inside her with a small cold instrument and the Lippes Loop came sliding out.

"Now what will you do?" the doctor said. "Would you like me to start you on the pill?"

"Not yet," she said. "Let me think it over for a while."

"Don't wait too long," he said. "You're a healthy girl. It can happen very quickly."

"All right," she said. "I won't." She gathered up her things and drove on over to Freddy's house to cook things in his gorgeous redwood kitchen.

"Now what will we do?" she said. "You think I ought to take the pill? Or what?" It was much later that evening. Nora Jane was sitting on the edge of the hot tub looking up at the banks of clouds passing before the moon. It was one of those paradisial San Francisco nights, flowers and pine trees, eucalyptus and white wine and Danish bread and brie.

Nora Jane's legs were in the hot tub. Her back was to the breeze coming from the bay. She was wearing a red playsuit with a red and yellow scarf tied around her forehead like a flag. Freddy Harwood thought she was the most desirable thing he had ever seen in his whole life.

"We'll think of something," he said. He took off his Camp Pericles senior counselor camp shorts and lowered himself into the water. He was thirty-five years old and every summer he still packed his footlocker full of tee-shirts and flashlight batteries and went off to the Adirondacks to be a counselor in his old camp. That's how crazy he was. The rest of the year he ran a bookstore in Berkeley.

"What do you think we'll think of?" she said, joining him in the water, sinking down until the ends of the scarf floated in the artificial waves. What they thought of lasted half the night and moved from the hot tub to to den floor to the bedroom. Freddy Harwood thought it was the most meaningful evening he had spent since the night he lost his cherry to his mother's best friend. Nora Jane didn't think it was all that great. It lacked danger, that aphrodisiac, that sugar to end all sugars.

"We have to get married," he told her in the morning. "You'll have to marry me. He walked around a ladder and picked up a kimono and pulled it on and tied the belt into a bowline. The ladder was the only furniture in the room except the bed they had been sleeping in. Freddy was in the process of turning his bedroom into a planetarium. He was putting the universe on the ceiling, little dots of heat-absorbing cotton that glowed in the night like stars. Each dot had to be measured with long paper measuring strips from the four corners of the room. It was taking a lot longer to put the universe on the ceiling than Freddy had thought it would. He turned his eyes to a spot he had reserved for Altabaron. It was the summer sky he was re-creating, as seen from Minneapolis where the kits were made. "Yes," he said, as if he were talking to himself. "We are going to have to get married."

"I don't want to get married," she said. "I'm not in love with you."

"You are in love with me. You just don't know it yet."

"I am not in love with you. I've never told you that I was. Besides, I wouldn't want to change my name. Nora Harwood, how would that sound?"

"How could you make love to someone like last night if you didn't love them? I don't believe it."

"I don't know. I guess I'm weird or abnormal or something. But I know whether I'm in love with someone or not. Anyway, I like you better than anyone I've met in San Francisco. I've told you that." She was getting dressed now, pulling a white cotton sweater over a green cotton skirt, starting to look even more marvelous than she did with no clothes on at all. Freddy sighed, gathered his forces, walked across the room and took her in his arms. "Do you want to have a priest? Or would you settle for a judge. I have this friend that's a federal judge who would love to marry us."

"I'm not marrying you, Freddy. Not for all the tea in China. Not even for your money and I want you to stop being in love with me. I want you to be my friend and have fun like we used to. Now listen, do you want me to give you back that car you gave me? I'll give you back the car."

"Please don't give me back the car. All my life I wanted to give someone a blue convertible. Don't ruin it by talking like that."

"I'm sorry. That was mean of me. I knew better than to say that. I'll keep that car forever. You know that. I might get buried in that car." She gave him a kiss on his freckled chest, tied a green scarf around her hair, floated out of the house, got into the blue convertible and away she went, weaving in and out of the lanes of traffic, thinking about how hard it was to find out what you wanted in the world, much less what to do to get it.

It was either that night that fertilized one of Nora Jane Whittington's wonderful, never to be replaced or duplicated as long as the species lasts, small, wet, murky, secret-bearing eggs. Or it was two nights later when she heard a love song coming out an open doorway and broke down and called Sandy Halter and he came and got her and they went off to a motel and made each other cry.

Sandy was the boy Nora Jane had lived with in New Orleans. She had come to California to be with him but there was a mix-up and he didn't meet her plane. Then she found out he'd been seeing a girl named Pam. After that she couldn't love him anymore. Nora Jane was very practical about love. She only loved people that loved her back. She never was sure what made her call up Sandy that night in Berkeley. First she dreamed about him. Then she passed a doorway and heard Bob Dylan singing. "Lay, lady, lay. Lay across my big brass bed." The next thing she knew she was in a motel room making love and crying. Nora Jane was only practical about love most of the time. Part of the time she was just as dumb about it as everybody else in the world.

"How can we make up?" she said, sitting up in the rented bed. "After what you did to me."

"We can't help making up. We love each other. I've got some big things going on, Nora Jane. I want you working with me. It's real money this time. Big money."

He sat up beside her and put his hands on his knees. He looked wonderful. She had to admit that. He was as tan as an Indian and his hair was as blond as sunlight and his mind as faraway and unavailable as a star.

"Last night I dreamed about you," she said. "That's why I called you up. It was raining like crazy in my dream and we were back in New Orleans, on Magazine Street, looking out the window, and the trees were blowing all over the place, and I said, Sandy, there's going to be a hurricane. Let's turn on the radio. And you said, no, the best thing to do is go to the park and ride it out in a live oak tree. Then we went out onto the street. It was a dream, remember, and Webster Street and Henry Clay were under water and they were trying to get patients out of the Home for the Incurables. They were bringing them out on stretchers. It was awful. It was raining so hard. Then I got separated from you. I was standing in the door of the Webster Street Bar calling to you and no one was coming and the water was rising. It was a terrible dream. Then you were down the street with that girl. I guess it was her. She was blond and sort of fat and she was holding on to you. Pam, I guess it was Pam."

"I haven't seen Pam since all that happened. Pam doesn't mean a thing to me. Pam's nothing."

"Then why was I dreaming about her?"

"Don't ruin everything, Nora Jane. Let's just love each other."

"You want to make love to me some more? Well, do you?"

"No, right now I want a cigarette. Then I want to take you to this restaurant I like. I want to tell you about this outfit I'm working for. I'll tell you what. Tomorrow's Saturday and I have to take Mirium's car back so I'll take you with me and show you what's going on."

"I've been wondering what you were up to."

"Just wait till you meet Mirium. She's my boss. I've told her all about you. Now come on, let's get dressed and get some dinner. I haven't eaten all day." Sandy had gotten out of bed and was putting on his clothes. White linen pants and a blue shirt with long full sleeves. He liked to dress up even more than Nora Jane did.

Sandy's boss, Mirium Sallisaw, was forty-three years old. She lived in a house on a bluff overlooking the sea between Pacifica and Montara. It was a very expensive house she bought with money she made arranging trips to Mexico for people that wanted to cure cancer with Laetrile. The Laetrile market was dying out but Mirium wasn't worried. She was getting into Interferon as fast as she could make the right connections. Interferon and Energy. Those were Mirium's key words for 1983.

"Energy," she was fond of saying. "Energy. That's all. There's nothing else." She imagined herself as a little glowworm in a sea of dark branches, spreading light to the whole forest. She was using Sandy to keep her batteries charged. She liked to get in bed with him at night and charge up, then tell him her theories about energy and how he could have all the other women he wanted, because she, Mirium Sallisaw, was above human jealousy and didn't care. Sandy was only twenty-two years old. He believed everything she told him. He even believed she was dying to meet Nora Jane. He thought of Mirium as this brilliant businesswoman who would jump at a chance to have someone as smart as Nora Jane help drive patients back and forth across the border.

Nora Jane and Sandy got to Mirium's house late in the afternoon. They parked in the parking lot and walked across a lawn with Greek statues set here and there as if the decorator hadn't been able to decide where they should go. Statues of muses faced the parking lot. Statues of heroes looked out upon the sea. Twin statues of cupid guarded the doorway.

Nora Jane and Sandy opened the door and stepped into the foyer. It was dark inside the house. All the drapes were closed. The only light came from recessed fixtures near the ceiling. A young man in a silk shirt and elegant pointed shoes came walking toward them. "Hello, Sandy," he said. "Mother's in the back. Go tell her you're here."

"This is Maurice," Sandy said. "He's Mirium's son. He's a genius, aren't you, Maurice? Listen, did you give Mirium my message? Does she know Nora Jane's coming?"

"We've got dinner reservations at Blanchard's. They have fresh salmon. Mimi called. Do you like salmon?" he said to Nora Jane. "I worship it. It's all I eat."

"I've never given it much thought," she said. "I don't think much about what I eat."

"Maurice takes chemistry courses at the college," Sandy said. "Mirium's making him into a chemist."

"That's nice," she said. "That must be interesting."

"Well, profitable. I'll make some dough if I stick to it. Sandy, why don't you go on back and tell her you're here. She's in the exercise room with Mimi. Tell her

I'm getting hungry." Sandy disappeared down a long hall.

Maurice took Nora Jane into a sunken living room with sofas arranged around a marble coffee table. There were oriental boxes on the table and something that looked like a fire extinguisher.

"Sit down," he said. "I'll play you some music. I've got a new tape some friends of mine made. It's going to be big. Warner's has it and Twentieth Century–Fox is interested. Million Bucks, that's the name of the group. The leader's name is Million Bills. No kidding, he had it changed. Listen to this." Maurice pushed some buttons on the side of the marble table and the music came on, awful erratic music, a harp and a lot of electronic keyboards and guitars and synthesizers. The harp would play a few notes, then the electrical instruments would shout it down. "Pretty chemical, huh? Feel that energy? They're going to be big." He was staring off into the recessed light, one hand on the emerald embedded in his ear.

Nora Jane couldn't think of anything to say. She settled back into the sofa cushions. It was cool and dark in the room. The cushions she was leaning into were the softest things she had ever felt in her life. They felt alive, like some sort of hair. She reached her hands behind her. "What are these cushions?" she said. "What are they made of?"

"They're Mirium's old fur coats. She wanted drapes but there wasn't enough."

"They're made of fur coats?"

"Yeah. Before that they were animals. Crazy, huh? Chemical? Look, if you want a joint there're different kinds in those boxes. That red one's Colombian and the blue one is some stuff we're getting from Arkansas. Heavy. Really heavy. There's gas in the canister if you'd rather have that. I quit doing it. Too sweet for me. I don't like a sweet taste."

"Could I have a glass of water," she said. "It was a long drive." She was sitting up, trying not to touch the cushions. "Sure," he said. "I'll get you some. Just a minute." He had taken a tube of something out of his pocket and was applying it to his lips. "This is a new gloss. It's dynamite. Mint and lemon mixed together. Wild!" Then, so quickly Nora Jane didn't have time to resist, Maurice sat down beside her and put his mouth on hers. He was very strong for a boy who looked so thin and he was pressing her down into the fur pillows. Her mouth was full of the taste of mint and lemon and something tingly, like an anesthetic. For a moment she thought he was trying to kill her. "Get off of me," she said. She pushed against him with all her might. He sat up and looked away. "I just wanted you to get the full effect."

"How old are you?"

"Sixteen. Isn't it a drag?"

"I don't know. I'd never have guessed you were a day over four. Three or four."

"I guess it's my new stylist," he said, as if he didn't know what she meant. "I've got this woman in Marin. Marilee at Plato's. It takes forever to get there. But it's worth it. I mean, that woman understands hair. . . ."

Sandy reappeared with a woman wearing gray slacks and a dark sweater. She looked as if she smiled about once a year. She held out her hand, keeping the other one on Sandy's arm. "Well," she said. "We've been hearing about you. Sandy's told us all about your exploits together in New Orleans. He says you can do some impressive tricks with your voice. How about letting us hear some."

"I don't do tricks," Nora Jane said. "I don't even sing anymore."

"Well, I guess that's that. Did Sandy fill you in on the operation we've got going down here? It isn't illegal, you know. But I don't like our business mouthed around. Too many jealous people, if you know what I mean."

"He told me some things . . ." Nora Jane looked at Sandy. He wouldn't meet her eyes. He picked up one of the canisters and took out a joint and lit it and passed it to Maurice.

"We have dinner reservations in less than an hour," Mirium said. "Let's have some wine, then get going. I can't stand to be late and lose our table. Maurice, try that buzzer. See if you can get someone in here."

"These are sick people you send places," Nora Jane said. "That you need a driver for?"

"Oh, honey, they're worse than sick. These people are at the end. I mean, the end. We're the last chance they've got."

"They don't care what it costs," Sandy said. "They pay in cash."

"So what does it do for them?" Nora Jane said. "Does it make them well?"

"It makes them happy," Maurice said.

"It makes them better than they were," Mirium said. "If they have faith. It won't work without faith. Faith makes the energy start flowing. You see, honey, the real value of Laetrile is it gets the energy flowing. Right,

Sandy?" She moved over beside him and took the joint from between his fingers. "Like good sex. It keeps the pipes open, if you know what I mean." She put her hand on Sandy's sleeves, caressing his sleeve.

"Do you have a powder room?" Nora Jane said. "A bathroom I mean."

"There's one in the foyer," Miriam said. "Or you can go back to the bedroom."

"The one in the foyer's fine." Nora Jane had started moving. She was up the steps from the sunken area. She was out of the room and into the hall. She was to the foyer. The keys are in the ignition, she was thinking. I saw him leave them there. And if they aren't I'll walk. But I am getting out of here. Then she was out the door and past the cupids and running along the paving stones to the parking lot. The Lincoln was right where Sandy had parked it. She got in and turned the key and the engine came on and she backed out and started driving. Down the steep rocky drive so fast she almost went over the side. She slowed down and turned onto the ocean road. Slow down, she told herself. You could run over someone. They can't do anything to me. They can't send the police after me. Not with all they have going on in there. All I have to do is drive this car. I don't have to hurry and I don't have to worry about a single thing. And I don't have to think about Sandy. Imagine him doing it with that woman. Well, I should talk. I mean, I've been doing it with Freddy. But it isn't the same thing. Well it isn't.

She looked out toward the ocean, the Pacific Ocean lying dark green and wonderful in the evening sun. I'll just think about the whales, she decided. I'll concentrate on whales. Tam says they hear us thinking. She says they hear everything we do. Well, Chinese people are always saying things like that. I guess part of what they say is true. I mean they're real old. They've been around so long.

It was dark when Nora Jane got to Freddy's house The front door was wide open. He was in the hot tub with the stereo blaring out country music. "Oh, I'm a good-hearted woman, in love with a good-timing man," Waylon Jennings was filling the house with dumb country ideas.

"I'm drunk as a deer," Freddy called out when he saw her. "The one I love won't admit she loves me. Therefore I am becoming an alcoholic. One and one makes two. Cause and effect. Ask Nieman. He'll tell you. He's helping me. He's right over there, passed out on the sofa. In his green suit. Wake him up. Ask him if I'm an alcoholic or not. He'll tell you." Freddy picked up a bottle of brandy from beside an art deco soap dish and waved it in the air. "Brandy. King of elixirs. The royal drink of the royal heads of France, and of me. Frederick Slazenger Harwood, lover of the cruel Louisiana voodoo queen. Voodoooooed. I've been voodoooooed. Vamped and rendered alcoholic."

"Get out of there before you drown yourself. You shouldn't be in there drunk. I think you've started living in that hot tub."

"Not getting out until I shrivel. Ask Nieman. Go ahead, wake him up. Ask him. Going to shrivel up to a tree limb. Have myself shipped to the Smithsonian. Man goes back to tree. I can see the headlines."

"I stole a car. It's in the driveway."

"Stay me with flagons," he called out. "Comfort me with apples, for I am sick with love. Nieman, get up. Nora Jane stole a car. We have to turn her in. Why did you steal a car? I just gave you a car." He pulled himself up on the edge of the hot tub. "Why on earth would you steal a car?"

So, first there was the night she spent with Freddy, then there was the night she spent with Sandy, then there was the night she stole the car. Then three weeks went by. Then five weeks went by and Nora Jane Whitttington had not started menstruating and she was losing weight and kept falling asleep in the afternoon and the smell of cigarettes or bacon frying was worse than the smell of a chicken plucking plant. The egg had been hard at work.

A miracle, the sisters at the Academy of the Most Sacred Heart of Jesus would have said. Chemistry, Maurice would say. Energy, Mirium Sallisaw would declare. This particular miraculous energetic piece of chemistry had split into two identical parts and they were attached now to the lining of Nora Jane's womb, side by side, the size of snow peas, sending out for what they needed, water and pizza and sleep, rooms without smoke or bacon grease.

"Well, at least its name will start with an H," Nora Jane said. She was talking to Tam Suyin, a Chinese mathematician's wife who was her best friend and confidante in the house on Arch Street where she lived. It was a wonderful old Victorian house made of boards two feet wide. Lobelia and iris and Madonna lilies lined the sidewalk leading to the porch. Along the side poppies as red as blood bloomed among daisies and snapdragons. Fourteen people lived in the twelve bedrooms, sharing the kitchen and the living quarters.

Nora Jane had met Tam the night she moved in, in the middle of the night, after an earthquake. Tam and her husband Li had taught Nora Jane many things she would never have heard of in Louisiana. In return Nora Jane was helping them with their English grammar. Now, wherever they went in the world, the Suyins' English would be colored by Nora Jane's soft southern idioms.

"And it probably will have brown eyes," she continued. "I mean, Sandy has blue eyes, or, I guess you could call them gray. But Freddy and I have brown eyes. That's two out of three. Oh, Tam, what am I going to do? Would you just tell me that?" Nora Jane had just come back from the doctor. She walked across the room and lay down on the bed, her face between her hands.

"Start at the beginning. Tell story all over. Leave out romance. We see if we figure something out. Tell story again."

"Okay. I know I started menstruating about ten days before I took the IUD out. I had to wait until I stopped bleeding. I used to bleed like a stuck pig when I had that thing. That's why I took it out. So then I made love to Freddy that night. Then Sandy called me, or, no, I called him because I heard this Bob Dylan song. Anyway, I was glad to see him until I met these people he's been living with. This woman that gives drugs to her own kid. But first I made love to him and we cried a lot. I mean, it was really good making love to him. So I think it must be Sandy's. Don't you? What do you think?"

Tam came across the room and sat down on the bed and began to rub Nora Jane's back, moving her fingers down the vertebrae. "We can make abortion with massage. Very easy. Not hurt body. Not cost anything. No one make you have this baby. You make up your mind. I do it for you."

"I couldn't do that. I was raised a Catholic. It isn't like being from China. Well, I don't mind having it anyway. I thought about it all the way home from the doctor's. I mean, I don't have any brothers or sisters. My father's dead and my mother's a drunk. So I don't care much anyway. I'll have someone kin to me. If it will be a girl. It'll be all right if it's a girl and I can name her Lydia after my grandmother. She was my favorite person before she died. She had this swing on her porch." Nora Jane put her face deeper into the sheets, trying to feel sorry for herself. Tam's hands moved to her shoulders, rubbing and stroking, caressing and loving. Nora Jane turned her head to the side. A breeze was blowing in the window. The curtains were billowing like sails. Far out at sea she imagined a whale cub turning over inside its mother. "It will be all right if it's a girl and I can name it Lydia for my grandmother."

"Yes," Tam said. "Very different from China."

"Who do you think it belongs to?" Nora Jane said again.

"It belong to you. You quit thinking about it for a while. Think one big grasshopper standing on leaf looking at you with big eyes. Eyes made of jade. You sleep now. When Li come home I make us very special dinner to celebrate baby coming into world. Li work on problem. Figure it out on calculator."

"If it had blond hair I'd know it was Sandy's. But black hair could be mine or Freddy's. Well, mine's blacker than his. And curlier . . ."

"Go to sleep. Not going to be as simple as color of hair. Nothing simple in this world, Nora Jane."

"Well, what am I going to do about all this?" she said sleepily. Tam's fingers were pressing into the nerves at the base of her neck. "What on earth am I going to do?"

"Not doing anything for now. For now going to sleep. When Li come home tonight he figure it out. Not so hard. We get it figured out." Tam's fingers moved up into Nora Jane's hair, massaging the old brain on the back of the head. Nora Jane and Lydia and Tammili Whittington settled down and went to sleep.

"Fifty-five percent chance baby will be girl," Li said, looking up from his calculations. "Forty-six percent chance baby is fathered by Mr. Harwood. "Fifty-four percent chance baby is fathered by Mr. Halter. Which one is smartest gentleman, Nora Jane? Which one you wish it to be?"

"I don't know. They're smart in different ways."

"Maybe it going to be two babies. Like Double Happiness Bun. One for each father." Li laughed softly at his joke. Tam lowered her head, ashamed of him. He had been saying many strange things since they came to California.

"You sure it going to be good idea to have this baby?" he said next.

"I guess so," Nora Jane said. "I think it is." She

searched their faces trying to see what they wanted to hear but their faces told her nothing. Tam was looking down at her hands. Li was playing with his pocket calculator.

"How you going to take care of this baby and go to your job?" he said.

"That's nothing," Nora Jane said. "I've already thought about that. It isn't that complicated. People do it all the time. They have these little schools for them. Day-care centers. I used to work in one the Sisters of Mercy had on Magazine Street. I worked there in the summers. We had babies and little kids one and two years old. In the afternoons they would lie down on their cots and we would sit by them and pat their backs while they went to sleep. It was the best job I ever had. The shades would be drawn and the fan on and we'd be sitting by the cots patting them and you could hear their little breaths all over the room. I used to pat this one little boy with red hair. His back would go up and down. I know all about little kids and babies. I can have one if I want to."

"Yes, you can," Tam said. "You strong girl. Do anything you want to do."

"You going to tell Mr. Harwood and Mr. Halter about this baby?" Li said.

"I don't know," she answered. "I haven't made up my mind about that."

Then for two weeks Nora Jane kept her secret. She was good at keeping secrets. It came from being an only child. When Freddy called she told him she couldn't see him for a while. She hadn't talked to Sandy since she called and told him where to pick up Mirium's car.

At night she slept alone with her secret. In the mornings she dressed and went down to the gallery where she worked and listened to people talk about the paintings. She felt very strange, sleepy and secretive and full of insight. I think my vision is getting better, she told herself, gazing off into the pastel hills. I am getting into destiny, she said to herself at night, feeling the cool sheets against her legs. I am part of time, oceans and hurricanes and earthquakes and the history of man. I am the aurora borealis and the stars. I am as crazy as I can be. I ought to call my mother.

Finally Freddy Harwood had had as much as he could stand. There was no way he was letting a girl he loved refuse to see him. He waited fourteen days, counting them off, trying to get to twenty-one, which he thought was a reasonable number of days to let a misunderstanding cool down. Only, what was the misunderstanding? What had he done but fall in love? He waited and brooded.

On the fourteenth day he started off for work, then changed his mind and went over to his cousin Leah's gallery where he had gotten Nora Jane a job. The gallery was very posh. It didn't even open until 11:00 in the morning. He got there about 10:30 and went next door to Le Chocolat and bought a chocolate statue of Aphrodite and stood by the plate-glass windows holding the box and watching for Nora Jane's car. Finally he caught a glimpse of it in the far lane on Shattuck Boulevard heading for the parking lot of the Safeway store. He ran out the door and down to the corner and stood by a parking meter on the boulevard.

She got out of the car and came walking over, not walking very fast. She was wearing a long white rayon shirt over black leotards, looking big-eyed and thin. "You look terrible," he said, forgetting his pose, hurrying to meet her. "What have you been doing? Take this, it's a chocolate statue I bought for you. What's going on, N.J.? I want you to talk to me. Goddammit, we are going to talk."

"I'm going to have a baby," she said. She stepped up on the sidewalk. Traffic was going by on the street. Clouds were going by in the sky. "Oh, my God," Freddy said.

"And I don't know who the father is. It might be your baby. I don't know if it is or not." Her eyes were right on his. They were filling up with tears, a movie of tears, a brand-new fresh print of a movie of tears. They poured down her cheeks and onto her hands and the white cardboard box holding the chocolate Aphrodite. Some even fell on her shoes.

"So what," Freddy said. "That's not so bad. I mean, at least you don't have cancer. When I saw you get out of the car I thought, leukemia, she's got leukemia."

"I don't know who the father is," she repeated. "There's a forty-six percent chance it's you."

"Let's get off this goddamn street," he said. "Let's go out to the park."

"You aren't mad? You aren't going to kill me?"

"I haven't had time to get mad. I've hardly had time

to go into shock. Come on, N.J., let's go out to the park and see the Buddha."

"He has blue eyes, or gray eyes, I guess you'd call them. And you have brown eyes and I have brown eyes. So it isn't going to do any good if it has brown eyes. Li said it's more the time of month anyway because sperm can live several days. So I've been trying and trying to remember . . ."

"Let's don't talk about it anymore," Freddy said. "Let's talk less and think more." They were in the De Young Museum in Golden Gate Park. Freddy had called his cousin Leah and told her Nora Jane couldn't come in to work and they had gone out to the park to see a jade Buddha he worshipped. "This all used to be free," he said, as he did every time he brought her there. "The whole park. Even the planetarium. Even the cookies in the tea garden. My father used to bring me here." They were standing in an arch between marble rooms.

"Let's go look at the Buddha again before we leave," Nora Jane said. "I'm getting as bad about that Buddha as you are." They walked back into the room and up to the glass box that housed the Buddha. They walked slowly around the case looking at the Buddha from all angles. The hands outstretched on the knees, the huge ears, the spine, the ribs, the drape of the stole across the shoulder. Sakyumuni as an Ascetic. It was a piece of jade so luminous, so rounded and perfect and alive that just looking at it was sort of like being a Buddha.

"Wheeewwwwwwwww," Nora Jane said. "How on earth did he make it?"

"Well, to begin with, it took twenty years. I mean, you don't just turn something like that out overnight. He made it for his teacher, but the teacher died before it was finished."

Nora Jane held her hands out to the light coming from the case, as if to catch some Buddha knowledge. "I could go see your friend Eli, the geneticist," she said. "He could find out for me, couldn't he? I mean he splices genes, it wouldn't be anything to find out what blood type a baby had. How about that? I'll call him up and ask him if there's any way I can find out before it comes."

"Oh, my God," Freddy said. "Don't go getting any ideas about Eli. Don't go dragging my friends into this. Let's just keep this under our hats. Let's don't go spreading this around."

"I'm not keeping anything I do under my hat," she said. She stepped back from him and folded her hands at her waist. Same old, some old stuff, she thought. "You just go on home, Freddy," she said. "I'll take BART. I don't want to talk to you anymore today. I was doing just fine until you showed up with that chocolate statue. I've never been ashamed of anything I've done in my life and I'm not about to start being ashamed now." She was backing up, heading for the door. "So go on. Go on and leave me alone. I mean it. I really mean it."

"How about me?" he called after her retreating back. "What am I supposed to do? How am I supposed to feel? What if I don't want to be alone? What if I need someone to talk to?" She held her hands up in the air with the palms turned toward the ceiling. Then she walked on off without turning around.

☙ ☙ ☙

Several days later Nora Jane was at the gallery. It was late in July. Almost a year since she had robbed the bar in New Orleans and flown off to California to be with Sandy. So much had happened in that time. Sometimes she felt like a different person. Other times she felt like the same old Nora Jane. That morning while she was dressing for work she had looked at her body for a long time in the mirror, turning this way and that to see what was happening. Her body was beginning to have a new configuration, strange volumes like a Titian she admired in one of Leah's art books.

It was cool in the gallery, too cool for Nora Jane's sleeveless summer dress. Just right for the three-piece suit on the man standing beside her. They were standing before one of Nora Jane's favorite paintings. The man was making notes on a pad and saying things to the gallery owner that made Nora Jane want to sock him in the face.

"What is the source of light, dear heart? I can't review this show, Leah. This stuff's so old-fashioned. It's so obvious, for God's sake. Absolutely no restraint. I can't believe you got me over here for this. I think you're going all soppy on me."

"Oh, come on," Leah said. "Give it a chance, Ambrose. Put the pad away and just look."

"I can't look, angel. I have a trained eye." Nora Jane sighed. Then she moved over to the side of the canvas and held the edge of the frame in her hand. It was a painting of a kimono being lifted from the sea by a dozen seagulls. A white kimono with purple flowers being lifted from a green sea. The gulls were carrying it in their beaks, each gull in a different pose. Below the painting was a card with lines from a book.

> "On some undressed bodies the burns made patterns . . . and on the skin of some women . . . the shapes of flowers they had had on their kimonos. . . ."
>
> *Hiroshima*, by John Hersey

"Hummmmmmmm . . ." Nora Jane said. "The source of light? This is a painting, not a light bulb. There's plenty of light. Every one of those doves is a painting all by itself. I bet it took a million hours just to paint those doves. This is a wonderful painting. This is one of the most meaningful paintings I ever saw. Anybody that doesn't know this painting is wonderful isn't fit to judge a beauty contest at a beach, much less a rock of art, I mean, a work of art."

"Leah," the man said. "Who is this child?"

"I used to work here," she said. "But now I'm quitting. I'm going home. I'm going to have a baby and I don't want it floating around inside me listening to people say nasty things about other people's paintings. You can't tell what they hear. They don't know what all they can hear."

"A baby," Leah said. She moved back as though she was afraid some of it might spill on her gray silk blouse. "My cousin Freddy's baby?"

"I don't know," Nora Jane said. "It's just a baby. I don't know whose it is."

I'm doing things too fast, she thought. She was driving aimlessly down University Avenue, headed for a bridge. I'm cutting off my nose to spite my face. I'm burning my bridges behind me. I'll call my mother and tell her where I am. Yeah, and then she'll just get drunker than ever and call me up all the time like she used to at the Mushroom Cloud. Never mind that. I'll get a job at a day-care center. That's what I'll do. This place is full of rich people. I bet they have great ones out here. I'll go find the best one they have and get a job in it. Then I'll be all set when she comes. Well, at least I can still think straight. Thank God for that. Maybe I'll drive out to Bodega Bay and spend the day by the ocean. I'll get a notebook and write down everything I have to do and make all my plans. Then tomorrow I'll go and apply for jobs at day-care centers. I wonder what they pay. Not much I bet. Who cares? I'll live on whatever they pay me. That's one thing Sandy taught me. You don't have to do what they want you to if you don't have to have their stuff. It was worth living with him just to learn that. I've got everything I need. It's a wonderful day. I loved saying that stuff to that man, that Ambrose whatever his name is. I'll bet he's thinking about it right this minute. YOU AREN'T FIT TO JUDGE A BEAUTY CONTEST AT THE BEACH MUCH LESS A WORK OF ART. That was good, that was really good. I bet he won't forget me saying that. I bet no one's said anything to him in years except what he wants to hear.

Nora Jane turned on the radio, made a left at a stoplight and drove out onto the Richmond–San Rafael bridge. She had the top down on the convertible. The radio was turned up good and loud. Some lawyers down in Texas were saying the best place to store nuclear waste would be the salt flats in Mexico. Nora Jane was driving along, listening to the lawyers, thinking about the ocean, thinking how nice it would be to sit and watch the waves come in. Thinking about what she'd stop and get to eat. I have to remember to eat, she was thinking. I have to get lots of protein and stuff to make her bones thick.

She was just past the first long curve of the bridge when it happened. The long roller coaster of a bridge swayed like the body of a snake, making a hissing sound that turned into thunder. The sound rolled across the bay. Then the sound stopped. Then a long time went by. The car seemed to be made of water. The bridge of water. Nora Jane's arms of water. Still, she seemed to know what to do. She turned off the ignition. She reached behind her and pulled down the shoulder harness and put it on.

The bridge moved again. Longer, slower, like a long cold dream. The little blue convertible swerved to the side, rubbing up against a station wagon. The bumper grated and slid, grated and slid. Then everything was still. Everything stopped happening. The islands in the bay were still in their places. Angel Island and Morris Island and the Brothers and the Sisters and the sad face of Alcatraz. An oil tank had burst on Morris Island and a shiny black river was pouring down a hill. Nora Jane watched it pour, then turned and looked into the station wagon.

A woman was at the wheel. Four or five small children were jumping up and down on the seats, screaming and crying. "Do not move from a place of safety," the radio was saying. "The aftershocks could begin at any moment. Stay where you are. If you have an emergency call 751-1000. Please do not call to get information. We are keeping you informed. Repeat. Do not move from a place of safety. The worst shock has passed. If you are with injured parties call 751-1000." I think I'm in a place of safety, Nora Jane thought.

The children were screaming in the station wagon. They were screaming their heads off. I have to go and see if they're hurt, she thought. But what if a shock comes while I'm going from here to there? I'll fall off the bridge. I'll fall into the sea. "The Golden Gate is standing. The approaches are gone to the Bay Bridge and the Richmond–San Rafael. There is no danger of either bridge collapsing. Repeat, there is no danger of either bridge collapsing. Please do not move from a place of safety. If you are with injured parties call 751-1000. Do not call to get information. Repeat . . ."

That's too many children for one woman. What if they're hurt? Their arms might be broken. I smashed in her side. I have to go over there and help her. I have to do it. Oh, shit. Hail Mary, full of grace, blessed art thou among women and blessed is the fruit of thy womb, Jesus. Womb, oh, my womb, what about my womb . . . ? Nora Jane was out of the car and making her way around the hood to the staton wagon. Holy Mary, Mother of God, pray for us sinners now and at the hour of our death. . . . She reached the door handle of the back seat and opened the door and slid in. The children stopped their screaming. Five small faces and one large one turned her way. "I came to help," she said. "Are any of them hurt? Are they injured?"

"Thank God you're here," the woman said. "My radio doesn't work. What's happening? What's going on?"

"It's a big one. Almost a seven. The approaches to this bridge are gone. Are the children all right? Are any of them hurt?"

"I don't think so. We're a car pool. For swimming lessons. I think they're all right. Are you all right?" she said, turning to the children. "I think they're just screaming." None of them was screaming now but one small boy was whining. "Ohhhhhhhh . . ." he was saying very low and sad.

"Well now I'm here," Nora Jane said. "They'll come get us in boats. They'll come as soon as they can."

"I'm a doctor's wife. My husband's Doctor Johnson, the plastic surgeon. I should know what to do but he never told me. I don't know. I just don't know."

"Well, don't worry about it," Nora Jane said. She set the little whining boy on her lap and put her arm around a little girl in a yellow bathing suit. "Listen, we're all right. They'll come and get us. The bridge isn't going to fall. You did all right. You knew to stop the car."

"I'm scared," the little girl in the yellow suit said. "I want to go home. I want to go where my momma is."

"It's all right," Nora Jane said. She pulled the child down beside her and kissed her on the face. "You smell so nice," she said. "Your hair smells like a yellow crayon. Have you been coloring today?"

"I was coloring," the whining boy said. "I was coloring a Big Bird book. I want to go home too. I want to go home right now. I'm afraid to be here. I don't like it here."

"He's afraid of everything," the little girl said. "He's my brother. He's afraid of the dark and he's afraid of frogs." "Ohhhhhhhhhhhhhhh," he cried out, louder than ever. "See," the girl said. "If you just say frog he starts crying."

"Celeste, please don't make him cry," the plastic surgeon's wife said. "I'm Madge Johnson," she went on. "That's Donald and Celeste, they belong to the Connerts that live next door and that's Lindsey in the back and this is Starr and Alexander up here with me. They're mine. Lindsey, are you all right? See if she's all right, would you?"

Nora Jane looked into the back of the station wagon. Lindsey was curled up with a striped beach towel over her head. She was sucking her thumb. She was so still that for a moment Nora Jane wasn't sure she was breathing. "Are you all right?" she said, laying her hand on the child's shoulder. "Lindsey, are you okay?"

The child lifted her head about an inch off the floor and shook it from side to side. "You can get up here with us," Nora Jane said. "You don't have to stay back there all alone."

"She wants to be there," Celeste said. "She's a baby. She sucks her thumb."

"I want to go home now," Donald said, starting to whine again. "I want to go see my momma. I want you to drive the car and take me home."

"We can't drive it right now," Madge said. "We have to wait for the men to come get us. We have to be good and stay still and in a little while they'll come and get us and take us home in boats. Won't that be nice? They'll be here as soon as they can. They'll be here before we know it."

"I want to go home now," Donald said. "I want to go home and I'm hungry. I want something to eat."

"Shut up, Donald," Celeste said.

"How old are they?" Nora Jane said.

"They're five, except Lindsey and Alexander, they're four. I wish we could hear your radio. I wish we could hear what's going on."

"I could reach out the front window and turn it back on, I guess. I hate to walk over there again. Until I'm sure the aftershocks are over. Look, roll down that window and see if you can reach in and turn the radio on. You don't have to turn on the ignition. Thank God the top's down. I almost didn't put it down."

Madge wiggled through the window and turned on the radio in the convertible. "In other news, actor David Niven died today at his home in Switzerland. The internationally famous actor succumbed to a long battle with Gehrig's disease. He was seventy-three. . . . Now for an update on earthquake damage. The department of geology at the University of California at Berkeley says — oh, just a minute, here's a late report on the bridges. Anyone caught on the Bay Bridge or the Richmond–San Rafael bridge please stay in your cars until help arrives. The Coast Guard is on its way. Repeat, Coast Guard rescue boats are on their way. The danger is past. Please stay in your cars until help arrives. Do not move from a place of safety. The lighthouse on East Brother has fallen into the sea. . . ."

"I want to go home now," Donald was starting up

again. Lindsey rose up in the back and joined him. "I want my momma," she was crying. "I want to go to my house."

"Come sit up here with us," Nora Jane said. "Come sit with Celeste and Donald and me. You better turn that radio off now," she said to Madge. "It's just scaring them. It's not going to tell us anything we don't already know."

"I don't want to come up there," Lindsey cried, stuffing the towel into her mouth with her thumb, talking through a little hole that was all she had left for breath. She was crying, big tears were running down the front of her suit. Madge climbed out the window again and turned off the radio.

"You're a big baby," Celeste said to Lindsey. "You're just crying to get attention."

"Shut up, Celeste," Madge said. "Please don't say things to them."

"I want to go to my house," Donald said. "I want you to drive the car right now."

"ALL RIGHT," Nora Jane said. "NOW ALL OF YOU SHUT UP A MINUTE. I want you all to shut up and quit crying and listen to me. This is an emergency. When you have an emergency everybody has to stick together and act right. We can't go anywhere right now. We have to wait to be rescued. So, if you'll be quiet and act like big people I will sing to you. I happen to be a wonderful singer. Okay, you want me to sing? Well, do you?"

"I want you to," Donald said, and cuddled closer.

"Me too," Celeste said, and sat up very properly, getting ready to listen.

"I want you to," Lindsey said, then closed her mouth down over her thumb. Starr and Alexander cuddled up against Madge. Then, for the first time since she had been in California, Nora Jane sang in public. She had been the despair of the sisters at the Academy of the Most Sacred Heart of Jesus because she would never use her voice for the glory of God or stay after school and practice with the choir. All Nora Jane had ever used her voice for was to memorize phonograph albums in case there was a war and all the stereos were blown up.

Now, in honor of the emergency, she took out her miraculous voice and her wonderful memory and began to sing long-playing albums to the children. She sang Walt Disney and *Jesus Christ Superstar* and Janis Joplin and the Rolling Stones and threw in some Broadway musicals for Madge's benefit. She finished up with a wonderful song about a little boy named Christopher Robin going to watch the changing of the guards with his nanny. "They're changing guards at Buckingham Palace. Christopher Robin went down with Alice."

The children were entranced. When she stopped, they clapped their hands and yelled for more.

"I've never heard anyone sing like that in my whole life," Madge said. "You should be on the stage."

"I know," Nora Jane said. "Everyone always says that."

"Sing some more," Donald said. "Sing about backwards land again."

"Sing more," Alexander said. It was the first time he had said a word since Nora Jane got in the car. "Sing more."

"In a minute," she said. "Let me catch my breath. I'm

starving, aren't you? I'll tell you one thing, the minute we get off this bridge I'm going somewhere and get something to eat. I'm going to eat like a pig."

"So am I," Celeste said. "I'm going to eat like a pig, oink, oink."

"I'm going to eat like a pig," Donald said. "Oink, oink."

"Oink, oink," said Alexander in a small voice.

"Oink, oink," said Starr.

"Oink, oink," said Lindsey through her thumb.

"There's a seagull," Nora Jane said. "Look out there. They're lighting on the bridge. That must mean it's all right now. They only sit on safe places."

"How do they know?" Celeste said. "How do they know which place is safe?"

"The whales tell them," Nora Jane said. "They ask the whales."

"How do the whales know?" Celeste insisted. "Who tells the whales? Whales can't talk to seagulls." Celeste was really a very questionable little girl to have around if you were pregnant. But Nora Jane was saved explaining whales because a man in a yellow slicker appeared on the edge of the bridge, climbing a ladder. He threw a leg over the railing and started toward the car. Another man was right behind him. "Here they come," Alexander said "They're coming. Oink, oink, oink."

"Here they come," Celeste screamed at the top of her lungs. She climbed up on Nora Jane's stomach and stuck her head out the window, yelling to the Coast Guard. "Here we are. Oink, oink. Here we are."

What is that? Tammili Whittington wondered. She was the responsible one of the pair. Shark butting

Momma's stomach? Typhoon at sea? Tree on fire? Running from tiger? Someone standing on us? Hummmmmmmmmm, she decided and turned a fin into a hand, four fingers and a thumb.

Here they come, Nora Jane was thinking, moving Celeste's feet to the side. Here come the rescuers. Hooray for everything. Hooray for my fellow men.

"Oh, my God," Madge said, starting to cry. "Here they are. They've come to save us."

"Oink, oink," Celeste was screaming out the window. "Oink, oink, we're over here. Come and save us. And hurry up because we're hungry."

❧❧❧

Crystal

❧❧❧

Miss Crystal's Maid Name Traceleen, She's Talking, She's Telling Everything She Knows

THE worst thing that ever happened to Miss Crystal happened at a wedding. It was her brother-in-law's wedding. He was marrying this girl, her daddy was said to be the richest man in Memphis. The Weisses were real excited about it. As much money as they got I guess they figure they can always use some more. So the whole family was going up to Memphis to the wedding, all dressed up and ready to show off what nice people they were. Then Miss Crystal got to get in all that trouble and have it end with the accident.

What they want to call the accident. I was along to nurse the baby, Crystal Anne, age three. I was right there for everything that happened. So don't tell me she fall down the stairs. Miss Crystal hasn't ever fall down in her life, drunk or sober, or have the smallest kind of an accident.

No, she didn't fall down any stairs. She's sleeping

now. I got time to talk. Doctor Wilkins be by in a while. Maybe he'll have better news today. Maybe we can take her home by Monday. If I ever get her out of here I'll get her off those pills they give her. Get her thinking straight.

How it started was. We were going off to Memphis to this wedding, Miss Crystal and Mr. Manny and her brother-in-law, Joey, that was the groom, and Mr. Lenny, that runs the store, and Mr. and Mrs. Weiss, senior, the old folks, and me and Crystal Anne and some of Joey's friends. We took up half the plane. Everybody started drinking Bloody Marys the minute the plane left New Orleans. They even made me have one. "Drink up, Traceleen," Mr. Weiss said. "Joey's marrying the richest girl in Memphis."

Miss Crystal started flirting with Owen as soon as the plane left the ground. This big Spanish-looking boy that was Joey's roommate up at Harvard. She'd already seen him up at Joey's graduation in the spring, set her eye on him up there. Well, first thing she does is fix it so she can sit by him on the plane. Me sitting across from them with the baby. Mr. Manny up front, talking business with his daddy.

Owen's telling Miss Crystal all about how he goes scuba diving down in Mexico. Her hanging onto every word. "I'm going to start a dive school down there as soon as I get the cash," he said. "I'm quitting all that other stuff. It's no good to work your ass off all your life. No, I want a life in the water." He poured himself another Bloody Mary. Miss Crystal had her hand on his leg by then, like she was this nice older lady that was a friend of his. He pretend like he don't notice it was there. Baby climbing all over me, messing up my uniform.

"To hell with graduate school at my age," Owen was saying. "I'm too big for the desks. I'm going back to Guadalajara the minute this wedding's over. Get me a wicker swing and sit down to enjoy life. You come on down and see me. You and Manny fly on down. I'll teach you to dive. You just say the word." Miss Crystal was lapping it up. I could see her fitting herself into his plans. It had been a bad spring around our place. It was time for something to happen.

"Go to sleep now," I'm saying to Crystal Anne. "Get you a little sleep. Lots of excitement coming up. You cuddle up by Traceleen."

The minute the plane landed there was this bus to take us to the hotel. I'll say one thing for people in Memphis. They know how to throw a wedding. The bus took us right to the Peabody Hotel. They had two floors reserved. Hospitality rooms set up on each floor, stayed open twenty-four hours. You could get anything you wanted from sunup to sundown. Mixed drinks, Cokes, baby food, Band-Aids, sweet rolls, homemade brownies. I've never seen such a spread.

The young people took over one hospitality room and the old people took up the other. Me and Crystal Anne sort of moving from one to the other, picking up compliments on her hair, getting Cokes, watching TV. I was getting sixty dollars a day for being there. I would have done it free. Every now and then I'd put on Crystal Anne's little suit and take her up to the pool. That's where Miss Crystal was hanging out. With Owen. He was loaded when he got off the plane and he was staying loaded. He was lounging around the pool telling stories about going scuba diving. Finally he sent out for some scuba diving equipment to put on a demonstration. That's the type wedding this was. Any of the guests that wanted anything they just called up and someone brought it to them.

It was getting dark by then. The sun almost down. Someone comes up with the scuba diving equipment and Owen puts it on and starts scuba diving all around the pool. He's trying to get Miss Crystal to go in with him but she won't do it. "Come on, chicken," he saying. "It's not going to hurt your hair. You'll be hooked for life the minute you go down. It's like flying in water."

"I can't Owee," she says. That's what she's calling him now. "I'm in the wedding party. I can't get wet now." Well, in the end he coaxed her into the pool, everyone hanging around the edge watching and cheering them on. All these bubbles coming up from the bottom where I guess she is. Mr. Manny standing with his back to the wall smoking cigarette after cigarette and not saying anything. Miss Crystal and Owen stayed underwater a long time. Crystal Anne, she's screaming, "Momma, Momma, Momma," because she can't see her in the water so I take her to the lobby to see the ducks to calm her down.

The ducks in the lobby of the Peabody Hotel are famous all over the world. There's even a book about them you can buy. What they do is they keep about thirty or forty ducks up on the roof and they bring them down four or five at a time and let them swim around this pool in the lobby. I was talking to this man who takes care of them and brings them up and down in the morning and the afternoon. We were on the elevator with him. He told Crystal Anne she shouldn't chase them or put her hands on them like some bad children did. "You have to stay back and just look at them," he said. "Just be satisfied to watch them swim around." So we go with him to take the old ducks out and put the new ducks in and that satisfies her and she forgets all about her momma up in the pool drowning herself to show off for Owen.

I kept seeing Mr. Manny standing against that wall with a drink in his hand. Not letting anything show. None of the Weisses let anything show. They like to act like nothing's going on. They been that way forever. My auntee worked for the old folks. She says they were the same way then.

Then it's dark and everyone go to their rooms to get ready for the rehearsal dinner. Miss Crystal's in the bathroom trying to do something with her hair. She can't get it to suit herself. She's wearing this black lace dress with no back in it and no brassiere. And some little three-inch platform shoes with that blond hair curling all over her head like it do when she can't get it to behave. Like I said, it'd been a long spring. All that bad time with Mr. Alan breaking her heart. Now Owen.

So she finishes dressing and then she orders a martini from room service. She's in such a good mood. I haven't seen her like that in a long time. We're in two rooms hooked together with a living room. I had on my black gabardine uniform with a white lace apron and Crystal Anne's in white with lace hairbows. We should have had our picture taken.

"Don't start in on martinis now," Mr. Manny said. "Let's just remember this is Joey's wedding and try to act right." I feel sorry for him sometimes. He's always having to police everything. Come from being a lawyer, I guess. Always down at the law courts and the jail and the coroner's office and all.

"I'm acting right," she says. "I'm acting just fine."

"Don't start it, Crystal." I move in the other room at that.

"I'm not starting a thing," she said. "You started this conversation. And you really shouldn't smoke so much, Manny. The human lungs will only take so much abuse."

Owen was waiting for us at the door of the dining room. He was really loaded now, laughing and joking at everything that happened. He was wearing this wrinkled-looking white tuxedo, big old shoulders like a football player about to bust out of it. He had half the young people at the wedding following him everywhere he'd go. Like he was a comet or something. That's the kind of man Miss Crystal goes for. I don't know why she ever married Mr. Manny to begin with. They not each other's type. It's a mismatch. Anybody could see that.

Well, this night was bound for disaster. It didn't take a fortune-teller to see that. I found Crystal Anne some crackers to chew on and in a little while everyone found their places and sat down. A roomful of people. I guess half of Memphis must have been there. They were all eating and making speeches about how happy Joey and his bride was going to be. She was a wispy little thing. But it was true about the money. Her daddy owns the Trumble Oil Company that makes mayonnaise. All her old boyfriends read poems they wrote about being married and Joey's friends all got up and talked about what a great guy he was. All except Owen, he got up and recited this poem about getting drunk coming home from a fair and not being able to find his necktie the next day. It got a lot of applause and Miss Crystal was beaming with pride. I'm sitting by Crystal Anne feeding her. The bride had insisted Crystal Anne must come to everything.

Then the band came and the dancing started. Mr. Manny, he's sitting way down the table talking to the bride's father about business, just like he's an old man, making jokes about how much the wedding must have cost. I felt sorry for him again. His jokes couldn't take a patch on that poem Owen recited.

Everybody ended up in the hospitality room about one o'clock in the morning. All except Miss Crystal and Owen. They're in his hotel room talking about scuba diving and listening to the radio. They've got this late night station on playing dixieland and I'm in there to put a better look on it. Crystal Anne's asleep beside me. Still in her dress. "Night diving's the best," Owen is telling us. "That's where you separate the men from the boys." He's lying on the bed with his hands behind his head. Miss Crystal's sprawled all over a chair with her legs hooked over the side.

So Mr. Manny comes in. He's tired of pretending he isn't mad. "Get up, Crystal," he says. "Come on, you're going to our room."

"I'm talking to Owen," she says. "He's going to take us diving in Belize."

"Crystal, you're coming to our room."

"No, I'm not. I'm staying here. Go get me a drink if you haven't got anything to do." She look at him like he's some kind of a servant. So he moves into the room and takes hold of her legs and starts dragging her. Owen, he stands up and says, stop dragging her like that, but Mr. Manny, he keeps on doing it. Miss Crystal, she's too surprised to do a thing. All I'm thinking about is the dress. Brussels lace. He's going to ruin the dress.

Then Mr. Manny he drag her all the way out into the hall and to the top of the stairs and they start yelling at each other. You're coming with me, he's saying, and she's saying, oh, no, I am not because I can not stand you. Then I heard this scream and I come running out into the hall and Miss Crystal is tumbling down those stairs. I heard her head hit on every one. Mr. Manny, he's just standing there watching her. You should have seen the expression on his face.

They don't put lawyers in jail for nothing they do. Otherwise, why isn't Mr. Manny in jail for that night? It's been two months since I ran down those stairs after Miss Crystal and hold her head in my lap while I waited for the ambulance to come. I've still got my apron, stained with her blood. And she's still in this hospital, crazy as a bat and they're feeding her pills all day and she don't recognize me sometimes when I go to visit. Other times she does and seem all right but you can't make any sense talking to her. All she want to do when she's awake is talk about how her head is hurting or wait for some more pills or make long-distance calls to her brother, Phelan, begging him to forgive her for turning his antelopes loose and come and bring her a gun to shoot herself with. And Mr. Manny. He's got her where he wants her now, hasn't he? Any day when he gets off work he can just drive down to Touro and there she is, right where he left her, laying in bed, waiting for him to get there. And my auntee Mae, that worked for the old people, the Weisses that are dead now. She says that's just how it started with LaureLee Weiss that ended up in Mandeville forever because she wouldn't be a proper wife to old Stanley Weiss. They ended up putting electricity in her head to calm her down. My auntee has been around these people a long time. She knows the past of them.

And there she is, Miss Crystal, that has been as good to me as my own sister. Lying on that bed. I'll get her out of there. Someday. Somehow. Meantime, she say, *Traceleen, write it down. You got to write it down. I can't see to read and write. So you got to do it for me.*

How to write it down? Number 1. Start at the beginning. That's what Mark advise me to do. So here goes. I remember when Miss Crystal first came to New Orleans as a bride. It was her second time around. There was this call from Mrs. Weiss, senior, and she say, Traceleen, Mr. Manny has taken himself a bride and I would like you to go around and see if you can be the maid. She has a boy she's bringing with her. She's going to need some help.

It's a day in November and I dress up in my best beige walking dress and go on around to Story Street which is where they have their new house. She's waiting on the porch and takes me inside and we sit down in the living room and have a talk and she tells me all about her love affair with Mr. Manny and how her son has been against the marriage but she decided to go on and do it because where they was living in Mississippi he was going to school with a boy that had a Ku Klux Klan suit hanging in his closet and they had meetings in the yard of the school and no one even told them not to. Rankin County, Mississippi.

Then I tell her all about myself and where I am from and she says are you sure you want to go on being a maid, you seem too smart for this work and I says yes, that's all I know how to do. She says, well, I can be the maid for a while but I'll have to get some education part time and let her pay for it because she doesn't believe in people being maids. I've got a lot of machines, she says. You can run the machines. When would you like to start?

I'll start in the morning, I said. I'll be over around nine.

The next day was Saturday but Miss Crystal hadn't even unpacked all the boxes yet and I wanted to help with that so I'd know where things were in the kitchen. I got off the streetcar about a quarter to nine and come walking up Story Street and the first person I run into is King Mallison, junior, Miss Crystal's son by her first marriage. My auntee Mae had already told me what he done at the wedding so I was prepared. Anyway, there he was, looking like a boy in a magazine, he's so beautiful, look just like an angel. He's out on the sidewalk taking his bicycle apart. He's got it laid out all over the front yard. It's this new bicycle Mr. Manny gave him for a present for coming to live in New Orleans.

"I'm Traceleen," I said. "I'm going to be the maid."

"I'm King," he said. "I'm going to be the stepchild."

So that is how that is and a week later the bicycle is still all over the front yard and there's about ten more taken apart in the garage and King says he's started a bicycle repair shop but it turns out it's a bicycle stealing ring and Mr. Manny's going crazy, he thinks he's got a criminal on his hands and Miss Crystal's second marriage is on the rocks. One catch. By then she is pregnant with Crystal Anne.

Number 2. This is a long time later. There has been so much going on around here I haven't had time to write any of it down. First of all Miss Crystal got home from the hospital. I had her room all fixed up with her Belgian sheets and pillowcases and flowers on the dresser and the television at the foot of the bed so we can watch the stories. She didn't even notice. She was so doped up. What she had from the fall was a brain concussion. So why did they give her all those pills? I looked it up in Mr. Manny's *Harvard Medical Dictionary* and it said don't give pills to people that injure their heads.

Then many days went by. Sometimes she would seem as normal as can be. Other days she's having headaches and swallowing all the pills she can get her hands on. Anytime she wants any more she just call up and yell at a doctor and in a little while here comes the drugstore truck delivering more pills, Valium and stuff like that. Then she'd sleep a little while, then get up and start talking crazy and do so many things I can't write them all down. Walk to the drugstore in her nightgown. Call up the President of the United States. Call up her brother, Phelan, and beg him to come shoot her in the head. Mr. Manny he can't do anything with her because she is blaming him for her fall and telling him he tried to kill her so he has got to let her do anything she likes no matter what it costs. But I can tell he don't like her taking all those pills any more than I do.

Meantime King came home from his vacation and start in school. Mr. Manny's having to help him all the time with his homework. Much as they hate each other they have to sit in there and try to catch King up. All this time he still hasn't caught up from the school he went to in Mississippi.

Then Miss Crystal she start talking on the phone every day to this man that is a behaviorist. He's hooked up with this stuff they got going on at Tulane where they are doing experiments on the brain. They got a way they can hook the brain up with wires and teach you how to make things quit hurting you.

Well, behind all our backs Miss Crystal she sign up to go down to the Tulane Hospital and take a course in getting her brain wired to stop pain. Then one afternoon after I'm gone home she get Mrs. Weiss, senior, to come and get Crystal Anne and she goes in a taxi cab and checks herself into this experiment place on Tulane Avenue and first thing I know about it is Mr. Manny calling me to find out where she's at. Then he calls back and says he's coming to get me and we're going to this hospital to see what she's up to. King overhears it and he insists on going along.

Here's what it's like at that place. A Loony Bin. All these sad-looking people going around in pajamas with their heads shaved, looking gray in the face. Everybody just crazy as they can be. This doctor that was in charge of things looked crazier than anybody and they had Miss Crystal in a room with a girl that had tried to kill herself. That's where we found her, sitting on a bed trying to talk this girl out of killing herself again. "Oh, hello," she said when we came in. "Tomorrow they're going to teach me to stop the headaches. I'm going to do it by willpower. Isn't that nice, isn't it going to be wonderful."

"Pack up that bag," Mr. Manny said. "You're not staying here another minute, Crystal. This is the end. You don't know what these people might do to you. Come on, pick up that robe and put it on. We're leaving. We're going away from here."

"Come on, Momma," King said. For once he and Mr. Manny had a common cause. "You can't stay here. The people here are crazy."

"I don't care," she said. She laid back on the bed. "I don't care what happens. I have to stop these headaches. Whatever I have to do."

"Please come home with us," I put in. "You don't know what might happen."

"Momma," King said. He was leaning over her with his hands on her arms. "Please come home with me. I need you. I need you to come home." That did it. He never has to ask her twice for anything. She love him better than anything there is, even Crystal Anne.

"My head hurts so much," she says. "It's driving me crazy."

"I know," he said. "When you get home I'll rub it for you." So then she gets up and goes over to the suicide girl's part of the room and explains why she's leaving and we close up her bag and the four of us go walking down the hall to the front desk. This is one floor of a big tall building that's the Tulane Medical Center. It's all surrounded by heavy glass walls, this part of the place. About the time we get to the desk a guard is locking all the doors for the night. Big cigar-smelling man with hips that wave around like ocean waves. Dark brown pants with a big bunch of keys hanging off the back. Light brown shirt.

"Come on," he says. "Visitors' hours are over. You've got to be leaving now."

"We're taking my wife home," Mr. Manny says. "She's checking out."

"She can't leave without authorization from the physician," the boy at the desk says.

Miss Crystal's just standing there, this little bracelet on her wrist like a newborn baby. Only she's Miss Crystal. Now she's getting mad. It had not occurred to her she couldn't leave.

"She's scheduled for surgery in the morning," the deskman says. "You'll have to have Doctor Layman here before I can release her."

"Release her!" Mr. Manny runs a whole law firm. He's not accustomed to anyone telling him what he can do. "She's not a mental patient. She can leave anytime she damn well pleases." I look over at King. He's got this look on his face that anybody that knows him would recognize. Look out when you see him look that way. He's very quiet and his face is real still. The guard has come over to us now to see what the trouble is. We're standing in a circle, with the crazy patients in their pajamas on chairs in front of a television, half watching it and half watching us. Then King he walks around behind the guard and takes his keys. So light I couldn't believe what I was watching. Then he moves closer and reach down and take his gun and back up over beside the television set. "Take her on out of here, Manny," he says. "You can pick me up on Tulane in a minute. Go on, Traceleen, go with them." Mr. Manny, he opens the door and Miss Crystal and Mr. Manny and I are out in the hall. King, he's standing there like in a movie holding that big old heavy-looking pistol.

Then we're out in the hall and down the elevator and running across Tulane Avenue to the parking lot. And we get into the car and circle the block and here comes King. He's locked the guard in the Loony Bin and thrown the keys away but he's still got the gun in his pocket. After all, he was born and raised in Mississippi. Then he's in the car and we are driving down Tulane Avenue. I will never forget that ride. Miss Crystal's crying her heart out on Mr. Manny's shirt and Mr. Manny and King are so proud of themselves they have forgotten they are enemies. That isn't the end.

When we got hime I put Miss Crystal to bed and Mr. Manny he starts going all over the house like he's a madman and throws out every pill he can find and then he comes and stands at the foot of Miss Crystal's bed and he says, "Crystal, get well. Starting right this minute you are not going to take another pill of any kind or call one more goddamn doctor for another thing as long as you live. I have had it. I have had all I can take. *Do you understand me. Do you understand what I mean?*"

"He's right, Momma," King says, coming and standing beside him. "We've had all we can take for now."

☙☙☙

Traceleen's Telling a Story Called "A Bad Year"

WHAT'S a story of this type for? What's any story for? To make us laugh I guess. Look at Mark, he tells a story, then he just busts out laughing, holding his hand on his knee the way he do. Mark's my husband, he's so sweet you wouldn't hardly know he is a man. Pick up the front of a Buick with no help. And sweet, sweet as sugar cane.

Sometimes I start telling a story that's sad and the first thing anybody says is how come? How come they went and did that way? Nobody says how come when you tell a funny story. They're too busy laughing.

How come? How come they went and did that way? That don't figure. That don't make no sense. Like Mr. Alter that come and stay with Miss Crystal all spring, then go home and shoot himself. 1976, I guess we won't forget that year. They wasn't in love either, not Mr. Alter and Miss Crystal. He was her business partner in that magazine. Francis, she called him. Francis said this and Francis said that. Mr. Manny got sick of hearing it.

Mr. Alter wasn't in love with Miss Denery either, that sleep with him when he was here. He wasn't in love with none of them that kept calling him up. Oh, he was a pretty man. I can't picture him with holes in his chest. It just don't make a bit of sense. He seem like such a happy man. Everyone in town calling him up whenever he was here, men and women. He'd just be wore out. He'd say, Traceleen, tell them I'm not here. Tell Miss Allene I'm taking a nap. Tell Miss Louise I'm gone to the coast.

How could he go and shoot himself with all those people loving him to death and wanting to talk to him all day? I couldn't blame them. He was the prettiest white man I ever did see in my life. And strong, strong as Mark. Didn't look like a poet. He looked more like a dock worker. All that curly black hair. And those big black eyes. Look like he just fill up a room with himself when he come in. Even Mr. Manny couldn't resist him even if he do get sick of Miss Crystal saying what he said all the time. "Stay another week," he'd keep saying. "There's nothing going on in the mountains. Stay with us. Crystal wants you here." Then Mr. Alter he'd unpack his bag and stay another week. March, April, May.

Miss Crystal, she just adore him. She'd even take care of Crystal Anne just to show off to him what a good mother she was. Mr. Alter, he loved little children. You didn't ever have to make them leave if he was around. He loved Crystal Anne and would let her rock on his foot while he talked, she'd hang on to his knee. But the one that loved him the most was King, Miss Crystal's son by her other marriage. King loved him the hardest of anyone. He started coming straight home after school and doing his homework and reading any book Mr. Alter recommended to him. He'd read it that day. Then too, Mr. Alter'd take him on walks and adventures. King was fourteen then, just the age for adoring someone. They went to all the cemeteries around town and made notes on the names for Mr. Alter's poems. They went together to a Martin Luther King march. And downtown to Ape Day when they had five Planet of the Apes movies in one day. They went to a jazz festival at the Catholic cathedral. All like that. They had become real close friends. How could you shoot yourself with a young man adoring you and copying every move you make? That's doing wrong, that's doing very bad even if he was a famous poet. Well, I shouldn't talk so loose like that. I shouldn't be the one to cast the stones.

How come him to do it to us I asked Miss Crystal a dozen times if I said it once. Every time she told me something different. Fame killed him, she told me once. He was famous but he didn't get any money for it. How was he supposed to act famous when he barely had a roof over his head?

It was those monks that raised him at that boy's school, she said another time. They took him down into the basement of that old place when he was a boy and told him darkness isn't any different from light. Benedictines. These old Germans in black robes. Right here in the modern world telling boys things like that. I blame them. No, I don't blame anyone. I don't know what caused it, Traceleen. Any more than you do. I don't know a thing. She ducked her head down like she was going to cry and I was ashamed to keep bringing it up but I went on.

It don't figure to me, I said. Walk into a bedroom and shoot himself in the chest with somebody else's pistol. How's that man supposed to feel? The one that owned the gun? What's he supposed to say when he comes home and his friend's on the floor, shot with his gun? Who's to blame? I tell you, I'm about to get mad at Mr. Alter. It's hard to go on loving someone that leads a Martin Luther King parade one day and three days later shoots himself to pieces with his buddy's gun.

Here's how it started. First it was March and I answered the doorbell one morning. Miss Crystal, she was at her dance class. And there was Mr. Alter standing on the porch wearing a Hawaiian shirt and smiling at me like I'm the one he came to see. He had gained some weight over the winter. Except for what I thought he looked just like the last time I'd seen him.

I came to surprise her, he said. Where is she? Where is the Duchess of Story Street? That's the kind of thing he'd say, laughing when he said it. Well, he came right in and got a glass of grapefruit juice and sat around the kitchen talking to me and then she came home and started screaming she was so happy to see him and they got out all their boxes of stuff about their magazine and started laying it out all over the dining room table. It's this magazine they're starting from scratch with some of Mr. Manny's money. It's a magazine for poetry and like that. No pictures.

Then they call up some people they know, poets,

people that their poems are going to be in the magazine, and pretty soon it's a crowd and they've moved into the living room and the music's playing. Jazz, that's all they like to listen to. They're all sitting on the floor, happy and drinking wine and talking all about poems and King comes home from school, he's fourteen, I already told you that, and he goes and sits on the floor by Mr. Alter and from then on he don't leave his side. March, April, May.

Now King's run off to a hippie commune because Mr. Alter shot himself and Miss Crystal's going crazy looking for him. It's the second time he's run off since the funeral. First time Mr. Phelan, he's Miss Crystal's brother that's a big-game hunter, he come up from his ranch in Texas to lead the search. And Mr. Manning, senior, that they call the old man, he's in town and everyone is bowing and scraping to him and he's some mad at Miss Crystal for taking his grandson off to live in New Orleans and letting him know people that commit suicide. And police cars are coming and going and detectives making reports. Miss Crystal, she can't even grieve over Mr. Alter for trying to find King. No one knows what to do. It's a mess. Where was I?

I'm telling too many stories at one time. What was it I set out to tell? I wanted to tell about Mr. Alter killing himself and how none of us could understand what caused it. I was trying to get to the part where Miss Crystal sent notices to all her friends and told them she wasn't going to any more funerals so if any of them was getting the idea of shooting themselves to count her out. That was the best part of that story.

Then I got off on King running away to the hippie

commune. We weren't sure exactly where. It would be the week they came to paint the outside of the house creme-colored. On top of everything else. Mr. Larkin, this Englishman painter, he's got a niece that's a famous tennis player. Anyway, he kept coming in, wanting someone to see if the color was okay. Finally he just went on and painted it. I think one of the policemen made the final decision.

They were all in the living room. The old man and Mr. Phelan and Miss Crystal and Crystal Anne, the baby, and Mr. Manny, Miss Crystal's husband. They had detectives out combing the United States. King had left behind this terrible note. Dear Mother, it said. All you ever did wrong was have me. Love King. Not even a comma.

Seems like they sat in that living room a year getting reports and making phone calls. I never thought I'd be glad to see Mr. Phelan but I was even glad he was there. He had on his black suit and a tie pin made out of a tiger claw he shot on a trip to Africa and he was in charge of things. The one they call the old man was just sitting on a straight chair asking questions. Day after day they sat there. The painters were all the way to the wall facing the Mertons' house when the case broke.

It was the old man that did it. All alone. One morning he got fed up with Mr. Phelan and his detective friends and he went outside and got into his old car and drove off. No one knew where he'd gone. Still don't know. He hasn't ever told a soul how he did it. He was gone about four hours. Then he came back in with a telephone number and they call it and sure enough it's a house down in Texas, not too far from Mr. Phelan's ranch, and

King is there. The boy that answered the phone said he was gone for the day, working in a taxidermy.

Then the men flew off in Mr. Phelan's plane to bring him back and Miss Crystal, she stopped crying and took a bath and even had something to eat.

King had arrived when I got there in the morning. Eating breakfast in the dining room. Like he hadn't ever run away. He smiled right at me through his scrambled eggs. It could have all stopped right there and that bad spring been behind us.

Only Mr. Phelan came in and took him in the den and held him down and cut off all his hair. There's been this big fight going on all year about whether Mr. Manny could make Miss Crystal make King cut his hair. It had got to be all they talked about up to the time when Mr. Alter came to visit. Now Mr. Phelan had his orders from the old man and in the end King was half bald.

Then Miss Crystal she got the gun and wave it at Mr. Phelan and said she was going to shoot him and I believed it. I thought she was going to. Mr. Phelan, he walk across the room as cool as a cucumber and take it out of her hand. Then King throw himself on Mr. Phelan for disarming her and it got out of hand. I never have seen anything like it.

In the end there was broken furniture and lamps and I don't know what all. And nobody is ever going to speak to anybody again and King's hair laying all over the den sofa and who you think got to clean all that up?

I had just got the vacuum plugged in when it started up again. Miss Crystal, by then she was back in the bedroom taking tranquilizer pills and King had gone to his room to sit on his waterbed and play the radio and Mr. Phelan was sitting in that Queen Anne chair in the living room reading a book and guarding the door. The doorbell's ringing off the wall and it's Mr. Big King from Meridian, that's King's daddy. He's just got wind of the runaway and he's boiling mad that he hadn't been called in. He came storming in mad as hell. Then he starts screaming for Miss Crystal to give him his boy she stole from him and he's calling her every name he can think of and Mr. Phelan rise up out of the chair and the two of them start scuffling, holding on to each other's arms and moving around the living room. I was scared to death but I couldn't stop watching. King's in the doorway and Miss Crystal fakes a faint in the front hall but nobody pays any attention to her. They've all seen that before. I would have gone to her but I couldn't cross the living room without taking a chance on getting knocked down. So I'm in the den behind the French doors and they're saying every kind of thing to each other. "What you done to his hair?" Mr. Big King's yelling. "I'm going to pull every hair out of your head for doing that to my son." I couldn't help but remember he'd been one of the main ones wanting Miss Crystal to make King cut it.

Mr. Phelan and Mr. Big King are yelling for a long time. Meanwhile, Miss Crystal she gets up since it's not doing any good to be laying on the floor and she yells at me to call the police.

"I'm leaving," King says. "This time I'm never coming back." Then he's out the front door and on his bike and gone and everyone stops and runs out on the porch after him but it's too late. He's gone. And he's got the old man's billfold with him, that was taking a catnap on the back porch and missed the fights. Everybody said there was hundreds of dollars in it. He can stay for months with all that money, they're saying. He can hide out anywhere. Except for his hair, Miss Crystal said. He can't hide that hairdo, can he? I'll find him, the old man said. He washed his face and hands and put on his shoes and took over. You moved him down here, Sister, and let him know all those poets and homosexuals and suicides and now you're paying for it. Well, your old daddy's still alive. Thank your stars for that. I've found him once this week. I'll round him up again. Get me a glass of sweet milk, Traceleen. And I'll be on my way.

What about me, Mr. Big King said. He's my boy. I'm going on the hunt. How about me, Dad, Mr. Phelan said. Don't you want me to go along and drive you? Then they're gone and I'm spending the rest of the day on the bed holding Miss Crystal and listening to her cry and Crystal Anne hasn't had any attention and the whole house a mess. 1976. I won't forget that year.

I love Miss Crystal. You know I do. I've told you that before. They're some people in the world, seem like they're just meant to be more trouble than other people. Demand more, cause more trouble and cause more goodness too. Someone's got to love and care for them. Got to study them, so we see how things are made to happen.

He's going to kill himself like Francis, she's saying over and over to me. Traceleen, you know he's going to do it. Now he hasn't even got his hair. He'll be dead before they find him. Just like Francis. Just like Francis Alter.

He's not going to kill himself, I tell her. I'm hoping it's true. He's got to live to get his revenge on Mr. Phelan.

As I said it I started thinking it sounded right. I never knew King to take an insult lying down before, I said, stroking Miss Crystal's hair with my hand. He'll be all right. They'll find him. We'll be seeing him again. Crystal Anne came and stood at the side of the bed and put her hand on her momma. King's gone, Momma, she said. King's crying.

This time the hunt went on for weeks. They combed every bar in town and every hippie commune in the South and moved out to the West. They bribed his friends for clues and put ads in the paper and Mr. Phelan prayed every day on his knees in the den and anyone that felt like it could join him. I joined in when I could. Mr. Phelan would make a first-rate preacher. He's got the voice for it. He can get into a prayer good as anyone I have ever seen. Mr. Manny, he'd come and kneel down but he wouldn't open his mouth. I thought it was nice of him to be there, him being of the Jewish race and all. Miss Crystal, she wasn't having anything to do with praying. All that bullshit's what got us where we are, she said. She stayed back in the bedroom talking to her cousin Harry on the phone and her boyfriend, Alan, that she gave up to save her marriage. She got to talk to him a lot during the emergency. Ordinarily, he won't even let her call him since she decided to stay with Mr. Manny. It's been hard on her.

We moved on into July and still no trace of King. Other parents that their children had run away are coming over all the time to have meetings. Oh, it's very sad, they're clutching letters they got and farewell notes and bits of information. But nobody's finding their children. It's a big country and our boy had nine hundred dollars and maybe more than that and credit cards. Every day we're praying he'll use one.

So July 10 came and went that is Crystal Anne's birthday. She got a green and yellow Sesame Street swing set and an ice cream cake made like a clown's face but no one's got the heart to celebrate. It's coming up to July 17, which is King' birthday. He'd be fifteen at seven-thirty in the morning, which is the exact time he was born by cesarean operation in Jackson, Mississippi. Fifteen years old. If he's still alive, Miss Crystal said. You ought to see the way she was looking by then. Look like she'd aged fifty years. Thin as a rail. Eyes like a praying mantis. Even her boyfriend, Alan, calling will not cheer her up. She won't even talk to him.

Then it's July 16 and I'm in the kitchen making shrimp creole from my auntee's recipe from Lafayette and who you think come walking in the side door almost six feet tall, look like he'd grown a foot and wearing a shirt hadn't been ironed and old torn-up shoes and smiling like he knows nobody's going to do a thing but hug his neck. "Where's my momma?" he says, when I got through hugging him to death. Then she was right there, her hair half full of curlers, Crystal Anne right behind her. And we all wrestle him around and sit him down and start putting food in his mouth. 1976. I don't want to go back there again. Too much happening. Too much going on. It was like a drought we had. Or a flood.

❧❧❧

Traceleen's Diary

ANOTHER time Miss Crystal's boyfriend, Alan, came over in the middle of the day and Mr. Manny caught them kissing in the front hall. Miss Crystal hadn't seen Alan in such a long time. She had give him up to save her marriage. She give him up the night Mr. Manny came home from his trip to Australia. I came to work one day and there she was, crying her heart out on the hall sofa, curled up in a ball getting the new chintz cover soaking wet. "I gave him up," she said, standing up, trying to stop the tears. "I did what I had to do." She lifted her hands and put them on my shoulders. We are eye to eye standing like that, the exact same height. Here's what she looks like, green eyes, hair like sunlight, something she does with her eyebrows, they come together when she's thinking, then her voice gets this serious note.

"I did what was best for King," she said. "I messed

him up enough marrying Manny. I can't change fathers on him again. Could I, Traceleen? The answer's no, you know it is."

"You could go on seeing Mr. Alan on the sly," I said. "You could see him in the afternoons."

"He won't see me anymore unless I move out today," she said. "He said either I pack up Crystal Anne and move to the Pontchartrain or it's all over. He won't share me with a husband. He's got too much pride."

"He might change his mind," I said. "When he gets to missing you."

"He won't change," she said. "He told me not to even call him on the phone."

Three months go by for Miss Crystal. Having to hide a broken heart. Then one day she can't stand it any longer. Miss Lydia had been here from California for a week, living in the guest room with Mr. Deveraux, the jazz poet, and I guess all that romance was catching. So one morning Miss Crystal call up Alan and he come right over and the minute he step in the front door he throw her down on the floor and start kissing her. In the front hall. Then who should come home from the office for a paper he forgot but Mr. Manny.

About this time here comes Miss Lydia down the stairs wearing a pink satin negligee, carrying half a bottle of wine, and wants to know who wants to go out for brunch at Brennan's with her.

This is a sample of what it gets like around here. Sometimes my blood's so high I can't catch my breath. This particular morning I'm standing in the dining room by the silver service. It's this silver service Miss Crystal's mother bring up here from Jackson and set it down on the sideboard and tell me to keep it polished. "This came from Philadelphia, Traceleen," she said. "It is a symbol of our family." "Yes, ma'am," I said. "I'll keep it shining." The next week Mr. Manny's mother come over for a visit and she notice it and that night she bring over a silver loving cup the synagogue give Mr. Manny's grandfather for being the rabbi and she set it down beside the silver service. The rest of the house is modern things. Miss Crystal she likes the modern world.

Back to what I was telling you. There's Mr. Alan and Miss Crystal on the floor and Mr. Manny coming in the hall. He was halfway in when I come in and stop by the silver service not knowing what's going to happen next. Miss Crystal, she's pretending Alan's fainted and she's kneeling over him, saying "Get up, Mr. Dalton, oh, what's happened to you." He had on these tennis clothes. That was lucky.

"I played three sets this morning," he said. "I guess I got dehydrated. Could I have some water? I've got to have water." Mr. Manny was standing about a foot away. He could have kicked in Mr. Alan's ribs but how was he to know for sure it was the thing to do. He hasn't ever seen Mr. Alan. He doesn't know him from Adam. "Good God, Crystal," he said. "What is going on here?"

Queen Esther saved it. She's our meter reader, a girl from Alexandria that's been on our route about a year now. She knocks on the door frame and comes in and stands by Mr. Manny. She's three inches taller than he is. Watusi blood, like Mark's mother. I can spot them a block away. It's the way the shoulders swing up high, like something swaying in the wind. So Queen Esther is there, in her gray uniform, holding her clipboard and Miss Lydia has gone for water and Alan is standing now, shaking his head. There's enough going on in the hall to last us about a year. "I'm fine," Alan says, not even taking the water, making his way out between Mr. Manny and Queen Esther. "I'll call you later about the policy, Mrs. Weiss. Whatever you want to do is fine with me."

"What's he selling?" Mr. Manny said, closing the door.

"Oh, some crazy new insurance," Crystal said. "Imagine the nerve of him, coming over here dressed like that."

"Is it all right if I go on downstairs?" Queen Esther said. "I'm behind already."

"Is anybody going to brunch with Peter and me or not?" Miss Lydia said. "I've got to call and see if they have a table."

"What did you come home for?" Miss Crystal said to Mr. Manny. "What do you need?"

"I need to get some papers," he said. "I left some papers here."

Then everything settle down like dust on a table and everybody keep their eyes to themselves and it's so hot that summer I think everybody in town going to melt and my heart beating so fast. Later, I'm riding home on the streetcar thinking about Miss Crystal, when she's going out to brunch, all dressed up looking so beautiful in a green and white dress and Miss Lydia beside her wearing lavender. Oh, Traceleen, you should have felt that kiss, she said. I can't live without him but I have to, don't I?

Here's what she did to make up for it. Spent half the night in a whorehouse trying to find out if it's true they rent young boys to homosexuals. I had to piece this story together from things she and Miss Lydia told me and Mr. Deveraux. That was all after the facts had happened.

First the three of them go out and get drunk at Brennan's and while they are there this writer friend of theirs comes up to their table and he's mad as he can be because he's trying to investigate if they are selling young boys to homosexuals from out of town. He thinks the Mafia is doing it. Or else he thinks some bars he is suspicious of are doing it. But he can't get any evidence. And somebody is making phone calls to him saying they will kill him if he doesn't stop trying to find out things he doesn't need to know.

So Miss Crystal volunteers to go to this bordello, that's what she calls it, and make friends with the owner and pretend she is an old hooker that quit to get married and Mr. Deveraux he is going along to protect her. Miss Lydia is not going to be any use to them because she is too large-boned to ever have been in that kind of business and wears short hair. Nobody would believe she is anything but a schoolteacher which is what she is. She just went along for the ride.

As soon as they get home from Brennan's they start planning what they're going to do. The writer has come home with them. He writes things about New Orleans for some newspaper in Philadelphia. He is sitting on the piano bench playing old love songs and talking about how mad he is about people selling anybody's body for anything, much less a child or a young person. So Miss

Crystal, what has she got to lose, she's got a broken heart anyway, she sits there hugging Crystal Anne and getting madder and madder. "What if it was King," she says. "If King was poor and black they'd have him for sure, beautiful as he is. No," she says. "Traceleen, call Mark and tell him you have to stay the night. I'm going down there and put a stop to this if it's the last thing I ever do."

That's how spoiled Miss Crystal is. She thinks she can do anything she wants to. She thinks she is invisible. "I will stay if you won't drink any more before you go off again," I said. "I won't be responsible for you getting killed."

"Traceleen's right," Miss Lydia says. "We can't go down there drunk."

"Let's go to the track and run," Miss Crystal said. "Let's go get into shape." So then they put up all the whiskey and put on their track suits and go over to the track and run until they have ruined their hairdos, then they come home and take a nap and change their clothes and get ready to go. By then Mr. Manny has come home and they tell him all about it and he says they are crazy and then he just gets a sandwich and goes back to his office.

Here is what happened. At nine o'clock they get in the car and go down to the French Quarter to this place called Lucky Andre's, which is one of the places Mr. Layton, he's the writer, thinks is where the sales of the boys is going on. He can't go with them because they know he is investigating them so he is going to be across the street in a hotel room waiting to call the police at a moment's notice if Miss Crystal and Miss Lydia and Mr. Deveraux don't come out right away.

Then the three of them go into the piano bar and start ordering drinks and pretending to be drunk and flashing a lot of money around so they will seem like they're crazy. Mr. Deveraux is supposed to be the one that will pretend he wants to buy a young boy but in the end he couldn't even pretend like it. He is a poet and too sensitive for this kind of work. They should have taken someone who had a different makeup.

Miss Lydia slipped off back to the room where they are playing Snooker and asked a few questions and found out where the stairs to the bordello was. So she goes back to the piano bar and tells Miss Crystal and Miss Crystal is so mad by then she's crazy and she says she's going to the bathroom and just goes right on up those stairs.

When she gets to the top there are two young girls sitting there on a bench talking to each other. Miss Crystal says they couldn't have been sixteen and she goes over to them and starts asking them questions about where they are from and what they are doing in that place this time of night. And one of them gets mad and socks her in the face.

The manager of the place come along. He's this big Italian-looking guy and he grabs her under the arms and wants to know what's going on. "I came here to stop this stuff," she said. "What do you mean having young girls up here in this dark old nasty place. You ought to be locked up in the jail forever . . . this place will be closed down . . . believe me now that I have seen this you will be sorry . . . this will be stopped."

She can't remember what all she told him. So he twists her arm half off, you should see the bruises, not to mention the place where the girl hit her with her fist and then he takes her into this big scary old room with a bed as big as the breakfast room, that's how she describes it later, and the bed has a velvet cover on it and about thirty pillows and there is a canopy over it. "It was the tackiest place I have ever been," she says. "Then he held my arms down and wants to know who sent me there and I said no one sent me, any decent person can't stand by when something like this is going on and he had better be letting me up because I am married to an important man who will have him in jail for life just for touching me."

But she is locked into that room and the man is big and scary. She says she never thought for a moment he would really hurt her or kill her but she could tell he wanted to. Meanwhile Miss Lydia and Mr. Deveraux have realized she must have gone upstairs and they are terrified and Miss Lydia runs across the street and has Mr. Layton call Mr. Manny and in the end there are policemen everywhere. Mr. Manny has called a judge he knows and there are policemen all over the place and Miss Crystal is let out of the room.

It's four in the morning when they get home. Mr. Manny has had it with being married to Miss Crystal even if they do have Crystal Anne. He packs him a little bag and goes to live in his summer house in Livingston. "I can't put up with any more," he says. "It is like a madhouse."

Wouldn't you think Miss Crystal would be just delighted and make up with Alan and have him move in and live happily ever after? No, that is not what happened. All she is interested in now is this whorehouse thing. It has taken up her whole mind. She is going to find out what is going on down there with selling young girls and maybe even children. She is going to find out about it and put a stop to it if it's the last thing she ever does. That's where we are now. Whole house has turned into an office. Mr. Manny over in Livingston in his summer house pouting, mad as he can be. Who can blame him? Crystal Anne running around the house in on everything. Almost time for school to start. King'll be coming home from his daddy's in Meridian. What will happen next?

Miss Crystal, she's like a diamond all these different sides to her. Turn her one way you see one thing, turn her another you see something else. Who am I, Traceleen? she said to me the other day. Sometimes I don't know who I am or why I'm here. Since that is so I might as well go on and fix it so they can't sell little children to people. Goddammit, I refuse to live in a city where something like that's going on. It's about to make a Christian of me. At least they listen when I call them up. Traceleen, do you realize that while I'm talking to you a child is being hurt somewhere. Somewhere in this town a child is suffering. This very minute in this very town!!

Then she gets up and walks around the room and starts talking on the phone again. Yelling at someone named Mr. Maglioso.

❧❧❧

DeDe's Talking, It's Her Turn

THE groom's mother's garden. You've never seen such roses. Tropicanas, President Hoovers, Queen Elizabeths, Sutter's Gold, Aurora's Dreams. A statue of Saint Francis beneath a Chinese elm.

I was the maid of honor. The minute Crystal called and asked me I went down to Bonwit Teller and bought a four-hundred-dollar beige chiffon dress and got my airline ticket for New Orleans. Who could stay away from anything Crystal Manning is up to? Well, I was going to be maid of honor in her second and final wedding and I had three jobs to do. Hold the flowers during the ceremony, keep Phelan Manning sober, and get King in a better mood. He's my godchild, Crystal's son by her first marriage. To Big King. That'll be over on the day they die. Meanwhile she was marrying Manny and moving to New Orleans to have a better life.

"I'll be able to send King up North to school," she said

on the phone. "I'll send him to Andover or Yale or somewhere. He'll get to use his mind."

"What makes you think he wants to go up North to school. I never noticed him being interested in school."

"I'm getting him out of Rankin County," she said. "I'm taking him to a place of higher concentration."

"You're taking him to a city to live a life he can't imagine when he's only twelve years old? Slow down, Crystal. Use your head. Think it over."

"Anything is better than Rankin County, Mississippi. You've forgotten. You've been gone too long. Well, are you coming down and help me out?"

"What's the date. When's the wedding going to be?"

"June the first. The first day of June."

So down I went. One morning I'm sitting at my desk at *Time* magazine researching an article on the Pentagon and that night I'm at a rehearsal party at the Royal Orleans and Phelan's reciting "The Call of the Yukon" to the rabbi and the matches on the table say *Manny and Crystal* in gold letters. *Many Congratulations!* The groom's mother stood in for the bride at the rehearsal and no one even cracked a smile. I was home.

"What's this marriage all about?" I said to Phelan the night before. He's Crystal's brother, a big-game hunter and real estate developer. He was the brains behind the Ross Barnett Reservoir. "I don't know what this marriage means."

"It means money," he said. "He's rich, DeDe. He's rich, rich, rich, rich, rich."

☙ ☙ ☙

"Why are you doing this, Crystal?" I said. "There's still time. You can still back out."

"He's rich," she said. "He's rich, rich, rich, rich, rich."

Things the groom's family gave King that weekend. Swiss army knife with ten blades, new bicycle, a Peugeot, ten-dollar bill, six shares of Walt Disney stock, twenty-dollar bill. "What am I supposed to do with this money?" he said to the groom's father.

"Spend it," the old man said. "Buy something for yourself."

He found an arcade a block from the hotel. Every time I looked for him he was there, sticking quarters into war game machines. "I don't care what she does," he said. "I'm going to Meridian to live with Daddy. I told her already. She knows."

"You'll change your mind when school starts. You got into Newman, didn't you? It's the best school in town."

"I saw it," he said. "The girls are ugly. The principal looks like a fairy. The yard's all dirty. There isn't any grass."

"Your mother loves you, King. She's doing this for you." He looked at me out of those steel eyes and stuck another quarter into his machine. "Don't be like this," I said. "Don't act this way."

"He's ugly," King said. "He looks bad. He's too short." Later he took the Swiss army knife and dropped it down the mail chute at the hotel. We heard it clanging as it fell. "It was an accident," he said. "I didn't think it would fit."

☙ ☙ ☙

A wedding at the groom's family's house. Six hundred dollars' worth of hothouse flowers all around the fireplace. Outside, those incredible gardens. A lily pond and two birdbaths and the statue of Saint Francis. Like a garden in a museum. The roses had these little laminated signs. I saw Crystal's mother eyeing them. "A Dorothy Perkins!" she exclaimed. "I haven't seen one in ages. Oh, I do love them so. Such a divine shade of pink."

Champagne in the garden before the wedding. "Come see the Max Graf," the groom's mother said. "It will only be blooming a few more days." I stood there in the morning sunlight. For a moment it all seemed so wonderful. She lucked up, I thought. She guessed right. I drank another glass of champagne. For a moment I believed in everything. The goldfish in the lily pond, Crystal's peau de soie wedding dress the exact color of her hair, the morning sun, the servants bringing champagne, the mothers bending together over the roses, their heads almost touching. King was standing beside them holding the garden shears. The groom's mother was pointing out dead branches for him to prune. "Oh, yes," she was saying. "There is one each of everything. I've been collecting for years. It's such a joy. My pride and joy."

King cut a tiny little cut in the pants of his new suit. We all ignored it. "He's my best little helper at home," Crystal's mother said. "He helps with everything. I don't know what I'm going to do with him way off down here in New Orleans."

"That Malmaison came from my mother's place on

Newcomb Boulevard," the groom's mother said. "I'll give Crystal a cutting as soon as they get settled."

"Oh, I wish you could interest her in gardening," Crystal's mother said. "It's such a comfort. It would be so good for her." The women stood up. Their hands touched. Hope beating its wings like a sparrow.

Then people were coming. Close kin on both sides, all the aunts and uncles, a few friends. There must have been thirty all together. The living room was big enough to hold twice that many. It was as cold as a chapel, the air conditioner circulating the smell of flowers and perfume. Champagne everywhere. Mrs. Manning in teal blue, Mrs. Weiss in pale pink, me in my four-hundred-dollar number from Bonwit Teller, Crystal in cream, half-drunk and nervous. The rabbi, fat and jolly, Phelan with his head bowed, pretending to respect all religions, the groom with his hands folded together at the waist. A thin redheaded woman struck a chord on a harp and the ceremony began. "Dearest friends," the rabbi said. He had made up a special ceremony for Crystal and Manny. "We have gathered together this morning for a very special reason. A reason that makes my heart sing."

But where was King? King was missing! Was I the only one who had noticed? "Now Crystal Louise and Emanuel Joseph, whom I held in my arms when he was a tiny baby, whom I had the joy to name, have come together here to be joined in holy matrimony. . . ." The rabbi went happily on. His jowls were moving up and down beneath his collar. He jowls were dancing a dance of matrimony. Beside me, Phelan had bowed his head all the way into his tuxedo buttons. Mrs. Manning had removed all expression from her face. If she minded Crystal being married by a rabbi she was too polite to let it show.

And where on earth was King? How in the world had I let him get away from me? The moment the ceremony was over I dropped the flowers on a chair and started searching. I tore through the dining room and into the kitchen and out a side door and found him right where I knew all along I was going to.

He was in the garden. He had finished off the Red Pinocchios and the Frau Karl Druschkis and started in on the Grandifloras. His new coat was draped over the statue of Saint Francis. From the back I could see his beautiful strong little shoulders working away. The path was littered with the remains of roses. He had cut them down to inches above the ground, had guillotined, had decimated, had sacrificed them. He didn't even look up when I screamed. He finished off a Marachal Neil. I ran to him.

"Why are you doing this?" I said. "How could you do this to us? How could you do it?"

"Don't they look nice, Aunt DeDe?" he said. "Won't she be surprised? Won't she be happy when she sees it?" I pulled him into my arms. His body was a statue. As cold and hard as marble. It would not let go.

But I kept trying. I hugged and hugged. I hugged as hard as I could. "Poor baby angel," I kept saying. "Poor baby. Poor baby angel heart."

"Won't she be surprised," he kept saying. "Won't she just love it when she sees it."

☙☙☙

Traceleen, She's Still Talking

ANOTHER time, Miss Crystal's brother Phelan bought this car in Germany and shipped it to New Orleans and we had to get it off the boat. There's more to getting a car off a boat than you'd imagine. In the end Miss Crystal had to call her cousin Harry that's a lawyer, and get him to call the owner of the shipyards and I don't know what all. That was just to get it off the boat. Before we even started driving it to Texas.

Miss Crystal is the lady I work for. I nurse her little girl, Crystal Anne, and I run the house. They're rich people, all the ones I'm talking about. Not that it does them much good that I can see. Miss Crystal's married to this man she can't stand. All the money in the world will not make up for that.

I'll say one thing for her though, she manages to have herself a good time. Her and her cousin Harry are always up to something. And Mr. Phelan, her brother that bought the car. He's always in on it too whenever he's in town. He's this big barrel-chested man that talks real low and looks at you out of the bottom of his eyes. Looks like he's sighting you down the barrel of a gun. He's always in Africa or getting married or something, sending Miss Crystal these clothes she don't wear. Lace dresses and negligees, satin pants, tennis dresses with little flowers appliquéd on them, like that. That's not her style. She like plain things. She never has flowers or writing on anything she wears.

I never had been to Texas before this trip. I'd heard all about it though. One time Mr. Phelan was in town and he got this screen and showed pictures of Texas, where he's got his ranch, and some of Brazil, where he'd been shooting jaguars. He had just got home from Brazil and he had all this jewelry with him made out of jaguar parts. He give Miss Crystal a necklace with a jaguar claw on it to make her play tennis better. She tried it a number of times but it never worked. She was so busy rubbing the claw for luck she forgot to look at the ball.

Finally she got so mad one day she just tore it off her neck, chain and all, and gave it to me. I put it away with the other stuff she gives me, newspaper clippings from when we get our name in the paper for having parties, silver spoons that get caught in the disposal, her old wedding ring. From her other marriage, to King's daddy. King's her son that smokes dope. She gave me the ring one day when she was drunk. I tried and tried to give it back but she made me keep it.

Anyway, it was Mr. Phelan that sent this car. He's her

brother but they're not a thing alike. Miss Crystal don't like him very much. She's always badmouthing him to Mr. Harry behind his back. Saying her daddy give him all her money. So now it's nine o'clock in the morning and they're calling her to come down to the docks and get this car he shipped over here. Then Mr. Phelan he calls from Texas and begs her to do it. "I can't," she says into the phone. "I've got a match at ten. I can't leave people standing on the court to be your errand boy, Phelan. It's your car, you come and get it."

Well, he finally talked her into it and she puts me in the car with the baby, Crystal Anne, and off we go to the docks. First we have to go in this little smelly office and this Cajun wants her to fill out some forms about who owns the car. Act like he think we're trying to steal it or something.

Well, she raises Cain about the forms and then she calls her cousin Harry and he comes over and gets it straightened out. Mr. Harry's a lawyer, but he only works part time. He doesn't keep regular hours or go in an office or anything. He just does enough to get by. So he dresses and comes on down, all the time we're sitting in that office and I'm trying to keep Crystal Anne from touching anything, everything's so dirty. So finally Mr. Harry comes in wearing this good-looking white suit, all shaved and looking like he owns the world. Miss Crystal's crazy about Mr. Harry. She's always in a good mood when he's around. So he comes and makes all these calls, then everything is okay. Crystal Anne, she's rubbed her hands all over the back of his pants but he doesn't notice it. Miss Crystal's in a better mood now that Mr. Harry has put the Cajun in his place.

What really cheers her up though is the car. "Look at that goddamn car," she says. "Isn't that car just like Phelan. Isn't that the tackiest thing you've ever seen in your life?" We're in a warehouse. Right down on the docks. It's noisy as it can be and this Cajun is driving down a gangplank in the biggest, shinest dark green car you have ever seen in your life. A Mercedes Benz number six hundred. It's as big as a hearse and heavy looking. "Just look at it," Miss Crystal says. She's laughing her head off. The driver had got out and was letting her look inside. "Where in the name of God did he get this car?"

"It's the biggest one they make," the Cajun said. "I've never seen one bigger and I unload them all the time." Mr. Harry had the explanation. "He got it from the head of the Mercedes company. It was being custom made for the president of the company. Phelan bought it right off the line and he needs someone to drive it down to Texas. Come on, leave the other cars here. Let's take it for a spin." He gave the Cajun a check and a twenty-dollar tip for putting up with Miss Crystal and the four of us got in the car. Crystal Anne needed changing in the worst way. As soon as we got inside I whipped off the old diaper and put on a new one. She'd been happy as she could be all morning, just good as gold, watching everything the way she do and chewing on her pacifier.

"How much do you think Phelan paid for this thing?" Miss Crystal said. "I bet it cost a fortune. He's gone too far this time, Harry. Even Phelan can't justify this car." She was playing with the radio dials, running the automatic antenna up and down outside the window.

"He needs it for his hunts," Mr. Harry said. "To meet

planes when people come down for the hunts. And he needs someone to get it down to Texas right away."

"Well, it won't be me," she said. "I'm not his errand boy. Let him fly up here and get it himself if he needs it so bad."

"He can't. Some men from Jackson are going down this weekend. They're paying two thousand dollars apiece to shoot a wild Russian boar. Phelan's got everything he owns in this operation, Crystal. You ought to want to see him make a go of it. Those animals he imported cost a lot of money."

"My money, Harry. My money. Every cent he spends is one more I'll never inherit. What kind of hunt? What's he up to now?" She turns her head and raises her eyes at me like only I can understand what she really means by anything.

"He's got the Lost Horizon stocked with game animals," Mr. Harry says, getting a serious expression on his face now he's talking hunting. All the men in Miss Crystal's family got that look. They put their elbows on their knees and their chins in their hand and put on that look whenever they got to talk about hunting anything, whether it's animals or King the time he ran away to the hippie commune. Scare me to death when they look like that. "He's got antelope and water buffalo and Russian boar. Well, the water buffalo aren't there yet but they're on their way. He's arranging African safaris for people that don't have time to go to Africa. It could be big, Crystal. He could get back all the money he lost in the duck decoy factory. He could make up for that land deal in Joburg."

"He's having safaris at the Lost Horizon? That little

scraggly piece of land? There aren't even any trees. I don't believe anybody would pay two thousand dollars to go down there for anything."

"You'd be surprised what people will do. I put some of my own money into it. So I think I'll just drive the car on down there for him, to protect my investment."

"Russian boar?" she said, like she couldn't believe she heard right. "He's importing Russian boar?"

"We better be getting Crystal Anne on home now," I say from the back seat. "I need to be putting her down for a nap." We were out in Jefferson Parish, almost to the lake, cruising along, it's like riding in a big green cloud, air conditioning so quiet you can hear yourself breathe, big old tires going thump, thump.

"I think I'll go with you to Texas," Miss Crystal says. "I'll take Traceleen and Crystal Anne and go along. It's a perfect time. Manny's out of town and King's in Meridian with Big King. I want to see this operation. This boar hunt. Honest to God, Harry, Phelan's outside the limits. He really is, you know he is."

"You just can't resist the car," Mr. Harry says, laughing and smiling, laying his hand on her knee. "You want to keep riding in it as much as I do."

"Let's don't forget to stock the bar," she says. "I want to really fill it up. Fix it the way it ought to be."

So the upshot of it is the very next morning Miss Crystal and Crystal Anne and Mr. Harry and me are driving out of town on eye-ten headed for San Antonio. "I've never been to Texas in my life," I said to Mark, getting my permission to go. Mark's my husband, sweetest man you'll ever know. He don't stand in anybody's way. "Go ahead," he says. "See the country. I'll be right here when you get back, right where you left me." That's how it always is with Mark and me. Miss Crystal, she can't believe my luck in men. My first husband was just as sweet as Mark. I've had two since Miss Crystal knew me, one just as sweet as the other. "Your turn'll come," I tell her when she gets low. "You'll find your true love before it's over." Well, it didn't happen on this trip to Texas.

The first thing that happened was we stopped on the outskirts of Baton Rouge and stocked up the bar. They must have put two hundred dollars' worth of whiskey in the car. One hundred ninety-six, seventy-eight, to be exact. I saw it on the cash register when Mr. Harry paid the bill. Crystal Anne, she picks up a plastic lemon and starts sucking on the cap so he bought that too. I started getting worried when I saw all that whiskey. Mr. Harry, he's got a bad head for whiskey and much as I hate to say it Miss Crystal's not much better. They started mixing drinks in these little silver cups that come with the car and by the time we're to Lafayette I'm driving. Miss Crystal and Mr. Harry in the back seat drinking and singing country songs and me up front with Crystal Anne strapped in her seat sucking on the lemon. "Don't let her swallow the cap, Traceleen," Miss Crystal said. "Keep an eye on her." As if I didn't have enough to do driving the number six hundred down the road and it starting to rain. I mean rain. We were just outside of Crowley when it started coming down. Coming down in sheets!

People from other parts of the country they see us on

television having our rains and floods and sometimes I wonder what they think it's like. Because the thing the television can't show them is the smell. Not a bad smell, a cold clean smell like breathing in water. We're below the sea in south Louisiana and when the rains come we're in the sea. The rain that day was the worst I've ever seen. I hadn't been driving ten minutes outside of Crowley when I knew we'd have to stop. "I can't see a thing," I said. "I can't see the road before me."

"Pull over," Mr. Harry said. "Let me take the wheel. Pull over on the side." I tried to. Crystal Anne was screaming and standing up in her seat belt. And the rain was coming straight at us like a hurricane. I thought I saw a place to pull over beside a bridge. I turned the wheel and the next thing I knew we were sliding down a wall of mud headed for an oak tree. We hit it broadside and came to a stop not ten feet from a river. "It's the Lacassine!" Mr. Harry yelled. "Goddamn, I've fished this river."

"Oh, my God," Miss Crystal said. She set down the glass she was holding and pulled Crystal Anne into the back seat. I'll say one thing for Miss Crystal. She's a good mother when she wants to be. "What are we going to do now, Harry?" she said. "What in the name of hell are we going to do?"

"I bet that door'll cost a couple of grand," he said. "At least two."

"To hell with the door," she said. "How are we getting out of here?"

"I'm not sure," he said. "Fix me another drink and let me think it over." So, there we were and it kept on raining. Every now and then I'd feel the car squench down in the mud, like it was settling. You could see me shudder every time it did it. Miss Crystal, she fixed me a bourbon and Coke. That helped a little. Crystal Anne had fallen asleep on her momma, just screamed a few minutes and went on off.

I guess this would be as good a time as any to tell you about the inside of the car. It was all made of leather, everything was leather. There wasn't anything that wasn't covered with leather but the dials. Even the refrigerator had a leather cover, softest, sweetest-smelling leather you could dream of in a million years, dark tan with here and there a black stripe.

Every place you turned there was a little hidden mirror. One beside each seat. I couldn't help but think of Mr. Phelan looking himself over while he'd be driving. The bar was in the middle so you could fix drinks from the front or the back and underneath was this nice little refrigerator that makes cubes the size of table dice. Net bags on the back of the seats for holding things. Just like on a Pullman. Oh, it was some car. And there we were, rammed up against a live oak and the rain coming down and no one knowing what to do next. "I'm for getting out and trying to make it up the bank," I said. "It's too big a chance to take, getting washed into the Lacassine inside a car."

"This car's not going anywhere," Mr. Harry said. "It weighs a ton. The best thing we can do is stay right here. Just sit tight till it stops raining."

"I think he's right," Miss Crystal said. "Let's just make another drink and eat some of this lunch you had the sense to bring." It *was* thanks to me there was anything to eat. I'd fixed a lunch of cream cheese sandwiches on Boston bread and radish roses and a little pie made of chicken scraps. Food tastes so good when you're in danger. We ate it every bite.

The highway patrol finally came and got us out. I never have been so glad to see a policeman. A black man, black as me, not coffee colored. "How you doing, ma'am," he said in the sweetest voice, sticking his head into the car. It was still raining but it was passing. "You hold on. We're bringing a rope for you all to hold on to going up the hill. We'll have you out of here before you know it." Then they came with ropes and took us one by one up the hill, Crystal Anne first, awake now and screaming her head off and in a while we're all up on the road and the policemen are writing everything down. The rain's slacking up but it's still falling.

Getting the car out was something else. They had to send for a wrecker and when that didn't pull it they had to get a tractor and lay boards on the hill and I don't know what all. Crystal Anne and I were sitting in the policeman's car watching and talking to him about everything. His people are from Boutte where Mark's from. Know everybody we know. Finally they got the wrecker and the boards all lined up and here come the car inching up the hill and back out onto the highway. Everybody clapping and cheering. The side that hit the tree didn't look too bad after all. Not as bad as I thought it was going to. Of course the doors won't open. All the men and policemen they're walking around the car, admiring it and commenting on it, talking about how much it cost and after a while Mr. Harry got into the driver's seat and turned the key and it started right up. Everybody cheered. "They make these things out of old tanks," Mr. Harry said, laughing up at the policemen. "Those Krauts can make a car. You got to hand it to them. They can make a car."

"Let's get going then," Miss Crystal said. She was starting to look pretty bad, her hair all coming out of her pageboy and her pants covered with mud. I can't stand to see her like that, hard as I work ironing everything she owns.

"Get in," Mr. Harry called out. "We're back on the road. We're on our way." So we all piled back into the car, this time I'm in the back with Crystal Anne and they're up front and as soon as we're out of sight of the policeman Miss Crystal tells me to reach in the refrigerator and hand her a bottle of wine. "No more hard liquor till we get to Texas," she said. "We've had enough trouble for one day."

Then it seem like we're driving forever. Like driving into a dream. First Beaumont, then Liberty, then Houston and we got to stop and let Mr. Harry get some Mexican food and call Mr. Phelan and tell him what's going on. Then someplace called Clear Lake where Crystal Anne went to sleep for the third time, this time for good. Then Almeda, then Salt Lick, then Seville. I'm memorizing the names to tell Mark. Then we're only six miles away on an asphalt road, then we turn onto gravel, then to dirt and we're there. Country as flat as a pancake and dry, hardly a tree in sight. It's the middle of the night and we're at this Mexican-style house all sprawled out in the moonlight, must have twenty rooms. Mr. Phelan's waiting for us in the yard, about six dogs with him. These big red dogs with skinny faces, like the ones Judge Winn have over on Henry Clay, look like they'd take your arm off. The minute I saw them I just held Crystal Anne closer to me.

"There he is," Miss Crystal said. "Wearing black. Look at those pants, Harry. Can you believe he's kin to us?"

Mr. Phelan always wears black. Every time he come up to New Orleans he's got on black. Look like that's his only style. This night he's got on a long-sleeve shirt with a big collar and his pants are sewn up the side with white stitching. His hair all cut off real short. Look like it's been shaved, and he's standing with his hands in his pockets, standing real still and not letting anything show on his face. If he's seen the side of the car he's not letting on. Mr. Harry, he turn off the motor and get out and hug his cousin. "Goddammit, Phelan," he says. "Put those dogs up. I've had enough trouble for one day without fooling with your dogs."

"They won't hurt you, Harry. They won't move unless I tell them to. Sit," he says to the dog pack. "Show Uncle Harry your manners." Every last one of them sit down on their hindquarters the second he say it.

"Hello, Phelan," Miss Crystal says, getting out. "Look in the back seat. There's your niece. Well, come on, stop acting like a movie star and look at what we did. It isn't all that bad." She walked around to the bashed-in side and he followed her.

"Who was driving?" he says. He still hasn't let on that he even cares.

"Traceleen," Miss Crystal says. "And Crystal Anne was in the front seat with her. It's a wonder she didn't crack her head open. It's a wonder we aren't all at the bottom of the river."

"You were letting Traceleen drive?" He let out his breath and moved in to put his hand on the bashed-in door. I moved back deeper into the back seat, keeping Crystal Anne between me and him. "Holy Christ, Crystal. You let the nigger maid drive my car? This goddamn car isn't even insured. Well, Jesus fucking H. Christ . . . I don't believe it . . . I can't understand . . ." He stopped and stuck his hands back into his pockets. He looked off into thc sky, this look coming onto his face like he is surrounded by a bunch of people that don't know what to do and he is tired of fooling with it and might just disappear into the night some day. "Never mind," he says. "I guess I'm lucky that it drives. I've got to use it tomorrow to pick up a party in San Antonio." He bent over and tried to stick a piece of chrome back on that was falling off. I felt sort of sorry for him for a moment. He'd been having a rough time lately from all I hear Mr. Harry and Miss Crystal say. Up to his ears in debt and all like that.

"Well, come on in," he was saying. "Come in and see the place." We all went in together. You've never seen such a sight as was in that house. No words will describe it. Every animal you ever heard of was in there. A full-sized baby giraffe, that's one thing. A big pile of elephant tusks. I don't kow how many. Lion heads and leopards and some kind of curved-horn sheep and several deer and this caped buffalo that almost killed him when he shot it. In between the animal heads was pictures of Mr. Phelan on his hunts. He's kneeling over animals in every picture. Like a preacher. Every way you'd turn there's another picture of him kneeling over something. I was thinking maybe if he was so broke he might think of starting him a museum.

"I want to go with you on the hunt tomorrow," I heard Miss Crystal saying. "I want to watch you hunt a Russian boar."

In the morning some new troubles started. Miss Lauren Gail. They were all around this big Mexican table eating breakfast and Miss Lauren Gail's with them now. She's Mr. Phelan's new wife. And her little girls, Teresa and Lisalee. Miss Lauren Gail's in a bad mood about the car. "He told me he bought a secondhand car over there," she's saying to Mr. Harry. "He didn't tell me he bought it from the president of Mercedes-Benz. All he does is lie to me. He lies when he could tell the truth. Crystal, remember that ring I wanted in that antique store in New Orleans, that I called you about? It was only eight hundred dollars. Eight hundred dollars, that's all, and he said we couldn't afford it and now he turns up with this car. How much did it cost, Phelan? I want to know how much it cost."

"I don't want to hear any more about the car," Mr. Phelan said. "That's a business car, Lauren Gail. And anytime you don't like what's going on around here you just take your feet out from underneath my table and hit the road . . . I mean it, Lauren . . . and take that expression off your face. I'm not going to watch you pout all day. That's it . . . start crying . . . because then I'll just go pack for you myself."

She straightened up her face and Mr. Harry tried to change the subject. He always is the peacemaker. "How many groups you had down here, Phelan?" he said. "Enough to start paying expenses?"

"We're doing okay. Rainey's got so much work he can't get caught up. He's got four heads waiting in the freezer. It's going to go, Harry, don't worry about that . . . I mean it, Lauren Gail," he says, looking her way again. "Don't pull that stuff on me when I have company." He's looking at her with his mouth set in a line.

Miss Lauren Gail she don't say any more after that and it all passes. In a little while she take her little girls and go off to her end of the house and Mr. Phelan he leads the way to show us around the ranch. We got to go see the stables and the cisterns and the lookout tower and then he takes us to see the hunt animals. First we got to go look at the antelope. They're in this corral with a barn behind it. "Haldeston shipped them from Wyoming," Mr. Phelan's saying. "We lost three on the truck and a couple since they got here. But they're all right. I think this crowd's going to make it. See that stallion over there. That's the horse. That's the ringleader. I'm saving him for myself."

"I thought you were letting them run," Mr. Harry said. "You told me you were going to keep them on the range."

"In time," Mr. Phelan said. "All in good time. Got to get them fattened up first. Come on, let's go look at the boar. That's the cash crop this year." He had the Russian boars in a special pen about a mile from the house. We got to drive across a field to get there. It's this pen behind a stand of pine trees, all surrounded by barb wire with some dogs outside and another fence around them. These dogs called mastiffs, all dusty and mean looking. Russian boar on the inside and mastiffs on the outside

There are six boar altogether. Two real small looking, the other ones look okay. They're all milling around. They don't look like anything worth two thousand dollars to me, dead or alive. Just look like old wild pigs anybody can see up around Crowley. Only these boar got gray fur, with black hair around their faces and legs. Where you get them from? I kept wanting to ask but I don't say it, I just hold on to Crystal Anne and keep my eyes and ears open.

"You're charging people two thousand dollars to shoot one of those things?" Miss Crystal says. "You've got to be kidding."

"It costs a lot to keep them," he says. "Have to air-condition the shed and God knows what else. They're very delicate. It's hard to keep them healthy."

"You've lost your mind, Phelan," she says. "Do you realize that?"

"Well, Sister," he says, shutting the door to the pen and turning around to take us back. "Nobody asked you to come down here and tell me how to live my life. I don't come up to New Orleans and stick my nose in your business, do I?"

"You've gone too far, Phelan. These pigs are just too far." She was right up to him now, almost touching. There couldn't have been an inch between them. It's busting loose, I thought. It's getting out of hand. I held on to the baby, holding in my breath. It was terrible, those mean-looking dogs leaning up against the fence and Miss Crystal, she's got this bad hangover anyway, she's right up in his face threatening him on his own ranch.

"I'm not the same person you used to kick around, Phelan," she says. "I'm a powerful woman, strong and powerful. I wouldn't mess around with me if I was you. I'm a different person than the one you used to know."

"That may all be so, little sister," he says. He hasn't moved an inch. He is still as he can be. "On the other hand, it's the same wall you're up against." I looked at him then and he did sort of look like a wall. I guess Miss Crystal thought so too because she took the baby out of my arms and started walking back to the car, holding up her head and swaying from side to side kind of devil-may-care.

We weren't in the big car this time. We were in a little steel-covered jeep made in England. It was fitted out with all kinds of hunting things. We all squeezed back into it and headed back to the ranch. Jack was driving. He's this black man Mr. Phelan took off to college with him when he was young. Call himself a chauffeur but he ain't no better than a slave. "Jack was the first black man to go to Ole Miss," Mr. Phelan's saying. "He was there a long time before James Meredith, weren't you, Jack? Jack was a KA, lived in the house with me. We even had him a pin made. Jack, you still got your KA pin? I want you to show it to Traceleen when we get back." Jack didn't say a word, just grinning from ear to ear.

☙ ☙ ☙

Then Mr. Phelan and Mr. Harry took the new car and drove off to San Antonio to get the men for the hunt and the rest of us spent the afternoon in the air conditioning listening to Miss Lauren Gail talk about Mr. Phelan won't buy her anything. "Don't say anything to the visitors about the pen with the boars in it," he had said to me, taking me aside when he was leaving. "We pretend the boar just comes charging out of nowhere. It makes it more exciting."

"Don't worry about me," I said. "I just came along to ride in the car."

Later that afternoon Mr. Phelan and Mr. Harry come back with these two men and they all sit around and have drinks and hot pepper cheese and then they have this Mexican dinner. You ought to see that dining room. Forty feet long, fireplace on either end. Every wall covered with animal heads, this big brown bear standing in one corner with his teeth showing and his claws out. Mr. Phelan's third wife shot it in Tennessee. Got her picture in a gun magazine for doing it. They got the story framed beside the bear in this glass frame that's really for holding recipe books. "Lauren Gail thought that up," Mr. Phelan said. "She should have been a decorator. Then she could have been in stores buying things all day long." He hugged her to his side and she put on this sad look like what's she supposed to do but take it.

In the middle of the room there's this big mahogany table and hand-carved chairs with chairseats embroidered with Mr. Phelan's coat-of-arms. He had a picture of it on the wall too, painted to match the chairseats. He kept asking Mr. Harry didn't he want him to get him a coat-of-arms for his house but Mr. Harry said no, he already had everything on his walls he needed.

These two men from Jackson they're having the time of their lives. One of the men was in the shoemaking business. He'd been playing chess with Mr. Phelan before dinner and he kept talking about how smart Mr. Phelan was. That he hadn't ever played anybody could beat him so fast. The other man, he used to have a tent factory but the government closed it down by driving him crazy telling him what all to do. He kept complaining about the government doing different things to him and getting drunker and drunker and Mr. Phelan kept pouring him wine and egging him on. "So I just closed the goddamn place and went to Vegas," he kept saying. "Fuck 'em. Fuck 'em. I just closed it down and went to Vegas. Fuck 'em. That's all I've got to say. Fuck 'em all."

I took Crystal Anne and went off to bed as soon as I could. I don't like her listening to talk like that. "Fock em, fock em, fock em," she's saying. "Fock em, Fock em, Fock em." She parrot everything she hear. What's going to happen when she shows up at nursery school talking like that? I could still hear them yelling while I'm walking down the hallway, talking all about the government and hunts they'd been on and what a wild Russian boar will do to you if you only wound it and don't kill it right and how you have got to shoot it just so or you'll mess it up for being stuffed. Mr. Phelan he was standing up when I left showing them a Russian boar nailed to a board, showing them where you have to make the bullets go in so you won't mess up the face.

"We're going on that hunt tomorrow, Traceleen," Miss Crystal said when she came to get in bed with Crystal Anne and me. She just climbed right in with us. First time I'd ever sleep with a lady I work for. That's how Miss Crystal is. Just act like she thinks she can make up the world. So she and Crystal Anne and me snuggle down into the covers. "Tomorrow you will see me in action, Traceleen," she said. "Crystal Anne, I want you to remember what's going to happen next." I thought it was the whiskey talking.

Now morning comes and they all have a breakfast of tequila and lemons and bread and butter. Mr. Phelan insist that's the right thing for hunters to have before they start a hunt. Miss Crystal, she's drinking it with them. Then she and Mr. Harry and one of the men from Jackson get into the English truck and Mr. Phelan and the other man and this one named Rainey that's the one stuffs the animals, they're next in the jeep and Jack and me and Crystal Anne bringing up the rear in the number six hundred. Jack, he's got on his cowboy hat and an African hunter's vest and he's been working on the bar. Got it fixed up more Mexican than we had it. Beer and tequila and some homemade drinks I never did learn the name of. So then we're ready and the sun's lighting up this big Texas field, looked like they hadn't had any rain in a year. Crystal Anne's she's real excited to be going somewhere so early in the morning and she's reaching up in the front seat trying to get Jack's attention and pulling on his hat.

Off we go down that dirt road and out onto the asphalt and then back onto dirt and up in front I can see Mr.

Phelan standing up behind the wheel pointing out things and talking. We come to a little used-up house by the road and we all stop and they come back to our car to get some more to drink and he's talking all about the boar and how tricky they are. Them men from Jackson hanging on to his every word. He should have been a preacher. I've thought that before.

So we pack back up and this time we take off across a stubble-covered field and cross a little ditch on top of some two by fours don't look like they'd hold a man much less a car, then we follow the ditch, it's supposed to be a creek but there's no water in it. It looks to me like we're just driving around the ranch. I can't see that we've gone three miles from home. We have another stop beside an old chimney that used to be a house and Mr. Phelan's got the binoculars out now, sighting through them and letting the men use them and they're sweeping the country he calls it. Then Mr. Phelan keeps on looking and looking at a spot over near a stand of pine trees and finally he takes down the binoculars and looks around on the ground for a while walking around and around in a circle looking for tracks. After a while he puts his arm around the tent man's shoulders and the two of them come over to our car and fix a drink. "We'll use that stand over there by the ridge. They've got to come this way sooner or later to get to water." He pointed east. "Over there's the only water source, a pond about a mile away. So we'll lay for them on the rise." He licked his finger and stuck it up into the air. "Yeah, the breeze is with us. They won't be able to smell us until they're here. They'll come before too long. They've got to have water. The only tracks are two days old. You're lucky,

Charlie. This breeze is going to win you a shot. You're a lucky man. I can tell that. I feel lucky just being with you." He leaned into the car. "Jack, you come over when we get set. Traceleen, you and the baby stay in the car. We're going up to the stand." His voice is real low now and he's pointing over to the east where the sun is getting up above the ground. There's this little rise of land look like it was pushed up by a tractor. With a board screen like for a bullfight in a movie. They're all real quiet now and put all the tequila glasses back in the car and take out all the guns and the men and Miss Crystal go walking off to the rise. Miss Crystal, she's at the edge, look like she's holding back. Off in the distance is the stand of pine trees in front of the wild Russian boar pen. I'm just hoping nobody will make a mistake and shoot at the car. "Now what's going to happen?" I ask Jack.

"Now the boys will let 'em wait awhile and get all hot and bothered. Then they'll let one of the boars go, back behind the trees, and it'll come charging out and as soon as it sees people it'll come running at them. Them boars go crazy when you let 'em loose, they'll run at anything."

"Then what?" I said.

"Then Mr. Phelan'll let somebody shoot and he'll shoot too in case they miss and then they'll keep letting them loose till everybody that paid gets to shoot one. Then they'll be through and Rainey'll put the boars in a tarp and take them off to be stuffed unless somebody wants to drive home with it tied to the hood of the jeep. Sometimes they do that." He stretched his arms and opened up the door. "Well, let me get my rifle out the trunk. He likes me to be standing by in case he should miss. You excuse me, Miss Traceleen. I got to get my gun out the trunk and load it up. I forgot to have it loaded." Then Jack pushes a button to open the trunk and he get out and goes around the back of the car to get his gun.

"Here's what's going to happen," I say to Crystal Anne, thinking I'd better tell her what it's going to sound like when they start shooting. So she won't be surprised. But I never got time to tell her because about that time it all busted loose. Someone at the pen has let a boar loose and he's coming across that field like a baseball. He's coming so fast my heart almost stopped. I feel Jack jump into the trunk of the car. He let out a big yell and jump right in on top of his gun and here comes Miss Crystal running down off the hill and she jump into the driver's seat and starts honking the horn as loud as she can and starts the car and then the car's moving and she's chasing the pig. Trying to save him or run over him one, I can't decide. Then the pig he takes off in the direction of the sun and we're chasing him in the car. Jack's in the back with the trunk top flopping up and down and Crystal Anne's laughing her head off, she thinks it's wonderful. I look out the window and there's Mr. Phelan, running after us with his gun in his hand. He's sprinting like a deer, heavy as he is. He's as mad as he can be.

Then we're on the asphalt and Miss Crystal's yelling. "Traceleen, roll up the window. Lock the doors." Jack's jumped out by then but the trunk top's still waving up and down and we're on the road. "Where're we going?" I say. "What's happening now?'

"Were going for the antelope pen," she says. "We're going to ram it down." Sure enough, she press her foot down on the pedal, lean into the wheel, the seat's too far back for her but she doesn't even stop to adjust it, and we're headed for the ranch. Mr. Phelan's still running after us, then I see him stop and help Jack up off the ground. We bust on down the road and turn on the gravel, one tire's sliding off in the ditch but Miss Crystal, she holds it on the road. I wish you could have seen her, sitting there behind the steering wheel in her fringed vest and her hunting pants with sandpaper on the knees and her khaki-colored hunting shirt, her hair all messed up and wild looking. If I live a million years I won't ever forget the look on her face that morning or the ride we had.

First we come to the automatic gate. What you call a Kentucky gate, you have to stop and pull a chain and it opens, then you got to close it by hand from the other side, but we don't close it this time. We bust on down the road over the cattle gaps and go on past the house without even slowing up, almost run over a couple of dogs, then we're to the antelope pen and Miss Crystal she just drive the car right into the gate, just ram it down. Then she backs up and rams it again. I could see it giving in and the radiator on the front of the car starting to smoke. This is no way to treat a Mercedes Benz number six hundred that cost twenty-six thousand dollars I couldn't help thinking. It would have been just as good to do it with the English truck. "Don't hit it on the front," I said, but she wasn't listening. "Hit it more to the side, with the fender." She don't even hear me. She just back up and ram it one more time. This time the whole gate and half the fence fall forward like they was made out of paper.

Then antelope are everywhere, all around us. For a minute it seem like the windows are covered with antelope faces, then they're gone, spreading out in every direction, their little white tails waving behind them.

The biggest one, the one Mr. Phelan call the horse, is taking off across the field behind the boar pen, two more following him. It's a field that stretches way off and ends in a wood beside where that little dry river runs. I watched those ones until they disappeared into the trees.

Then we're backing out over the boards and Miss Lauren Gail and her little girls and all the kitchen help are running out into the yard to see what's happened. The radiator's really smoking now, but Miss Crystal she backs and turns and pulls up in front of the kitchen stairs to yell to Miss Lauren Gail. "Send my clothes to New Orleans," she yells out the window. "Tell Harry I'm sorry I had to leave him here." Then we're barreling back down the dirt road and through the gate and onto the asphalt.

"You think we ought to drive it with that steam coming out in front?" I said.

"It will run," she says. "If we don't stop it will get us where we're going." We make it through the gate and turn onto the main road and here comes Mr. Phelan in the jeep headed right at us. "God in Heaven," I'm yelling. "Here he comes. What if he shoots?"

"I'll run over him if he shoots at me," she says. "I'll knock his goddamn jeep off the road." She was gripping the wheel like it was a horse she was riding. She was *driving* that car. I held Crystal Anne in my lap. When we passed Mr. Phelan I laid my head down so I wouldn't have to see him. I was sure he would shoot out our tires but I guess even Mr. Phelan knows better than to shoot at people. We passed him on that narrow road with a swoosh, so close I could hear him screaming. I guess he could see the steam coming out the radiator. I was wondering if Miss Crystal caught his eye.

She had planned it all before it happened. Well, not the exact way but near enough. She had put a bag for Crystal Anne into the car and had her pockets stuffed with money and credit cards and we drove to San Antonio at ninety miles an hour and cruised into the parking lot at the airport and got out and left the car sitting there with steam coming out the bottom and the top. It had made it to San Antonio but I heard later that all it was good for after that was to sell in Mexico. I sure hated to leave that car like that. I ran my hand across the leather dashboard as I was getting out, admiring one last time the way the leather parts fit into the steel so fine you couldn't tell where one began and the other ended. Even the button on the dashboard looked special, like it had grown there. Look like a navel on a baby, I was thinking. Or a navel orange.

We got a ticket on a United Airlines 747 and started for home. We were traveling first class, traveling in style. That's how Miss Crystal does things. She's always saying she's going to stop and save some money but she can't ever seem to find the right place to stop.

We strapped ourselves into these nice big seats, with Crystal Anne sitting in the middle and Miss Crystal leaned back and took a moment's rest for the first time since she'd opened her eyes that morning. She still had on her hunting clothes. Looked like some famous actress that had been on a location shot. She reached over and touched me on the arm. "We're going home in triumph, Traceleen. What a trip. I could never have followed my conscience today if you hadn't been there to help, you know that, don't you?"

I accepted the compliment. I knew it was the truth. Nobody can get anything done all by theirself. That's not the way the world is set up.

"It is very sad," she said to me later, when the plane was in the air, and we had been served some French Columbard wine and were having our lunch. "When you cannot love your one and only brother. It breaks my heart, Traceleen, here he is in the modern world and still killing things all the time. Like he was from another century. He was such a smart little boy. He was destined for better things."

"I wouldn't waste too much time feeling sorry for Mr. Phelan," I said. "He looks to me like he does about what he wants to do."

"You're right," she says. "That wine was making my mind soft. Listen, Traceleen, let me tell you a story about what he did to me one time. I was thinking about it this morning while I was getting up my courage, waiting for the boar to come. This was a long time ago, when I was eight years old and he was twelve." She took a big sip of her French Columbard wine and started telling the story.

"It was one Sunday, in Indiana, right in the middle of the Second World War. It was in this Spanish house we had. There was this living room, with very high cathedral ceilings, and I came downstairs one Sunday and there was Phelan, sitting at Momma's cardtable driving an airplane. There were footpedals for his feet and a steering wheel and a dashboard with all sorts of dials on it. It was a special kind of plane where the pilot is also the bombadier and Phelan was flying over Japan, dropping bombs on cities and ammunition dumps.

"Ack, ack, ack, his guns would roar. Ziiiiiinnnnnnn-ggggg, as the bombs fell. Then he would lift up into the clouds barely escaping the zeroes. I almost fainted with envy when I saw him. It drove me crazy. Finally I went over and asked him if I could fly it and he said no, it was against the law because I wasn't a pilot.

"So I went to my room and got my new Monopoly set and brought it out and offered to trade. 'No,' he said. Then I went back into my room and got my butterfly collecting kit and I brought that out and still he wouldn't let me have a turn.

"All day I kept adding to the pile of things beside the fireplace and still Phelan flew on and on as if I wasn't even there. Ack, ack, ack, the guns would roar. Ziiii-nnnnnnnggggggggg.

"Finally I went to my room and came out with the binoculars my great-uncle Philip Phillips had used in World War I and I said, 'Phelan, I will trade you these binoculars for the plane.'

"He got up from the pilot's seat and took the binoculars and the Monopoly set and my rubber printing stamps and several other things that interested him and we shook hands on the deal. At our house a deal was a deal forever. If you shook hands it was over. So Phelan took my stuff and I sat down at the plane and reached for the steering wheel. It was only an old piece of cardboard he had painted. I put my feet down on the pedals. They were two old shoeboxes with cardboard springs. Traceleen," she said. Her voice was rising. "Traceleen, are you listening? Can you hear me? This is everything I know about love I'm telling you. Everything I know about everything."

"Momma," Crystal Anne said, laying her hand on her momma's cheek to calm her down. "Momma's talking."

❧❧❧

Acknowledgments

Excerpts from "The Love Song of J. Alfred Prufrock" by T. S. Eliot reprinted by permission of Harcourt Brace Jovanovich, Inc. from *Collected Poems 1909–1962*. Copyright 1936 by Harcourt Brace Jovanovich, Inc.; Copyright © 1963, 1964 by T. S. Eliot.

"Pictures in the Smoke" and an excerpt from "Inventory" by Dorothy Parker reprinted by permission of Viking Penguin Inc. and Gerald Duckworth & Company Limited from *The Portable Dorothy Parker*. Copyright 1926 by Dorothy Parker; Copyright renewed 1954 by Dorothy Parker.

"Jade Buddha's Red Bridges, Fruits of Love" has previously appeared in *The Atlantic*. "Music" (under another title) and "The Gauzy Edge of Paradise" have previously appeared in *Mademoiselle*.